A WISH TO DIE
A WILL TO LIVE

About the Author

Frank Senauth was born in Guyana, South America, and in 1959 he immigrated to London, where he worked and studied. In 1973 he and his wife felt that Canada held better prospects for them, and they subsequently immigrated to Winnipeg, Canada. He worked at several jobs until he was able to start his own real estate business. In 1986 he retired from business and decided to try his hand at writing, following the ambitions of his youth. Having the leisure to pursue a writing career, he joined several schools in children's and adults' writing in Canada and the States.

The author feels that his writing has changed somewhat throughout the years, and that he has learned to write for his audience rather than for himself. After developing his prose, he felt ready to take on the world with his fascinating writing, and his first idea for a novel was *A Wish to Die – A Will to Live*.

The author wishes to wholeheartedly thank Minerva Press and all its staff for their work in the publication of his novel, bringing his book to life and making his dream come true. He hopes you will enjoy his work.

Forthcoming from Minerva Press is the sequel to Frank Senauth's first novel, entitled *A Time to Live – A Time to Die*.

Chapter One

John Stone awoke slowly from a deep sleep. His eyes gradually flickered open, and he was able to inhale the smell of antiseptic in the hospital room. Then he heard the clanging sounds of carts being wheeled outside his room. His eyes traveled slowly around the room, then peered at the dimmed lights in the ceiling. His head was light and his mouth was dry, and his whole body felt stiff. Then he realized that he was in a hospital room. John was tall, slim, black hair, brown eyes, and he was considered as handsome. He was admired by many women, but his one and only love was his beautiful wife, Mary Stone.

He shook his head slowly as he remembered that he was shot in the chest. He couldn't remember anything else. He breathed slowly in and out, and felt the surging pain in his chest. Then he realized they had operated on him to save his life. He was alive, and lying in a hospital bed. He didn't know where.

John didn't know what had transpired since he was shot in the chest and become unconscious. They had found him and brought him to the hospital for emergency surgery. They had several tubes in his arm. He was lying still in his bed. He tried his best to focus on what had happened. Where was his family? They should have been there in the hospital to greet him, but somehow they were not there. He thought that was strange. He didn't know what had happened to them. His thoughts kept spinning and he couldn't think straight or find the right answers to his immediate thoughts.

Suddenly the door of the room clicked open, then he saw for the first time the young nurse who was assigned to him. She came to his bedside, and looked down at him with a smile. She wore a white uniform with a tag on the right side of her upper breast pocket; it read, 'Nurse Hill'. John looked up at her, then slowly read the tag on her uniform. At first he thought she looked like someone out of a heavenly dream. She was tall, slim and her face was white and beautiful. He kept a steady glance at her to make sure she was real. He wanted to make sure he wasn't dreaming.

"I see you're awake, Mr. Stone. How do you feel?" she asked softly.

"I feel awful, nurse. Where am I?" he asked softly.

"You were brought here this morning to the St. Mary's Hospital for emergency surgery. Dr. Zale operated on you. You were really lucky that your next-door neighbor found you outside on the sidewalk. He immediately called 911 and covered you up with two blankets, otherwise, you would have died outside in the cold," Nurse Hill explained.

"You said my next-door neighbor called 911?" John asked.

"Yes."

"Why didn't my wife call 911?" John asked. His whole body became numb at that moment, and he was sure that something was radically wrong.

"Nurse Hill, where's my family?" John asked nervously.

Nurse Hill just looked at John sadly.

"Nurse, if you know something, please tell me," he pleaded. "What's happened to them?" he kept saying.

"Mr. Stone, I'll get Dr. Zale for you. He'll be able to explain to you about your family," she said quickly, and went out of the room.

John was now certain that something was terribly wrong. He was too weak to bring himself to think that the worst was yet to come. But somehow he knew he couldn't escape the news that the doctor was about to tell him.

John remembered some of the aspects of what had happened that morning. He had been shot twice by a burglar who broke into their house. He had heard a noise downstairs and gone to investigate. He took his handgun with him, and was overpowered by the intruder. He was knocked out at the bottom of the stairs. When he became conscious, he saw the burglar coming down the stairs. The intruder had John's gun in his right hand and a ski-mask in his left hand. John leaped at him and was shot twice in the chest. He fell to the floor, then the gun was thrown at his side. He saw the gun and slowly picked it up and went after the burglar, who had gone through the front door and onto the sidewalk. He fired once at the burglar, then he collapsed onto the sidewalk outside his front door, and was out cold.

John became restless, and tossed his head slowly from side to side in bed. There were tubes in his arms, and he couldn't move his body as he would have liked.

"Where's that doctor?" he whispered to himself.

Shortly afterwards, Dr. Zale entered the room. John looked at him steadily as he approached his bedside. The doctor wore a white coat and glasses. He was an elderly man with some gray hair on his head, partly bald, slim and short.

"Mr. Stone, I'm Dr. Zale. How are you feeling?" the doctor said, as he gazed down at John. The doctor bore a serious expression on his face. John saw at once from the expression on the doctor's face that the news was going to be bad, bad news. His whole body shook like a leaf and he was still cold and numb all over. The news was not out as yet, but yet John felt as if he had just died a sudden death.

"Well Doctor, tell me?" John asked sharply.

"Mr. Stone, I know what you want me to tell you, but what I have to say will be very painful for you. Your situation, in short, is critical. I don't want to alarm you further," Dr. Zale said slowly.

"Doctor, please don't keep me in suspense. Tell me what I want to know, and if it's displeasing to me, I'll be the only one to suffer some more," he said quickly.

Dr. Zale gazed at John for a few seconds, then he looked away. Then he looked sadly at John.

"You want to know about your family?" Dr. Zale asked.

"Yes, Doctor, please do tell me," John insisted.

"Your family," the doctor said, then shook his head slowly.

"What are you trying to tell me, Doctor?" he asked bluntly.

"I'm sorry to tell you this, Mr. Stone, but your family is no more," Dr. Zale told him gently.

"What do you mean?" John cried out.

"They didn't survive the shootings," Dr. Zale said.

"What shootings?" John cried loudly.

"They didn't survive the shootings in your home," Dr. Zale explained.

"You mean my family were all killed?"

"Yes. I'm sorry to say they're all dead," Dr. Zale said sympathetically.

"They're all dead? Why didn't you let me die, too, so I could be with them?" John cried. The tears came slowly down his cheeks.

Then he got enough strength to filter out a loud scream into the room. Nurse Hill came quickly into the room with a small tray.

"Just as I expected," Dr. Zale said to the nurse. He took the syringe, and plunged the needle into the top of the little bottle, which contained a sedative, and when the required dose was in the syringe Dr. Zale administered it into John's arm. "This will make you sleep, Mr. Stone. You need your rest and you'll need all your strength to cope with this terrible situation."

"They're all dead..." John kept saying. His head was tossing from side to side. Then the room became darker and darker until he fell into a deep sleep.

"Poor man. His whole family wiped out. I hardly think he'll want to live after this," Dr. Zale told the nurse. "Keep an eye on him, Nurse Hill," the doctor added and left the room.

"Yes, Doctor," she said, and took John's pulse. "I feel badly for you, Mr. Stone. You'll need lots of love and attention, and I'll give all I can," she said to herself, then she wiped the sweat off his face. "You're a really handsome man. I could really go for someone like you. What am I saying? I'm just dreaming," she whispered.

*

The following morning, John woke up. He felt weak and his head was light like a feather. He looked around the room slowly, and everything came back to him gradually. That word was still in his memory, 'Dead!' 'Dead!' "They're all dead. I'm all alone. I can't live without them," he muttered to himself.

He didn't try to speak or think. He felt if he didn't do either, his whole burden would go away and his whole life would be the same again, but after a while he realized that it would be a physical impossibility for his life to be the same again.

Nurse Hill came into the room quietly and went to his bedside. She looked down at John. He kept his eyes closed when he heard her enter the room. He felt by doing so he'd keep his private thoughts to himself.

"I know you're awake, Mr. Stone. Please, look at me," she said softly.

John heard her loud and clear. Her voice was soft and sweet and he felt that its sound was bringing him back to reality. He slowly opened his eyes, and the first thing he saw was her pretty face, and her blue eyes. He forced a smile at her.

"Did anyone ever tell you that you have a pretty face?" he asked slowly, half winking at her.

"Yes, but not like this," she said, smiling. "I'm glad you're back with us, Mr. Stone. I must say, without any question, that you're a handsome guy," she teased, bending over him.

"Thank you. It's a pity I won't have anyone to admire me any more," he said sadly, without looking at her.

"It's not the end of the world. You'll find someone to love you again," she told him. "Now, it's time for your breakfast, so you can get back your strength."

"Yes, ma'am. You're so nice to me. You really make me feel at ease. Thank you," he said, moving his fingers.

"That's what I'm here for, Mr. Stone. I'm here to take care of you, and that I'll do. I promise you."

"Nurse Hill, I'd like you to get in touch with my in-laws, Mr. and Mrs. Young of Moorestown, Pennsylvania. They'll have to know about their daughter and their grandchildren," John told her sadly, and closed his eyes. He re-opened them after a few seconds.

"Mr. Stone, you shouldn't be dealing with this just yet. You'll have to get your strength up. I'll get you some breakfast," she said and started to leave the room.

"They live in Moorestown. Please get in touch with them," he said as she left the room. Then he closed his eyes. He wanted to think for a few minutes before the nurse got back. He didn't hear Nurse Hill when she came back into the room and stood at the side of his bed.

"Mr. Stone, don't go to sleep on me again," she said.

"Just thinking, Nurse Hill," he said and opened his eyes. Then he felt sad that he was now all alone, and didn't have a family to comfort and love him any more.

"Are you ready for some light food?" she asked.

John shook his head. Then he felt the tears coming down his cheeks. He hadn't cried for a long time. Now he had no choice but to cry for the family he loved; he knew he'd never see his beloved family again or hear their sweet voices once more.

"You have to eat something to get your strength up," she urged.

"How can I eat at a time like this?" he said softly.

Nurse Hill put the tray down, and wiped the tears away from his face. "You really loved them," she said softly.

"They were my whole life. Now, I have no life!" he cried, and shifted his right hand from side to side.

"They loved you, and they would have wanted you to live for their sake. That's why you have to get strong and fight for your life. You only have one life to live," she told him as she wiped his face with a tissue.

He smiled at her. "For your sake, I'll eat something," he said, looking at her steadily.

"Now you're making sense, Mr. Stone," she said, smiling. Then she started to feed him like a baby.

When Nurse Hill left the room, John had time to think.

"Mary, David and Cindy – all gone," he kept saying, repeating himself. "Why did I live? Why didn't I die with them?" he cried, and shook his head several times.

Fifteen minutes later, Nurse Hill returned to the room. She brought some juice for him, and pulled up a chair and sat at his bedside.

"You're back so soon, Nurse?" he asked politely.

"Yes. I brought you some juice. I just wanted to tell you that we left a message on the Youngs' answering service, stating that it's an emergency and they should call the hospital immediately."

"Thank you, Nurse. I don't know how I'm going to repay you," he said, looking at her steadily.

"You're welcome. I know you'll think of something, Mr. Stone," she told him with a smile.

"Call me John. Mr. Stone makes me feel old," he told her, as though he'd known the nurse for a long time.

"Well, my first name is Karen, but I like to be addressed as Nurse Hill," she said in a professional way.

"I understand, Karen. Nurse Hill."

Nurse Hill assisted him with some juice. He swallowed it slowly, and all he could think about was her pretty face, and her soft touch. Gradually he felt his confidence returning to his weak body.

"You're my best patient. You eat and drink everything that I give you," she said with a smile.

"I'm only able to be my best by looking at your pretty face. You've a very nice touch for your patients, as I said before," John teased.

"I didn't know my face had that effect on you," she said and gazed at John. "It must be awful the way you feel, Mr. Stone."

"I don't know what I'm going to do, Nurse. Are you married?" he asked.

"No. I don't even have a regular boyfriend. Why do you ask?"

"Well, you don't know what it is to be attached to someone you love," he said softly.

"No, I don't. You loved her very much?"

"Yes. Mary was my whole life. We were just thirteen when we met and fell in love with each other. We eloped from Moorestown at the age of eighteen. We got married and started our family, David and Cindy. Mary was a very loving and thoughtful person. She was always willing to help anyone in need. I loved her so much," he told her. When he looked up at her, he saw the tears gliding down her cheeks.

"You're crying."

"Yes, I'm crying for you. What you said was too emotional for me to hide my feelings. I know it will never be the same for you again, but you'll find love again some day. I'll pray for you, Mr. Stone, so you'll be able to see your way brightly," she said softly.

"You remind me so much of Mary," he said, looking at her steadily.

"I'd better get to my next patient. You need some time to rest. I'll be back to see you later," she said, wiping the tears away from her eyes.

"Yes, I'll be here. I have nowhere to go," he said. He closed his eyes and all he could see were the pretty faces of his family. They were smiling at him, and he wasn't in a position to smile back at them. He realized they were only a figment of his imagination, and he'd never be able hear or see them alive again in this lifetime.

*

It was the third week of July, 1976, when John and Mary Young graduated from Moorestown High School. He was madly in love with her. His dream was to get married to her when they were over the age of eighteen.

John was tall and slim, with black hair and brown eyes. His girlfriend, Mary, always told him that he was handsome. She was slim, fairly tall and had long brown hair, green eyes, and a fair complexion. She was always neatly dressed. Her body was fully developed. John was always excited when he was near to her. She was his best friend and she made him happy. He enjoyed her company. He knew that Mary would be his wife some day, and that no one would change his feelings for the woman he loved so much. He wanted to be with her for the rest of his life. He realized that would never happen unless they took their destiny into their own hands. That was when John made plans to leave the farm and everything else behind, and to start life from scratch in a new city.

John lived with his family on the Stones' farm, which was four miles away from Moorestown, Pennsylvania. His father was James Stone, his mother was Sofie Stone, his brother was Harold, and his sister was Rose. He was the youngest.

John loved his family, but he didn't want to spend the rest of his life on the farm. He didn't want to be a farmer. He knew he had to do something about it quickly and get the situation going his way.

John remembered the 3000 acres of their prime farm land, with the red and green farmhouse which looked like something out of an old western movie. He had hoped some day that a producer or director would put their farmhouse into a western.

He remembered the warm summer days, the tapping of rain on the roof, and the cold nights in winter.

The next day, John approached his mother in the kitchen for some advice. She was a tall, attractive, stout woman in her forties. He knew that she'd be sympathetic to his cause.

"Mom, I thought it best to speak to you first. I'm in love with Mary and we want to get married. I'd like to speak to Dad about the way I feel," he told her.

"I know the way you feel, John. You'll have to do what works for you. I'll inform your father that you want to speak to him this evening," she said, then gave him a sudden hug.

That evening John met his father in the family room. He looked down at his parent, who was sitting in his favorite chair, reading an old newspaper. His father was a tall, broad man in his forties. He was stern and hard-working.

"Dad, I'd like to speak to you man to man," John told him seriously.

His father looked up at him, removing the newspaper from his view. "Your mother told me you wanted to speak to me. It sounds serious," his father said, looking up at him.

"Yes, sir, it's rather personal."

"I'm listening."

"I remember when I was just about nine years old, you took me horseback riding. We always went to our favorite spot on the northern side of the farm. You told me one day that I'd be master of this farm. I was too young to understand what you really meant, but now I do," John told his father.

"Where's all of this leading to, John?"

"I'm in love with Mary Young. We want to get married and leave Moorestown."

"The Youngs' daughter?"

"Yes, sir."

His father shook his head twice. "I was under the impression that you'd go to college, and some day you'd be the next Stone of this farm," he told him bluntly.

"I understand the way you feel about me, Dad, but you have to understand that I need to live my life in my own way."

"And what way is that, son?" Mr. Stone asked bluntly.

"Well, sir, I'm grateful for all the good things you have done for me. I'll always love you and be proud of you as my father, but I have to get married to Mary and leave the farm," he said quickly.

"You should think this over very carefully, son. It's a big step you're taking. What about Mary's parents? How do they feel about all of this?" his father asked.

"Mary is now eighteen and she's old enough to make up her own mind. She doesn't need her parents' consent to get married," John told him frankly.

"You should slow down, son!"

"You got married to Mom when you were just seventeen."

"That's true, but that was different."

"How different, Dad?"

"I had my parents to support me. If you get married to Miss Young and leave Moorestown, you'll have no one to support you. No career, no job, and no money to live on," his father explained.

"I realize that, sir, but I'm positive I can make it away from the farm, and without any help from you."

"You're an adult now, son. I can't stop you from doing whatever you want to do. It's your life. Don't throw it away."

"I'm sorry, Dad. I know you wanted me to be the master of this farm one day, but that's not for me," John confessed.

"Your brother Harold will now become master of this farm," his father told him bluntly.

"A good choice, Dad. Harold is a good man and a hard worker. I know he'll make you proud," John told his father, then left the room.

The next afternoon, John met Mary at Ruby's Cafe in Moorestown. They had met there several times before, but this time it was different. They sat at their usual table by the window. They ordered two burgers and fries, and two soft drinks. The joint was small. Some kids and adults hung out there and bought light snacks.

"It seems from the expression on your face, John, that we both have the same bad news," Mary told him.

"What did your parents say?" John asked.

"They strongly objected. They stated quite clearly that I was too young to get hitched. They want me to go to college before thinking about matrimony. What are we going to do, John?" she asked seriously.

"We'll think of something, hon," John told her.

"My parents like you. You remember that Saturday afternoon when I invited you for supper?"

"I remember. They thought I was just a simple little farmboy, but I proved them wrong."

*

John was invited to supper that Saturday afternoon at the Youngs' residence. He sat with the family around the dining table, and all the food was on the table ready for serving.

"Mrs. Young, I have to say something before I share this delicious meal with all of you," John said, then closed his eyes and clasped both of his hands. "Great One above, bless this family, especially Mrs.

Young for slaving over a hot stove to prepare this delicious meal in front of us. Amen," John said softly, then opened his eyes. He saw everyone looking at him curiously. "Thank you, Mrs. Young," John told her, smiling.

"And thank you, John. I wish my family felt the same way you do," she told him cheerfully.

"Thank you, Mom," Mary said.

"Thank you, Mom," Alice said.

"Thank you, Mom," Mr. Young said.

"It was so nice of all of you to compliment me. So now let's eat," Mrs. Young said, smiling.

*

"That was very funny what you did, but we all appreciated your keen sense of humor. Do you remember when you invited me to the farm that weekend?" Mary asked.

"Yes, I remember. That was the time when I proposed to you, hon, and we had our first and very special kiss."

*

That weekend John had invited Mary to the farm. He took her horseback riding that afternoon. They rode to his favorite spot on the northern side of the farm. When he was a small boy, his father used to take him to that very spot. There were several apple trees and two large pine trees, and a large pond at the side. In summer the family would hold picnics, and they would invite some of the other farmers in their area. When his father brought him to that special spot, he'd lift him up so he could see all around the Stones' farm.

"Son, all of this will be yours some day. You'll be master of this farm."

When John arrived at his favorite spot on the farm with Mary, he dismounted from the saddle. Then he went to help Mary off her horse, but before he could get to her, she tried to dismount from the saddle herself and fell to the ground. John rushed quickly to her assistance. He sat on the grass, then raised her up in his arms.

"Mary are you hurt?" he asked nervously.

"No, I'm not hurt, John," she replied, smiling.

"I thought for a minute you were hurt, Mary," he said quickly. Then he held her in his arms and, without thinking, he kissed her.

"What was that for?" she asked cheerfully, then she looked surprisedly at him.

"I love you, Mary. You're the only girl for me," John told her quickly.

"I love you too, John, and you're the only boy for me," Mary said, smiling.

"Then we'll get married when we're eighteen," he told her.

"That's a date, John."

"Is that a yes, Mary?" he asked cheerfully.

"Yes, John," Mary said with a big smile on her face.

"Well, let's seal it with a kiss," he suggested in a teasing way. She closed her eyes, then John kissed her to seal their date with matrimony.

*

"Mr. Stone, you're having a dream. Wake up!" Nurse Hill said softly. She held his left hand, which was nearest to hers.

John didn't move immediately, then he suddenly opened his eyes and gazed at Nurse Hill.

"Mary, she was here. It was so plain. I held her hands and kissed her," John slowly told Nurse Hill.

"It was just a dream, Mr. Stone. You're now back in the real world with us," she assured him.

"I can't help thinking about the past," he said sadly, gazing at her.

"You can't forget the past because it's part of your life," she told him, still holding his hand.

"It's so good you're here to comfort me, Nurse Hill," he told her frankly.

"It's my job to make you feel comfortable. I came to tell you that your in-laws are on their way. They'll be able to take some of the burden off your shoulders. This is a dreadful time for you. You need all the help you can get," she told him.

"You're right, Nurse Hill. I can't do this on my own," he cried. "I love my family. I love them so much, and now they are all gone."

Repeatedly, John shook his head from side to side. "Now they're all gone and I'm left all alone," he kept saying to himself.

"You'd better get some rest and take it easy. I'll be back to see you shortly," she told him and left the room. John closed his eyes and tried his best to block out the bad memories in his brain.

Chapter Two

John woke up after his nap that afternoon. His in-laws, the Youngs, hadn't arrived as yet. He knew he had to face them whether he was willing or not. His family was completely wiped off the face of the earth, and he was left all alone. He realized that the Youngs would be devastated when they got the bad news that their daughter and grandchildren were all gone, never to be seen alive again. He shook his head at the thought of them receiving such dreadful news.

He waited impatiently for the door of the room to click open, and each minute seemed longer than usual. He closed his eyes and started to think of something nice. Then he remembered his graduation dance in June, 1976.

*

John arrived at 6.30 that Friday evening at the Youngs' house to pick up Mary, his sweetheart. He had borrowed his father's Ford truck that he had washed and polished during that day for the occasion.

He wore his brown suit, white shirt, brown tie, and brown shoes. He held a corsage in his left hand while he rang the doorbell nervously. The door opened shortly afterward. Then he came face to face with Mary's father.

"Good evening, Mr. Young. I came to escort Mary to the graduation dance," John said, smiling.

"And a good evening to you too, John. Please come in! Mary will be with you shortly."

"Thank you, sir," John said, then entered the house. The door closed behind him, and Mr. Young led him into the living room. This was his third time to come to the house. He took a seat on the large sofa. Mr. Young sat on the small sofa opposite John. Then he looked at John for a few seconds as if he was sizing him up.

"John, Mary told us that both of you are planning to get married. Can you tell me something about that?" Mr. Young asked.

"Yes, sir, we've been planning for a few years to get married. You know teens' dreams? We made arrangements two years ago to get married when we turned eighteen, but that was just a dream on our part. We're too young for matrimony," John told him, smiling.

John observed the expression on Mr. Young's face as if he didn't believe what he had told him.

"Well, sir, did you ever make any plans in respect of the woman of your dreams when you were a teen?" John asked, and kept his fingers crossed on his right hand.

"Well," Mr. Young said and smiled at John. He didn't want to answer the question.

"I know it's sort of personal, and I don't expect you to tell me, sir," John said, smiling.

"John, I must say that you have a knack of making a person feel at ease," Mr. Young told him with a slight smile on his face.

"Thank you, sir. That means a lot to me coming from you, and you have nothing to worry about."

A few seconds later, Mary and her mother came into the living room. John saw them and got up to face them. His eyes were fixed on Mary. She was beautiful in his sight.

"Good evening, Mrs. Young," John said, smiling and still looking at Mary.

"And good evening to you too, John. Your date is beautiful and ready for you," Mrs. Young told him.

"A beautiful corsage for a beautiful lady," John told Mary, then gave her mother the corsage. Her mother took it and pinned it onto Mary's white gown.

"Well, the dance will be over if you two love birds don't stop gazing at each other and get going. I hope you'll take good care of our daughter, and don't do anything I wouldn't do," Mr. Young teased.

"Yes, sir, I'll take good care of Mary. We'll be back before eleven thirty."

John held Mary's right hand and they slowly made their way out to his truck that was parked at the side of the road. He opened the passenger's door for her to enter the truck. Then he entered the driver's side of the truck. Then he gazed at her for a few seconds.

He couldn't take his eyes off her. She looked so different in her white gown, and white shoes to match. She had a new hair-do that gave her pretty face a new look.

"I'm sorry, hon, that we'll be going to the prom in my father's old truck," he told her.

"It doesn't matter, John, as long as we're together," she said, and squeezed his hand.

"You smell so good, hon, and you look so beautiful. I really feel like driving off into another dimension with you," John teased. Then he started the engine and drove down Main Street to the Moorestown High School.

"I never knew that you felt like that, my hero, John," she said with a giggle.

John realized that he loved Mary because she was a thoughtful and a loving person. She always wanted to help her friends, and she'd say the right things to them. He felt at ease with her. She was his sweetheart as well as his best friend. His greatest hope was that some day she'd be his wife, but he realized that was just a wish that was yet to come.

John drove into the school's parking lot and parked his truck, then he switched off the engine. Then they sat there for a few minutes, gazing at each other like two love birds.

"What did my father say to you, John?" Mary asked.

"He wanted to find out my intention towards you."

"What did you tell him?" she asked.

"I told him we were planning a long time ago to get married. I told him in such a way as if we were just planning and nothing else," he told her.

"My dad is an accountant and he's pretty smart. You can't pull the wool over his eyes," she said frankly.

"Well, hon, let's go in and say hello to our friends, then we can dance the night away," he told her quickly.

"Good idea, John."

They made their way into the school. John held Mary's hand, then he gazed around the gymnasium, which was specially decorated for the occasion. There were assorted ribbons, balloons, soft lights, and a disco band on the stage. The evening was set for them to have a good time. There would be dancing, drinking and lots of food.

That evening John and Mary danced in the gymnasium to most of the disco music, whether it was slow or quick. After each slow dance, John became more attached to his sweetheart. It was as if he was searching for something that was missing from their friendship. He knew that they were in love. But how much in love? The answer didn't come to him as quickly as he would have liked.

At 10.30 that evening, John took Mary outside to his truck. He had his own bright ideas about her and he wanted to express it in his own loving way.

"Are we leaving now, John?" Mary asked in the truck.

"No, hon," he replied and rolled down his window.

"Oh, I get it, you want to play cool like the other couple over there," she said.

"You got it right, hon," he said, then took her into his arms and kissed her passionately. "I wanted to do that all night," he told her quickly. "But I had to be a perfect gentleman in front of all our friends. Now, I can afford to be bad," he told her softly in her ear.

After a few minutes of lovemaking to Mary, John pushed his right hand under her gown, and ran it up and down her smooth legs. Then after a while, Mary pulled his hand out.

"Bad boy," she said, slapping his hand several times.

"I'm sorry, hon. But you're so gorgeous that I couldn't help myself," he said politely.

"Thank you, John. You shouldn't be sorry at this point. I liked it, but we can't go around doing stuff like that as yet," she told him. "Please don't be annoyed with me, John," she added, then she kissed him.

"I can never be annoyed with you, hon," he told her.

"I think it's time for you to take me home, my hero. They'll be looking out for us to get back before midnight," she told him.

"Yes, ma'am," John said, then started up the engine of his truck, and pulled out of the school's parking lot.

John realized that his feeling for Mary had grown stronger throughout the years. When she was near to him, he wanted to hold her and crush her in his arms. He felt his love for her was getting out of control. He knew he had to make an effort to simmer down his feelings for her, otherwise he might lose her for good. He couldn't take any chances of that happening.

Ten minutes later, John pulled in front of Mary's residence, then he cut off the engine.

"Well, here we are, hon," he said, looking at her.

"The lights are still on in the house. I must go now," she said, then bent over and kissed John.

"Good night, hon. We'll talk soon," he said quickly.

"And thank you for a very enjoyable evening, John. I'll be thinking of you all night," she said teasingly.

"Me, too," he said, then he went out of the truck, and opened the door for Mary. He helped her out of the truck and kissed her good night. He gazed at her as she ran up the front stairs, then she turned back and waved goodbye to him. He waved back at her. Then he stood there on the sidewalk, and watched as the front door closed behind her.

"We'll be together soon. I love you, Mary Young. I want you badly. I can't help the way I feel. I love you too much," he whispered to himself.

*

John opened his eyes when he felt Nurse Hill's soft hand rubbing against his left hand.

"I'm sorry to get your attention this way, Mr. Stone, but there's a Detective Lang outside. He wants to know if you're strong enough to speak to him. I took the liberty of telling him you're not well enough," she told him.

"I'm not strong enough, but I may as well speak to him. Show him in!" John said.

Nurse Hill went out of the room and showed the detective into John's room, then she left the two men to converse. Detective Lang was tall, broad shoulders, and partly bald. He was smartly dressed in a dark suit.

"Mr. Stone, I'm Detective Lang from homicide division. I'm investigating the murder of your family. How are you feeling?" he said, looking over John's bed.

"I've had better days," John replied, smiling.

"Is it that bad?"

"Yes. Now to you, Detective Lang."

"I'd like you to tell me what really happened on Wednesday morning, the 3rd of November. Fill in the blanks that I don't already know," Detective Lang said, then got out his notebook and pen out of his jacket pocket. Then he was ready to take notes.

John related his story to Detective Lang, and he took it all down in his notebook, then he looked at John for a few seconds before asking him any more questions.

"You were knocked out at the bottom of the stairs by the burglar. You didn't know what had happened to your family when you became conscious. You didn't know if they were dead or alive," Detective Lang read from his notebook.

John shook his head. "I really don't know what happened to them. I feel bad about the whole situation. I should have been there to protect them, but instead I couldn't save them. It's my fault," John cried, not looking at Detective Lang.

Mr. Stone, each one of your family was shot and they all died from a gun shot wound."

"I believe it was my gun they were shot with."

"How do you know that?"

"The burglar took my gun when he hit me over the head. When the burglar came down the stairs with my gun, I was conscious. We struggled. He didn't have his ski-mask on. It was in his left hand, and the gun was in his right hand. I saw his face as we struggled, then the gun went off twice in my chest," John explained painfully. Then he closed his eyes.

"They're all gone," he said four times.

"Can you describe the burglar?"

"I can never forget that ugly face. His face was long, with a small scar of the right side of it. The man was tall, in his thirties, and he had long black hair. That's all I can remember. I hope you find him and put him away for a long time for what he has done to my family," John said slowly.

"We'll put out an all points bulletin on this burglar whom you described. We're holding the keys for your residence, so if anyone wants to get inside, they'll have to get in touch with me," Detective Lang said, and put his card on the small table beside John's bed.

"Thank you for coming, Detective Lang."

"Thank you, Mr. Stone. I may need to speak to you again at a later date when you're strong enough, then you can go through a mug shot book to see if you recognize that burglar," Detective Lang said and left.

John felt the surging pain all over his body. Detective Lang had brought back memories of his beloved family, who were lying in the morgue. He had no idea why his life had turned upside down.

Nurse Hill came into the room and stood over John. He knew she was there and he opened his eyes, and looked up at her. He had a sad expression on his face.

"I came in to see how you're coping. I saw Detective Lang leaving," she said, looking down at him.

"Not very good. Detective Lang was asking me questions about what happened that morning. It all came back to me," he said, and shook his head in disgust.

"It will be question after question, and you wouldn't have a chance to rest," she said softly.

"I guess it's his job to ask me questions."

"But you're not well enough to answer all those questions. The questions will only upset you. You'll have to get your rest, so you can get well," she said, and left the room.

John's thoughts kept spinning from side to side. He didn't know how he was going to face his in-laws, the Youngs. He realized that they would be devastated when they found out what had happened to their daughter and grandchildren. He felt fully responsible for his family's demise. He couldn't save them from the bad man who had broken into their home.

Nurse Hill came into the room with a tray, and on it was a special diet for John. John came back to his natural self when she came into the room. He looked up at her and wanted to forget all the bad things that kept spinning in his head.

"How are you feeling now? Now, you must try to eat something, and get some rest," she said, smiling.

"If my wounds don't kill me, the strain will. I now have to face my in-laws," John said softly.

"I forgot to tell you that the Youngs left a message that they are on their way."

"I'm afraid they'll blame me for this," he said nervously.

"Well, Mr. Stone, you'll have to take one step at a time. Now, take your broth, so you can get your strength back," she said and placed the tray at his bedside.

"You're so good to me, Nurse Hill. I don't know what I'll do without you," he said, looking at her steadily.

"You make me sound like someone special, and that's nice," she said, smiling.

"Anything else that I need to know?" John asked.

"Oh, yes, your next-door neighbor, Mr. Roberts, called to see how you are. He was the one who found you outside, and saved your life," she said, shaking her head.

"I was lucky he found me when he did. I have to thank him when I'm well again," John said, as he swallowed his diet.

*

Later that evening, John opened his eyes, and the two figures beside his bed became clearer. Mr. and Mrs. Young were sitting down at his bedside. Mrs. Young was short and slim. She wore a long blue dress. Mr. Young was tall and slim, and he wore a brown suit. They were both in their late forties. John saw the tears coming down Mrs. Young cheeks. He just gazed at her and he didn't know what to say. They both looked tired and sad. He realized that the grief had hit them hard where it really hurt.

"We didn't want to wake you, John," Mr. Young said, shaking his head.

"John, my baby is gone, and all my grandchildren. Why did this have to happen to them?" Mrs. Young cried.

John focused his attention on Mrs. Young. "I've asked myself that question many times, and I was unable to get the right answer," John said slowly.

"How in the name of heaven did this happen to them?" Mr. Young asked sternly.

John shook his head. "I didn't know how I'd face you both after all of this. I feel partly to blame," John said, then he told them the story about the burglar.

"But you're not to blame," Mr. Young said.

"But it was my gun that killed them and I feel responsible. I couldn't save them. I would have been better off if I were with them," John said sadly.

"You had the gun for your protection," Mr. Young said.

"Some protection!" John said.

"At first, I blamed you for my baby's death, but seeing you suffer like this in this bed, I can't really blame you, John," Mrs. Young cried, then wiped her face with a tissue.

"I hope the police arrest this brute who did this to our children," Mr. Young said.

"I don't know for sure, Mr. Young, but I feel the brute is long gone, and the police will be unable to find him. But I'll know that ugly face anywhere," John said, looking at Mr. Young.

"You're lucky to be alive, John," Mr. Young said.

"Yes, I'm lucky. I have my next-door neighbor to thank for me being here. He called 911 for me."

"Now, we'll have to figure out what to do," Mr. Young said.

"I'm too weak to even think, so both of you will have to help me to make the funeral arrangements," John explained.

"John, don't worry. We'll stay for a while, and we'll make all the necessary arrangements," Mrs. Young said.

"I'm sorry, but this is going to be a very emotional task on your part. But in my state I need all the help I can get," John said.

"It's a task we have to face whether we like it or not. Mary is our baby, and the children are our grandchildren," Mr. Young hinted.

"I loved my family and now they're all gone. I can't face myself, and I don't think I can live with myself now. It's too much for me to even think about all that's happened," John cried, not looking at his in-laws.

"We'll let you rest now, John. We'll be staying at the City's Hotel. Alice will be coming down tomorrow, so she can attend the funeral. We'll be in touch," Mr. Young said.

"You take care, John," Mrs. Young said, then they left. When they were out of the room, John closed his eyes, and tried his best to go to sleep. He couldn't bear to face his heavy burden.

*

The following day, Pastor Boyd from the First Baptist Church came to see him. He sat at John's bedside. He was a tall, stout, black man, in his fifties. He wore a black suit and black tie, and he was partly bald in the middle of his head.

"Brother John, I came as soon as I heard what happened. I'm really sorry for the loss of your family, so sorry," Pastor Boyd said slowly in a coarse voice.

"Thank you for coming, Pastor Boyd. I really need your spiritual help and guidance at this very moment. My life is no more to be," John said slowly.

"It was last night one of the brothers called me and told me about your tragedy. I'll do everything in my power to help and comfort you from your deep hurt, Brother John," Pastor Boyd said. "Now, let's pray. May the Lord give Brother John strength and courage to face his great loss, the loss of his beloved ones. And may his loved ones be always in his memory. Amen."

John felt the tears running down his cheeks, then he shook his head. "I should have died with them, also, then I'd be together with my family," John cried.

"Brother John, you have to be strong, and face this tragedy like a man. You have to live for your family. They would have wanted you to live for their sake. There's no other way you can face it. I'll pray for you. What can I do to help in your time of need, Brother John?"

"My in-laws, Mr. and Mrs. Young are staying at the City's Hotel. It would be nice for you to visit them, and help them to make the arrangements for my family to be buried in the Philadelphia Cemetery. Please help me, Pastor Boyd. You married us, you baptized us, and now you have to do your solemn duty to bury them," John said sadly.

"I'll do my best to help you, Brother John."

"Pray for me. I feel like my soul is lost and never to be regained."

"Don't say that, Brother John. God will help you to regain whatever you feel you have lost. Bless you, Brother John!"

"Thank you for coming, Pastor Boyd."

"We'll be in touch, Brother John," Pastor Boyd said, then left.

*

Four days later, a bright and sunny November morning. It was the day that John mostly dreaded. It was the funeral of his beloved family. He was still in his hospital room. Nurse Hill helped him to get dressed in his black suit, black tie, white shirt, and black shoes, which she had picked up from his home the day before. She wore a black dress, a white overcoat, white stockings and white shoes. She was accompanying John to the funeral. He was still weak and had to be pushed in a wheelchair.

Nurse Hill sat next to John in the chauffeur-driven limousine which followed the three hearses from the funeral home. His in-laws, the Youngs, followed behind. The tears trickled down his cheeks.

"How could this have happened to me? I'm alive and they're no more," John cried, looking at Nurse Hill. He felt close to her for the first time. He knew she had become his friend, and the time was now right for them to be on a first name basis.

"John, please don't make this harder on yourself. We'll get through this together," she said, and held his hand. "I promise you," she added.

"I can't help the way I feel, Karen. I'm glad you're my friend, especially at a time like this," he said, edging closer to Nurse Hill for some comfort. Then he smiled slightly at her.

"Karen, I didn't realize that I called you by your Christian name for the first time. You're so good to me. I can never repay you for all that you've done in my time of need," he said, sobbing on her shoulder.

"John, I'm glad to be here for you. I'm not speaking as your nurse, but as your true friend," she said, putting her arms around him in his time of sorrow.

The limousine slowly pulled into the Midway Cemetery. It was a large 2000 acres of burial site. The tombs and the graves were neatly kept in the cemetery. All the vehicles were parked on the road inside the cemetery. John waited inside his limousine until everyone else got out of their vehicles and the caskets were displayed alongside the three graves. Nurse Hill got out of the limousine, and got the wheelchair from the back of the vehicle. Then she helped John into it, and pushed him to his place at the gravesides. Then she stood behind him. John looked around and saw some members of the First Baptist Church. Mr. and Mrs. Young and their daughter, Alice stood on the left-hand side of John. Pastor Boyd stood on the right-hand side of John. John glanced at Alice, who was now a teen, and whom he had not seen for many years. She was sobbing. Then he looked at Pastor Boyd, and signaled to him to go ahead with the eulogy.

"Brother John and Sister Mary became members in my church in 1976. Shortly after that, I married them. When their children were born, I baptized them. Then this dreadful thing happened to them and they were swept away into heaven in their prime time of life. They'll be missed by all their relatives and good friends who loved them," Pastor Boyd said. Then he looked at John for a few seconds, and he shook his head twice.

"Thank you, Pastor Boyd, for your very nice final words, sending my beloved family on their journey of no return. I also want to say my final goodbyes to them, but before I do, I'd like to hum Mary's favorite song, *Danny Boy*. She had a sweet voice when she sang this song to David and Cindy at bedtime," John said. Then he started to hum the song, and to his surprise, the Youngs joined in with him. They hummed on for a few minutes, then they stopped.

"That was specially for all of you, Mary, David and Cindy. Mary, I'll always love you wherever you are. David we played ball in the back yard; you are the son that I love and will never forget. Cindy you are the daughter that any father would have loved to hug, and that's how I'll always remember all of you. You are the greatest family any husband could have had. I love all of you wherever you are. Good-bye my family, goodbye," John said with the tears running down his cheeks. Then he gave the order for the caskets to be lowered into their respective graves. When that was done, he was given some earth by a grave digger. John held the earth tightly in his left hand, then he threw some earth with his right hand on each casket.

"Dust to dust, earth to earth; may God bless each soul forever," Pastor Boyd said loudly.

"Bless their souls. Good-bye my family," John whispered to himself, then he bowed his head for a few seconds, and said a small prayer for his beloved family, whom he knew he would never see again. He'd only be able to see them in his imagination. And without his family, he felt completely empty inside. His whole world of excitement would cease. He didn't know how he was going to survive in an empty world of his.

Pastor Boyd went over to the Youngs and gave them his condolences, then he offered his condolences to Brother John, then he left the cemetery.

Mr. and Mrs. Young and their daughter Alice went over to John, who was still looking dazed in his wheelchair.

"We'll be going back today to Moorestown, John," Mr. Young told him. Then Alice and her mother bent over and kissed John on the cheek. "John, take care and if you need anything, let us know," Mrs. Young told him.

"Good-bye. We'll be in touch," he told them sadly.

John sat in his wheelchair for a few more minutes. He just wanted to think. "Good-bye, my family. We'll meet again some day," he said sadly to himself. Then Karen went in front of him and looked at him sadly. "Do you wish to leave now, John?" she asked softly. John looked at her with tears in his eyes, and shook his head up and down.

Chapter Three

John Stone was taken back to his hospital room after the funeral. Nurse Hill helped him to change his clothes and got him back into bed. He just lay in his bed; he wanted to be alone. He had just buried his family and didn't have an appetite. His eyes were clouded with grief and he felt empty inside. No words could describe the way he felt. The grief had left him numb and cold all over his body. With all the grief he felt, his earnest wish was to die at that very moment.

Then Nurse Hill brought him something to eat.

"I don't want to eat," he told her sternly.

"You have to get your strength up, John; you can't let yourself go to the dogs," she told him as a friend.

"It's like a bad dream, the worst day of my life," he said slowly, choking from his tears.

Nurse Hill sat down with the tray, and started to feed him, and for some strange reason he didn't object. He just swallowed whatever she put in his mouth. She had a way with him that he couldn't resist. She was the shoulder that he leaned on, and it was like everything she said to him he had to obey. When she felt he had enough to eat, she got up with the tray, and smiled at him.

You'll be okay, John; you need your rest," she said.

"You're a great help to me. You make it so easy for me to cope with my problems; you care. Thank you," John said, then closed his eyes. He wanted to just lay there and think of the past.

"I'll be here if you need me, John," she said, and left the room.

*

It was Thursday, the first week of August 1976. John and Mary sat close to each other on the bus to Philadelphia. John wore a shirt and jeans. Mary wore a blouse and jeans. They had taken a small amount of clothing, which was in the baggage compartment of the bus.

"John, we've done it," Mary said, holding John's hand tightly.

"Yes, hon, we're now together, and no one is going to keep us apart. I love you and that's all about it. My mother drove me to the bus stop with the truck, then she gave me some money. She told me she loved me, and if things didn't work out, I should come back home," John told Mary slowly.

"I told Alice, my sister, that I was leaving and she wished me all the best. My parents were out at work, and I left them a short note on the kitchen table for them to read when they got home. 'Dear Mom and Dad, I'm leaving with John to make a new start in Philadelphia. We love each other. Please don't worry about me, I'll be all right. John will take care of me. I trust him with my life. I love you both. Please forgive me for running away like this. Love, Mary.'"

"What did your sister, Alice, say when you told her you were leaving?" John asked.

"She said she realized that some day we would have had to part. I'll miss her, but now I have you, and I love you," Mary said cheerfully.

"I love you too, hon, and I'll take good care of you," John said, still holding her hand tightly.

"This is really a trip we'll never forget," Mary said.

"We have a few hours before we reach our destination, so we'll just pretend we're on a day trip to some nice place. We can relax and think about all the good things we're leaving behind; our family and our good friends," John said softly.

"Don't remind me, John, but that's a good idea. I'll close my eyes and think," Mary said, and lay her head against his shoulder.

The bus was nearly filled up, and only two seats were vacant. There were some mothers and children on board and some older folks who were going on a day trip. John felt sad when the bus passed through the town and onto the main highway. He stared at the passing farms, pastures and large houses which were just outside the highway.

John's eyes felt tired, and he closed them, and his thoughts kept spinning in his brain. He remembered when he was eight years old; his father used to take him horseback riding. They'd go to their favorite spot on the farm. John was always the talkative one. He'd ask his father question after question, and his father would try to give him the correct answers to his questions, but answers only John would understand as a child. His father would show him the farm as far as he could see.

*

"All this will be yours some day, son. You'll be master of this farm," his father would say to him every time they went to that spot on the northern side of the farm.

"What's a master, Dad?" John asked.

"Well, son, a master is a person like me, who owns land and property. If I were going to rent out this land and farmhouse to someone else, I'd be called a landlord," his father explained.

"Landlord, that sounds nice, Dad, but I'd rather to be the master of this farm some day," John said, looking at his father cheerfully.

"That's my boy, my favorite son," his father said, smiling.

"Isn't Harold your favorite son too, Dad?"

"Harold, Rose and you, you are all my favorites."

"You don't want to admit it, Dad, but I'm your favorite son," John said, holding his father's hand.

"You're too smart for me, son. You're just like me. That's why you're my favorite," his father confessed, smiling.

"I was right all along, Dad. You were trying to pull one over on me," John told him.

*

John couldn't believe that he was heading on a bus with Mary to a strange place that he'd never been to. He kept his eyes closed, and he tried to remember some of the pieces he was leaving behind. Mary's parents had moved from Littlerock to Moorestown four years ago. John met Mary Young for the first time at the Moorestown School. He was shy at first and he'd just smile at her, then one day they just hit it off. John told her all about his family and his life on the farm. Then he'd listen to her carefully as she told him about her childhood days, and the time spent with her younger sister, Alice. John knew that it was love at first sight, and he'd have to keep his feelings to himself until the right moment arrived.

John opened his eyes and looked at Mary, who was awake.

"Did you have a nice dream?" she asked.

"It was more than a dream. It was real. It was the first time when we met. Then I invited you to the farm, and we kissed for the first time. Then after that you invited me to your home. I showed your parents that I wasn't a farm boy," John explained to her.

"And you really showed them you were intelligent and friendly. You were my sort of guy, and I was really proud of you that evening," she told him.

The bus arrived in the City of Philadelphia at 4.30 that afternoon. John's eyes were peering over the outside scenery. He felt like a new person in a new magical place where he'd start a new life, and bring to life a new family. He noticed the buildings were large, and the people were dressed differently to the people in Moorestown. When the bus pulled into the bus station, they got off it, and collected their belongings from the baggage compartment. Then they headed down Main Street. They had no idea where they were going or where they were going to stay. They were strangers in a new world, and they knew no one in this new world of theirs.

"We'll have to find somewhere to eat, hon," John told Mary, as they walked slowly along the sidewalk.

"Yes, I'm starving," Mary said, looking at all the buildings as they passed. Then after walking a few more blocks, they came upon Paul's Cafe on Main Street. The area consisted of several restaurants and fast food joints. They looked through the front window before entering the building, and saw only two customers sitting at two tables. John pushed the glass door open, then they entered the building, and headed for a corner table. The inside of the building was small, with ten tables scattered around the room, and at the back of the room there were four built in counter stools for customers to sit on.

John threw his bags at the corner of the table. Mary took a seat at the table. John went to the counter to order whatever was available on the menu.

"Hi, I'm Paul, the manager, and welcome to Philadelphia."

"Hi. How did you know that we're new customers?" John asked.

"Well, I know all my customers that come in here. I have never seen you before, and I see you have some baggage at your table."

"You're very observant, Paul. I'm John, and that's my fiancée, Mary. Now you know us," John said, smiling.

"What would you like to order, John?"

"Anything you can whip up for us quickly."

"Fries, burgers and coffee?"

"That would be fine, Paul."

"My assistant is out. She's having a baby."

"A baby?" John asked. Then he went back and sat with Mary.

"It seems that Mr. Paul, the owner needs some help."

"He does?"

"Yes. His helper is out. She's having a baby. You know what that means?" John asked, making faces at Mary.

"Well, I'm available for any work," Mary said, smiling.

"We'll have to make friends with Paul, and maybe he'll be able to give us some information where to find a place to stay. We need some digs," John said.

"Good idea, John," Mary said. "And here he comes," Mary added, and forced a smile.

"Hi, Paul, I'm Mary."

"Nice to meet you, Mary," Paul said and placed their order on the table. "Sorry to keep you waiting," Paul said, looking at Mary.

"John said that you may need some help. I used to work part-time in the local cafe in Moorestown," Mary told Paul.

Paul sat down with his new customers while they ate their burger and fries. "Yes, I do need some help, but I can only pay minimum wage," he told Mary.

"Well, I just need a job. I'll work hard for you," she pleaded.

"So where are you folks staying?"

"As you know we're new here, and we don't know anyone. Maybe you would know where we can find a place to stay," John said.

"Let me think. Mrs. Big is a regular customer in here. She told me just last week there was a small suite for rent in her apartment. She's just a tenant, not the owner. She lives in the Blackwater Apartments, the second floor, suite 11," Paul told them.

"How do we get there?" John asked as he ate his burger.

"You can take the local bus outside here, then you get off two miles up Main Street when you come to Wall Street. Cross the road to your left, then two blocks on Wall Street; you'll come to the Blackwater Apartments," Paul explained.

"Thank you, Paul," Mary said, smiling.

Paul turned to John. "And you can apply at Eagle Lumber for a job. It's close to the apartment. They are always searching for new workers."

"Thank you, Paul. You've been a great help," John said.

"Well, good luck," Paul said, then he went to serve another customer, who was at the counter.

John and Mary finished their meal and drank their coffee. Then John went to pay for their meal. He thanked Paul for his hospitality.

Then they took the number two bus up Main Street, and got off at Wall Street. They hurried over the road, and walked slowly down Wall Street. Then John saw the sign which said, 'Straight on for Blackwater Apartments.'

"We're on the right track, hon," John told Mary, then he took her bag in his left hand. He knew she was tired. They came upon the Blackwater Apartments four blocks away. They made their way onto the sidewalk of the main building. The surrounding areas consisted of several large apartment buildings, houses, small business and factories. John realized that area was a working class neighborhood. He looked up at the old apartment building from the outside, and it stood up like a monster on five acres of land. The car park was on the northern side of the building, and only one truck was parked there. The paint in front of the building was peeling; it needed some major work to bring it back to life. John realized the building was run down.

They slowly went up the stairs to the second floor to suite 11, which was the first suite on that floor. John dropped his bags at the side of the passage way, then he knocked on the suite door several times. He waited and there was no answer.

"Maybe Mrs. Big is out," Mary said.

"Well, we'll wait on the stairs," John told her.

"We'll sit here and wait. We have no place to go and lots of time," she said and forced a smile.

Several minutes later, the door next to suite 11 popped open, and an elderly woman came to John and Mary. She looked at them for a few seconds, then she smiled.

"Are you waiting for someone?" she asked.

"We came to see Mrs. Big," Mary told her politely.

"Mrs. Big went out shopping. She'll be back within the next hour. Was she expecting you?" the resident asked calmly, looking at John, then at Mary.

"No. We're from out of town. We were told that there is a vacant suite here in the apartment. We really need a place to stay," Mary pleaded with the resident.

"There's a vacant suite here, but the owner, Mr. Ward, likes to rent to elderly people like myself," she told Mary, looking at her.

"We're tired, hungry and we have very little money in our pockets," Mary told her sadly.

"You poor dears. Why don't you come into my suite and wait for Mrs. Big. Then maybe we can think of something for both of you," she told them, shaking her head.

"Thank you," Mary said.

"Emily is my name," the resident told them.

"I'm Mary and this is John, my fiancé."

"It's a pleasure meeting you, Miss Emily," John said, smiling. John knew he had to put his charm on Emily.

"Bring your baggage in and make yourself comfortable," Emily said, then led them into a small living room. The room was lit by a table lamp. There were a large and a small sofa in the room and two small chairs, a small coffee table with a lamp, a large ready made carpet on the floor, and only two large pictures on the northern side of the wall.

"Have a seat. I'll make you some tea and sandwiches," Emily said, then went off to the kitchen.

Shortly afterwards, Mary went after Emily who was in the kitchen. Emily was an elderly lady in her late sixties. She was tall, slim and lived by herself.

"Can I help you, Miss Emily?" Mary asked politely.

"Well, you can cut the bread in slices. And you'll find some cooked ham in the fridge. Where did you say you came from?" Emily asked as she put the kettle on the stove.

"Moorestown, Pennsylvania, ma'am."

"What are you going to do here?" Emily asked.

"Well, this is a big city. We want to find work and settle down here. Maybe raise a family," Mary said, smiling.

"This is a nice place to live. I'm sure you'll do well here," Emily said, looking at Mary.

"I hope so. Our lives depend on it," Mary told her.

"You're a very pretty young lady."

"Thank you, ma'am."

"What did your parents say when you told them you were leaving?"

"Well, to tell you the truth, I didn't tell them I was leaving. I'm eighteen now; I can do as I please."

"Good for you, Mary. Take a stand," Emily said.

John and Mary left thirty minutes later when Mrs. Big arrived in her suite. They thanked Emily for her hospitality. John knocked on the suite door. Then, a few seconds later, an elderly woman appeared in the doorway. She looked the young couple up and down for a few seconds. She was stout, tall woman in her late sixties and she lived alone.

"Mrs. Big?" John asked, looking at her.

"Yes. Can I help you?" she asked.

"Yes, Mrs. Big. I'm John and this is my fiancée, Mary. We were sent to you by Paul, the owner of the cafe on Main Street. He said you may have a suite for us to rent," John said politely.

"Why don't you come in and we can talk about this inside," she said, then led them into her living room.

"We were at Miss Emily's waiting for you. She was good enough to offer us snacks while we were waiting," Mary said.

"She's a good person and my good friend," Mrs. Big said. Then she gazed at John in the light for a few seconds.

"Is there anything wrong, Mrs. Big?" John asked.

"What's your last name?" she asked eagerly.

"Stone, ma'am."

"I thought so. You remind me of someone I once knew. Does Charles Stone mean anything to you?" she asked quickly.

"Charles is my uncle, but we haven't seen or heard from him in years," John told her.

"Your uncle was a member of my church. He didn't like the farm, so he came here to start a new life. He got married to a member of the church. They had two children, a girl and a boy. His wife got sick, then she passed away. Charles couldn't bear to live here any more, so he moved to New York City. I never heard from him again," Mrs. Big explained. "He was such a nice man," she added.

"So you knew my uncle? I never knew him. He went away before I was born," John told her.

"So you've followed in your uncle's footsteps, and left the farm also," she said, smiling.

"Yes, ma'am! I want a better life for myself and my family. Mary and I are very much in love. We want to get married as soon as possible. We want to make our home here in Philadelphia," John explained excitedly.

Mrs. Big gazed at the couple for a while, then she shook her head. Her face lit up and she clasped her hands.

"Is anything wrong, Mrs. Big?" John asked.

"Nothing is wrong. It's just the opposite. It's my lucky day. Someone told me I was going to receive some young relatives, but I never knew it was going to come true," she told them with a smile.

"But we're not your relatives, Mrs. Big," John said.

"We may not be relatives now, but I'm quite sure later on we'll become relatives," Mrs. Big said lively.

John smiled at Mrs. Big's little joke. He didn't understand what she meant. He felt she knew more than she was telling them, but he didn't press for any answers.

"So you guys really need a place to stay?" she asked.

"We certainly do, Mrs. Big," Mary said.

"Mr. Ward, the owner, was supposed to send someone over to do the repairs in suite 13, but he hasn't. That's the vacant suite. He likes to rent the suites out to elderly people, but that's about to change. It's about time we got young blood in this apartment," Mrs. Big said sternly.

"So you really want us to have this suite?" Mary asked.

"Yes. I want to help both of you, but you'll have to help yourselves also."

"We're prepared to do anything to help, ma'am," John told her.

"That's the spirit. I'll get the keys and show you the suite, but you won't like what you see," she said and led them to suite 13. She opened the door, and turned on the lights. John and Mary went through the passageway, and into connecting doorways, leading to each room, living room, bedroom, kitchen and bathroom.

"Take a good look, kids," Mrs. Big shouted after them. Then she stood by the entrance door to wait for them.

They slowly inspected the suite. They came upon the kitchen area, the stove was old and dirty with grease. They opened the fridge and it was filled with mildew, and a stinky odor came from it. Mary put her left hand over her nose, then quickly closed the door with her right hand.

"What a terrible smell," she told John.

They went over to the kitchen cupboard, then she slowly opened the door of the cupboard half way, and a large black roach crawled out of the cupboard, and it fell to the kitchen floor.

Mary went into a panic when it dropped by her feet. She quickly went into John's arms. He held her tightly in his arms.

"There now, hon, you're not afraid of a little roach," John said, trying to calm her down. Then she looked up at him and smiled.

"Let's move on, hon," he told her.

They went to the bedroom area which consisted of an old bed, a small dresser, and a small table in the corner of the room. The living room consisted of a couch, a coffee table. The kitchen consisted of a fridge, a stove, a small table and two chairs. The small bathroom, which was at the side of the kitchen, consisted of an old-fashioned four leg bathtub, and an old-fashioned toilet, and there was no wash basin.

John noticed the paint on the ceiling and walls were peeling, and there were cracks all over the suite. The rug on the floor needed cleaning, and the linoleum in the kitchen had holes. The suite smelled of a rank odor. John and Mary hurried to the door way where Mrs. Big was standing.

"How did you like your self tour of the suite?" Mrs. Big asked.

"This place is like a place from another time. I can't believe that poor people have to live in places like this," Mary told Mrs. Big.

"Don't take Mary seriously, she has a vivid imagination. I can fix this place up just like new," John told Mrs. Big.

"I'm glad that someone knows what he's doing. We really need a man like you around here, John. Please be that man, and make this suite your home," Mrs. Big said, smiling.

"Well, Mrs. Big, we have no choice because beggars can't be choosers," John told her as they headed back to her suite.

"You're so right. Now that we have that all sorted out, I'll get you guys some supper," Mrs. Big said and closed the door.

"Mrs. Big, why are you so good to us? You hardly know us," Mary said as they walked into Mrs. Big's suite.

"It's just the way I feel. I feel the good one above has sent you two young people to me for a reason, then it's my duty to guide you both into the right direction. I must let you into my little secret, I feel as though I have know both of you for a long time. I really can't explain the way I feel. I feel both of you are going to be here with me for a long time," Mrs. Big tried to explain, looking at John and Mary. Then both John and Mary went over to Mrs. Big, and gave her a friendly hug.

"Thank you," she said, trying her best to hold back the tears from her eyes. Then she took her newly acquired friends to the kitchen and seated them around the kitchen table. Then she went to work and whipped some supper for her two acquired children.

"You guys better eat my supper, so you can get your strength up. It's now nearly nine o'clock and we'll have to do some cleaning in your suite, if you're going to stay there for the night," Mrs. Big told them.

John turned to Mary and smiled as he ate his supper.

"Why are you smiling at me?" Mary asked.

"I'm just thinking of you trying to clean that apartment and you're afraid of a little roach," he told her, still smiling.

"You can laugh all you want, John, but I'm not going to let a little roach scare me again," she said quickly, and tapped him on the shoulder.

"We'll see. I'll be at your side just in case you need me, hon," he teased.

"I like that. You kids really make me feel like a real Mom," Mrs. Big told them with a little giggle.

"Well, Mrs. Big, from the way you're treating us, we'll let you be our adopted Mom. How's that?" John said, looking at her.

"That's fine with me, kids," Mrs. Big replied, smiling.

Chapter Four

Four days later, John was discharged from St. Mary's Hospital. He went to recuperate at his home on 45 Blexley Avenue. His first day there was the worst. He kept seeing himself being shot at the bottom of the stairs, and the burglar's face kept appearing in his memory. He felt sad and weak and he couldn't think straight. He felt the house was closing in on him, and the rooms were becoming smaller by the minute. He couldn't understand why.

He sat in his favorite chair in the living room that was on the first floor. He knew that Nurse Hill would come after work to see him that same evening. They'd become good friends and he trusted her. He knew she was really helping him to get back on his feet, and also helping him to regain his mental attitude. He didn't need her love, but only her shoulder to lean on until he was able to stand on his own two feet. He centered his mind on some of the good things that had happened to him in the past.

*

Mary and Mrs. Big were doing the cleaning in suite 13, at the Blackwater Apartments that first night. Then, John had a sudden urge to call his mother on the phone. He asked to be excused, and went to the ground floor where there was a public telephone. He pushed his left hand into his pants pocket, and pulled out some coins. "I hope I have enough coins," he whispered to himself. Then he slowly inserted the coins into the slot of the public telephone, and dialed the number slowly to the farm; he waited for the telephone on the other side to ring, and it was picked up after the second ring.

"Hello, Sofie Stone speaking."

"Mom, this is John. I just wanted you to know that Mary and I have arrived safely in Philadelphia. We met this nice lady. Her name is Mrs. Big. She's helping us with a place to stay. She told me she knew Uncle Charles. They were friends from the same church. Everything is working out just fine for us, Mom," he told her eagerly.

"I'm glad you found a place to stay, and a friend to assist you, John. I'll be praying for you every night. I love you and I miss you. I wish you were here, but you have your own life to live now," she told him quickly.

"Mom, from what Mrs. Big told us, I suspect she knew Uncle Charles more than she was willing to tell us."

"Well, listen carefully to what I have to say. There was a rumor going around years ago that Uncle Charles had an affair with a young woman in Philadelphia, and she had a baby girl from him. She didn't have the means to take care of the child, so when Uncle Charles got married to someone else, she gave him the baby girl to raise. Then his wife had a baby boy. The woman's first name was Sandra, and I don't know her last name. So if Mrs. Big's first name is Sandra, she'd be that woman," his mother explained.

"Thanks, Mom. I'll check it out. I love you, and give my regards to Dad, and the rest of the family."

"Before I forget, Mary's mother called me. She wants to know where you and Mary went to. I told her if you call, I'll let you call her. Take care of yourself, John, and call me soon again," she said and hung up.

John pulled out all the coins he had in his pocket and counted them, then he knew he had enough change to make another call. He inserted some of the coins and dialed the Youngs' number, then the phone on the other side rang once, and it was picked up. "Mary, is that you?" Mrs. Young asked quickly.

"Hello, Mrs. Young. This is John. My mother told me you called, and you were worried about Mary."

"Where's Mary?" she asked sternly.

"She's with Mrs. Big, our friend here at the apartment. Please don't worry Mrs. Young. Mary will be calling you soon. She doesn't know that I'm calling you."

"Where did you all go to?"

"We're in Philadelphia, and I don't want you to come looking for Mary. She's eighteen and she knows her own mind."

"I know that, John. I know you love her, and you'd be taking care of her, but you'll have to understand that she's my little baby," Mrs. Young cried.

"I understand Mrs. Young, but you'll have to realize that she can't always be your little baby. It's time for you to let go, and let her live her own life."

"John, I'm pleading with you! Please take good care of my baby! Give her my love, and I hope she calls me soon," Mrs. Young said nervously.

"And you give my regards to Mr. Young and Alice. When we're settled, you'll have to visit us."

"If you need anything, John, let us know."

"We're all right for now, Mrs. Young. We'll be in touch soon," John said and hung up.

John went back to Mrs. Big's suite and found Mary and Mrs. Big drinking tea.

"You're just in time for tea, John. We did all the cleaning while you were away," Mrs. Big told him. John sat down next to Mary, and she poured him a cup of tea.

"Well, what happened?" Mary asked.

"I phoned my mom and told her we arrived here safely. We found a nice place to stay, and we also found a nice friend, Mrs. Big."

"Why thank you, John," Mrs. Big said.

"And what else, John?" Mary asked with her eyes wide open. John hesitated, and gazed at her steadily.

"Well, did you call my mom?" she asked.

"Yes."

"I thought so. So?"

"When I called my mom, she told me your mother had called her. So I called your mom. I told her we arrived here safely. I told her you'd call her soon. She sends her love," John told her.

"Thank you for calling my mother, John. I didn't have the courage to call her myself, but I'll make it my point of duty to call her tomorrow," Mary said sadly.

Mrs. Big turned to John and Mary. "Well, you kids must be tired. It's past midnight. I'll get you some bedding for your bed. I'm up at seven in the morning, so you're welcome to come for breakfast," she told them.

Mary got up and gave Mrs. Big a hug. "Thank you Mrs. Big. Thank you for all the help. You're just like my Mom," Mary told her with a smile.

"Thank you, child."

They took all their stuff to suite 13. Mrs. Big followed with the bedding, and she threw it onto the bed.

"Well, you kids have fun, and I'll see you in the morning. I must get to bed. It's past my bed time," Mrs. Big said and left the suite.

Mary looked at John, and started to make up the bed.

"Just don't stand there, John, help me, so we can get to bed," she said jokingly.

"Well, that's what a husband is for, to help his wife," John said, smiling.

"Husband?" Mary asked.

"Not legal, but to be. If you know what I mean, hon?"

"I know what you mean, hon. You're not going to get away with it, hon. You see I'm onto you, hon," Mary told him quickly.

John went quickly over to Mary and kissed her. "That's for seeing through me, hon," he said.

"I know why you're trying to be nice to me, but it's not going to happen," she told him.

"You can't blame a guy for trying," he said, smiling.

"Yes, in your dreams, John," she said with a smile.

Mary finished making up the bed, then she went into the bathroom, and got changed into a short, blue negligee. Then she went into bed, and got underneath the sheets. She didn't move for a few seconds, and when she did turn onto her side, the bed spring on her side went down. John was changing into his pajamas, and saw what happened. He started to laugh at the whole incident.

"What's so funny?" Mary said without looking at him. "Come on and help me out of here," she pleaded with him. John went quickly to her assistance. He helped her out of the bed. Then he bent under the bed. "It's just two springs came loose," he told her, and inserted them back into their rightful holes on the bed frame. He raised up and faced Mary. "Now my fair lady? The bed is now fixed."

"Fixed!" she said vexedly. "I left my nice and comfortable bed at home to end up in this dump," she added. John realized that Mary was upset. He went over to her and took her into his arms.

"Hon, I'm sorry that we have to start off like this, but we'll have better days to come, so smile for me," he told her softly.

"I'm sorry, John. I'm just tired," she said and got into bed. John turned off the lights and got into bed with Mary.

"John, we have made it this far, and we're now together. I know you may get mad at me for what I am about to say. I'm going to put this spare pillow between us," Mary told him.

"What do you want to do that for?" John asked.

"To answer your question, I'm a young woman, and I haven't been touched by any man before, so I want to keep it that way until we're married. In the meanwhile, you'll have to control yourself. Maybe take some cold showers daily," Mary told him sternly.

"Now we're together, hon, are you giving me the brush off?" John said jokingly.

"No, John, we're together for keeps, but I don't want you to take advantage of me at this early stage."

"I understand, hon. Don't worry your little head. I'll be a perfect gentleman to you. Say no more," he declared.

"While we're on the subject, I'd like to know something about you," Mary said.

"I thought you knew everything about me. What would you like to know?" he asked.

"Something personal," she answered.

"How personal?"

"Are you horny?" she asked shyly.

John started laughing at Mary's question.

"What's so funny?" she asked.

"Now that you ask, I never really thought about it."

"Do you get wet dreams?" she asked.

"Yes, sometimes."

"And I suppose you get these wet dreams because of me."

"How do you know that, hon?"

"I know a little about human nature," she told him.

"We're on the right track, hon."

"I have to ask you a pertinent question while we're on the subject," Mary said.

"What's it this time, hon?"

"Well, how big is it?" she asked.

"How big is what?"

"You know?"

"Oh, that. It's about twelve inches," John told her.

"*That* big? I don't think I'll get married to you, John. You'll kill me with your twelve inches of flesh," she explained.

"Just kidding, hon. It's only six inches."

"That's more like it, John. Don't you kid about a thing like that. So if you got a chance on me, how many times would you be able to do it?" she asked.

"I really don't know, hon. I never tested it out on anyone before. You're going to be my first. I may be able to do it once or twice. We don't want to overdo it," John explained.

"Well, you'll have your chance very soon, and only then we'll know the answer to that," Mary said.

"And when is that, hon?" he asked.

"That will be when we're married. Then you'll be able to poke me as often as you like. You may even die on the job if you become dedicated to a life of sex," she said jokingly.

"Don't say that, hon. I'm going to live for just that. Now that I told you about myself, I feel that it's your turn to tell me some of your dark secrets, hon."

"This is embarrassing. But what do you wish to know?" she asked.

"Well, did you ever have any wet dreams?" John asked.

"I had one recently, and it was my first. I was in bed, and you came from nowhere. I felt you on top of me, and you were poking me between the legs. You were giving me such a heavenly feeling that I suddenly came to a climax. I opened my eyes and called out your name. But you were just in my imagination. I couldn't believe what had happened. I felt between my legs, and my panties were all wet and only then I knew I had a wet dream," Mary explained slowly.

"All this talk about sex is turning me on, hon," John told her eagerly.

"Well, John, all you get for being a good boy is a good-night kiss, so brace your tender lips for it."

"Yes ma'am," John said, and bent over and kissed Mary.

"Goodnight, John. We're just like buddies, telling each other our secret delights," Mary told him with a chuckle in her voice.

"Good night, hon, sleep tight."

Shortly afterward, Mary shook John from his side of the bed. "John, look on the floor," she said with her hand on his shoulder.

John took a quick look and turned to Mary. "Don't be afraid, hon. You're looking at mice and roaches roaming on the floor. I was trained on the farm to get rid of such pests, so tomorrow I will," John told her sternly.

"Good for you, John. Now I can go to sleep," she told him quickly. "John, do you think we have made a mistake coming here?" she asked.

"It's too early to tell, hon. Now, go to sleep," John said, then he started to say his prayers.

"He says his prayers too," Mary whispered.

"Yes, I do, and you should too," he insisted.

He heard Mary saying her prayers, then he dozed off into a deep sleep.

"Don't try anything on me while I'm asleep," Mary said softly to John, but all she heard was his snoring.

"I hope these nasty little pests don't come up here and attack me," she said to herself and slowly went to sleep.

*

The following morning, after breakfast, John left the apartment and walked three blocks east to Audrey Avenue, then he came upon Eagle Lumber. He gazed at the front of the building, and felt that whoever was managing the building wasn't doing a very good job. The front of the building needed cleaning, and most of all it should have been painted in a bright shade of paint to attract more customers.

John saw all the lumber around the yard, and the building stood in the middle of 15 acres of land. He entered the store and no one was around to serve him, so he walked slowly from aisle to aisle, viewing the items and the prices. This was the first time he went shopping for supplies for himself. He felt the items could have been displayed on the shelves in a better fashion. He pretended that he was the manager of the store, and he formed in his mind how he'd manage the business. While he was daydreaming, he didn't hear the footsteps that came up behind him.

"Can I help you, sir?" a man's voice asked.

John quickly turned around to face a tall, elderly man who was dressed in a dark suit. They both looked curiously at each other for a few seconds.

"I suppose you're the manager?" John asked, smiling.

"Yes, I am. Ted Johnson at your service."

"John Stone and I'm new here," he said, smiling.

"I realized that when I saw you going around and around the store," the manager told him.

"Well, to tell you the truth, Mr. Johnson, when you came up from behind me, I was daydreaming of working here. I really need a job, any job," John pleaded.

The manager smiled at John. "Daydreaming of taking over my job, I suppose," the manager said jokingly.

"How did you know that?" John asked.

"I know. I used to daydream the same way when I was your age. Did you say your name was John Stone?"

"Yes, sir."

"I used to know a Charles Stone," the manager said.

"He was my uncle. He left the farm before I was born, and I didn't know him," John explained.

"I'd like to help you, John. What can you do?"

"My father taught me carpentry and painting. At the high school I learnt salesmanship, and to be a salesman, you have to be thoughtful and friendly," John told him.

"I must say that those are very good qualities, and now all you need is a start, John," the manager told him in a friendly voice.

"You mean I'm hired, sir?"

"Well, I'm curious to see what you can do. There's a lady in aisle 5. Her name is Mrs. Good, and she can never make up her mind what she wants. I want you to go to her and try to sell her something, anything in the store. I'll be looking on to see how you'd handle the situation," the manager told John with a half smile.

"Well, sir, I thought you'd give me something more challenging, but that seems easy enough," John said with a smile and went to aisle 5. He knew that he had to make a good impression on the manager. He realized his chance of getting a job at the store depended on how he handled himself for the next five minutes. John came up from behind Mrs. Good, and he gave a sudden cough. She turned around, looked and smiled at him.

"Good morning, Mrs. Good," John told her, smiling.

"And good morning to you, young man. I suppose you are new here, and you have the advantage over me. I don't know your name," she told him.

"My name is John Stone, ma'am."

"Are you related to Charles Stone?"

"Yes, ma'am. He was my uncle."

"You said was. Is he still alive?" she asked.

"I really don't know, ma'am. We haven't seen or heard from him in years. Now that we have that out of the way, Mrs. Good, how can I help you?" John asked in a friendly voice.

"Well, young man, I'm thinking of decorating a few rooms in my house. When Mr. Good was alive, I didn't have to bother with this. He did all the handy work," she explained sadly.

"What rooms are you thinking of decorating?"

"The kitchen and the living room. I can't make up my mind what color to paint them in," she said hesitantly.

"What color do you have now, ma'am?"

"A light gray."

"I feel that you have had that gray long enough, and it's time for you to have a new and exciting color in those rooms. A color that will bring life to your rooms."

"What color would you suggest?"

"Well, ma'am, since you're relatively still young, you'll have to live with the new modern colors. I'd suggest an off-white, and any room with this color would look brighter and larger. And in the future if you want to sell your house, you'll get a good price for it," John explained.

"Well, young man I didn't expect this sort of friendly service. How many gallons of paint should I buy?"

"To be on the safe side, you should get two gallons for each room. I don't want you to think that I want you to do the whole house, but if you do two rooms, you'll feel guilty."

"Why should I feel guilty?" she asked.

"Well, when you decide to do the kitchen and living room, the rest of the house will be a drag to you," John told her.

"You're right young man, I should do the whole house, so I wouldn't feel guilty, but..."

"Don't tell me you need some help?"

"Yes. How did you know that? You're reading my mind," she said, smiling.

"You told me your husband did all the handiwork. If I can be of service, I'll come around to your place to do any repairs, fill in any cracks in the ceilings and the walls. Then you'll be ready for painting; this will make your house look beautiful once again."

"But what you're asking me to do will cost me big bucks," she said reluctantly.

"That is so, ma'am, but in the long run you'll be better off. If you have to sell your house at any time, you'll get back every penny with interest. Mr. Johnson can make arrangements for you to pay your bill by small monthly installments," John told her, smiling.

"Well, thank you, son. That's a good idea."

John took Mrs. Good to the manager, Mr. Johnson, and told him about the proposal.

"I never knew you had such a proposal until your handsome salesman was able to convince me," Mrs. Good told Mr. Johnson.

"Well, Mrs. Good, we're here to please you," Mr. Johnson told her, then he took John aside to speak to him.

"I'm sorry if I jumped the gun, Mr. Johnson, but I told you I can sell anything you have in this store, including the store," John told Mr. Johnson with a half smile on his face.

"When I asked you to help Mrs. Good, I wanted to see how you'd handle the whole matter. Maybe you'd sell her something in the store. I never expected that you'd convince her to decorate her whole house, and buy all the building materials from us, and we'd do the job for her. We don't have such a service at the present moment, John," Mr. Johnson explained quickly.

"Just one minute, sir, you do have such a service now. When you hire me, I'll be that service," John told him sternly.

"But to put such a service in operation, you'd need help. You can't do all the work on your own."

"You have lots of help in the mill, and any one of your helpers will be glad to earn extra money in this new project. I'll train someone myself," John told him convincingly.

"And for a minute, I thought you'd need training. We have a deal if this service of yours works," Mr. Johnson told John. Then they shook hands.

"Thank you, sir, and you haven't seen anything as yet."

54

They both went over to Mrs. Good. "John will be at your service, Mrs. Good. We'll deliver all the materials necessary to do the job. John will come around to your place, and he'll see how best he can help you."

"Thank you, Mr. Johnson," Mrs. Good said, smiling.

Mr. Johnson turned to John and the two men's eyes met, then they both smiled at each other. John realized that he was now home free. He was now hired.

"Well, you should thank, John. He'll be the one to make your home beautiful."

"Don't thank me just yet, Mrs. Good. I'll be seeing you later," John told her.

Mr. Johnson took John around the building and showed him the different areas. He also introduced him to Hector Saunders, who worked in the lumber yard. Hector was going to become John's helper. Hector was a Native Indian, who was tall, slim and dark.

John told Hector about the project and he'd make some extra money. Hector was interested and willing to help John in whatever way possible. John sensed that Hector was a bit jealous because he was going to be a helper to a newcomer in Eagle Lumber.

*

John shook his head as he came back to reality. Then he stood up from his favorite chair, and went to the passageway at the bottom of the stairs. He could see himself clearly being shot twice by the burglar. He stood there nervous and powerless for a few seconds Then he had the urge to speak out his thoughts. He clasped his hands together and slightly closed his eyes. Then he saw the burglar's face clearly. He opened his eyes.

"Why did you have to take my family away from me? I love them. Now, I'm all alone. Why didn't I die with them? So I'd be with them forever. My life without them isn't worth living; I'd be only living in an empty world," John said sadly to his imaginary burglar in the passageway.

Chapter Five

John went back to his favorite chair in the living room and eased himself into it. He didn't want to think any more. He just wanted to relax. He closed his eyes and fell into a light sleep. Then shortly afterwards, he heard a buzzing in his ear. It was like a bee trying to wake him up. He shook his head to shake it off, but the buzzing still continued. He opened his eyes, and tried his best to make himself alert. Only then he realized that someone was ringing the doorbell. Someone was at the front door. He knew Karen was going to come to see him, but he didn't know she was going to be that early. He jumped up and went to the front door. He looked through the glass, and saw Karen. He opened the door quickly to let her in.

"Karen!" John said surprisedly.

"Yes. I hope you haven't forgotten your favorite nurse. I was ringing the doorbell for a good while. I was afraid something had happened to you in the house," she told him eagerly.

"I am sorry, Karen. I just had a bad dream just before you came," he said, then they both went into the living room.

"I know it's tough on you, living in this house. It would only bring back memories of the past. You need to live somewhere else, John," Karen advised him.

"This is my home and part of my life is here. I just can't abandon my home where my family lived and died," he snapped.

"I didn't mean it that way. I'm sorry," Karen told him. Then she smiled at him.

"I should be the one to tell you I'm sorry – after you're so good to come over here to cheer me up," John said softly, and he forced a smile at Karen.

"You have a very nice home, John," she told him.

"I did all the decorations and the renovations. I did it all for them. Now they are gone forever."

"Please, John, don't dwell on the past."

"I can't forget, it's part of my life," he said sadly.

"I understand, John," she said, then they both sat down on the large sofa.

"I'm glad you are here, Karen."

"Why is that?" she asked, smiling.

He held her hand. "Detective Lang came to see me this morning, and asked me more questions. After he left, I started to think hard on the whole situation. I'm afraid he thinks that I am the one who did it," John explained.

"Did what?" she asked.

"Murdered my family," he snapped.

"But, John, you loved your family! I know you would never harm them. How could he think you did it?"

"I feel it's only a matter of time before they arrest me, and put me in prison. All the evidence points to me. It was my gun, and I took out new life insurance policies on my family a few months before. No one saw the burglar who broke into this house," John explained to her.

"I think you're convicting yourself before hand, John. I know it's a difficult situation, and I'll do my best to help you," she told him sympathetically.

"I wish it were that simple, Karen, but thank you."

Karen prepared supper for John, and after supper they sat on the sofa, and talked for several hours, then she left for her apartment. John was left alone, and he had time to think, and that he did. He remembered the first few weeks when he and Mary had arrived in Philadelphia, and they had made arrangements to get married.

*

It was a bright Sunday morning in September. It was the morning that John and Mary were going to be joined together in the Philadelphia Baptist Church on Main Street. The church was packed with all the members, and for some strange reason the word had got around that the newcomers were going to get married after the Sunday church service.

The church was brightly lit, and flowers were placed all over the building, which were donated by the members. It was a special day, a special service, and also a special wedding of the young couple, John and Mary.

John, Mary and Mrs. Big sat in the front pew. John wore his brown suit, white shirt, brown tie, and black shoes. Mary wore her white Sunday best dress, and white shoes to match her dress. Mrs. Big wore a blue dress, and blue shoes to match. All eyes were on John and Mary, and the members were whispering about them.

Pastor Boyd went into the pulpit, then all eyes were centered on him. He looked down at the members for a few seconds. "Good morning, Brothers and Sisters. As you know today is a special day for John and Mary. They are going to be joined this morning in holy matrimony. John and Mary, please stand," he said, looking down at them.

They both stood up with a bright smile on their faces, and faced the members of the church.

"John and Mary became members last week, and they don't have any relatives here, but they're lucky to have you Brothers and Sisters as their friends. As you know our service only lasts for 45 minutes, but today it will only be for 30 minutes, and after that we'll have the marriage ceremony of John and Mary. Whoever wants to stay and witness the ceremony may do so," Pastor Boyd explained.

Thirty minutes later the service was finished; Pastor Boyd went in front of the church. All the members stayed to witness the marriage ceremony of the young couple. The organist played 'Here comes the bride'. Then John, Mary, Mrs. Big and two flower girls came forward to the front of the church. The two flower girls stood on each side of the party. The ceremony was about to begin.

"Before I start this wedding ceremony, John and Mary would like to read a love passage to each other," Pastor Boyd said, smiling.

"Mary, my poor life wouldn't be worthwhile without you. I love you and I want to be with you forever. I am sorry our parents are not here to witness this ceremony, but we're together and we're happy," John told Mary.

"John, I know the way you feel about me. I feel the same way, too. I love you with all my heart, and I'll be all you expect. I'll be your wife, your friend, and most of all the mother of your children. My parents are not here, John, but you are. I'll always love you," Mary told John, smiling.

Pastor Boyd waited until the music stopped, then he smiled at John and Mary.

"Well, Brother John and Sister Mary, this is the great moment you have been waiting for to enter into holy union," Pastor Boyd said.

Then the whole congregation became silent.

"Dearly beloved. We are gathered here today to witness this wedding ceremony of Brother John and Sister Mary. Please join hands. Do you, Mary, take John to be your lawful wedded husband? For better or for worse, for richer or poorer, in sickness and in health, till death do you part?"

"Yes, I do," Mary answered.

"Do you, John, take Mary to be your lawful wedded wife? For better or for worse, for richer or poorer, in sickness and in health, till death do you part?"

"Yes, I do," John answered.

"Who giveth this woman away?" asked Pastor Boyd.

"I do," Mrs. Big replied, and she gave the ring to John.

"You may put the ring on her finger," Pastor Boyd said.

John takes Mary's right hand, and put the ring on her middle finger.

"Mary, I give you this ring as a symbol of my everlasting love for you," John said, smiling.

"John, I accept this ring as a symbol of our vows. In the name of the Father, the Son and the Holy Ghost. Amen," Mary replied, smiling.

"Let anyone who knows why this couple should not be joined together in holy matrimony speak now or forever hold his or her peace," Pastor Boyd said and waited for a few seconds, and no one stood up.

"Now that Brother John and Sister Mary have exchanged vows and the ring in the name of God, with the powers vested in me, I hereby pronounce you husband and wife. Brother John, you may kiss the bride." John took Mary in his arms and kissed her. Pastor Boyd shook their hands and some of the members came to the front of the church to congratulate the couple, and wish them all the best. Then the Pastor took the wedding party to his office at back of the church, so they could sign the marriage register.

After the signing of the register and photographs were taken, Mrs. Big took the couple to her apartment. It was the wedding day of her two children, and she wanted to give them a special treat. She prepared a delicious meal for them. Then, later that afternoon, she gave them an envelope with some money to pay for the local hotel room she had booked for their honeymoon. It would be a one-night stand of love and delight for Mr. and Mrs. Stone. It would be a night they'd never forget.

John and Mary arrived at the Mayday Hotel on Main Street. They booked in at six thirty that evening. They had supper in the dining room, then they both had a glass of white wine, as it was a special occasion for them. They had to seal their marriage with a drink. The hotel had several guests in the dining room, but John was so thrilled with his new wife that he didn't see or hear anyone else in the dining room. He only concentrated on his beautiful wife sitting in front of him, and he realized that soon he'd be able to poke her on his honeymoon.

"John, I am ready to go up to our room," Mary told him with a smile.

"It's what I wanted all the time, and now I'm nervous," John told her.

"Me, too. But we're married now, and we'll have to get this over with," she said quickly.

Then they slowly went up to their room on the second floor. John unlocked the door and opened it. He looked at his young bride for a few seconds. His eyes were lit up and there was a big smile on his face. Then he glanced at Mary up and down.

"I know what I am supposed to do with my bride," he told her softly. Then he picked her up and carried her over the threshold, then he put her down carefully inside the room, and closed the door behind them. He returned to her and held her tightly in his arms, then he kissed her passionately.

"Well, this is a start to what is yet to come," he told her softly.

"John, you are so romantic. Let's see what you do next. Surprise me!" she told him, smiling. "I'll change my clothes. I'll be back in a second," she said and went into the bathroom.

"I thought you were supposed to get undressed for this occasion!" he shouted after her. Then he started taking off his clothes quickly, and he was left in his underpants. He folded his clothes neatly, and put them onto the nearby chair. Then he went into the double bed. He just lay back and he imagined that in the next few minutes he'd be doing an act of love to consummate his marriage. He realized the thought of lovemaking was something to be cherished.

The light was dim in the room. He saw a dresser, a clothes closet and two chairs.

A few minutes later, he saw his beautiful bride step out of the bathroom. She had on a short, see-through black negligee. He lifted the cover to let her into the bed, then she took her rightful place beside him.

"Well, hon, this is it," John told her nervously.

"Well, John, it is up to you now," Mary told him.

"What do I do? I have never done this before," he said quickly.

"There's always a first time, John, so use your imagination," she said with a giggle.

"What imagination?" he whispered.

"Your sexual imagination," she blurted.

"Well, give me a clue. How do I go about this?"

"For starters, strip me. Take off my negligee and pull off my panties. Is that enough of a clue for you to dwell on?" Mary asked him quickly.

"So that's my clue?"

"Yes. Enough talk! Action!" Mary said boldly.

John plucked up enough courage to do the impossible. He slowly peeled off her black negligee, then he gracefully removed her silk panties. He felt nervous and his hands trembled under the covers as he stripped his bride. His heart was beating faster than usual and he felt the blood running up and down his body. He started to rub his left hand on her chest, then he played with the nipples on her hard breasts. He didn't know how to handle the situation, and he just kept on doing what he thought was best and excited him.

"You're doing fine, John. Just continue playing with my body parts. It feels great," she told him. "The real thing is between my legs, so go for it," she urged.

John slowly moved his hands down her body, and tentatively between her legs. He touched it gently for a few seconds, and it felt small and moist.

"It's so small, hon," he told her shyly.

"It is small and sweet, and it's all yours to take, John. You can do whatever you like with it as soon as you're ready," she told him in a state of ecstasy.

"How do I know when I am ready, hon?" he asked, gasping for breath.

"You'll know, John, because you'll have six inches of hard flesh ready to enter me. I am sorry, John," she said softly.

"Sorry for what?" he asked anxiously.

"For not giving you some sex all those nights," she told him. "Now is your chance to poke me hard," she demanded.

"They say good things come to those who wait," he told her.

Mary laughed at what he told her. "Well, let's not wait any longer. Take me!" she said, and held tightly onto his shoulders. It was a sign for him to mount on top of her. John held Mary in his arms and kissed her passionately, then he was ready to take the plunge. He gently mounted on top of her. She didn't move. She just kept still, and waited for the moment of truth to arrive.

"John, I want this to be real. I want us to have a baby of our own. Now, please take me and give me all that you have. I love you, John. This is what you have been waiting for all these months," she said, her hands around his body, gripping him tightly, and panting for breath.

John heard what Mary said about a baby, but he knew that before they could make a baby, he'd have to know something about sex. He tried several times to enter Mary, but without success. In a way he was partly glad that he had made little progress. He loved Mary too much, and he couldn't bear to hurt her for his enjoyment. He dismounted from her, breathing heavily in and out.

"John, what's wrong?" she asked.

"I don't know. I can't seem to get it right," he told her nervously. "It's more difficult than I thought, and I don't know anything about sex. I don't want to hurt you, hon," he told her softly.

"Don't be discouraged. This is something new to us. You have to try again. I know you don't want to hurt me because I am a virgin. But to love me, John, you'll have to hurt me, so get back on top of me and try again," she demanded.

He did as Mary told him and gently mounted back onto his partner's warm, soft body.

"You are doing fine, John. I'll help you to find me, so you can penetrate into my vagina," she told him softly.

"I understand, hon," he said. His body was trembling on top of hers, then he slowly penetrated into her vagina. Mary screamed a little as she felt some pain inside of her.

He held tightly onto her and he felt as if he were in another dimension. His movements were slow at first, then they accelerated according to the way he felt. Then, after a few minutes, they both came to a final climax. John considered himself at that moment as a man and Mary as a woman. They were bonded at that moment by love. They were no longer children of the past, but adults of the future.

"John, I love you, and that was beautiful, so please do it again. I'm all yours," she insisted.

"I love you too, hon. And that's a good idea. We'll have to make up for lost time," he said. "I know now that practice makes perfect," John added quickly, and mounted back onto his wife for another session of lovemaking.

They left the hotel early the next morning, and went back to their apartment. After freshening up, John left for work at Eagle Lumber. He'd daydream at work about when he and Mary were having sex the night before on their honeymoon. He felt so out of place for the first time. He knew for sure that he'd have to practice on Mary after work, and sex would be his passion from then on. He felt it was something that was so sweet and it grew on you. He felt that no way would he be able to put it off.

That evening John heard a knock on his suite door. He got up from where he was sitting in the living room, and opened it. He looked up at the gentleman in front of him.

"Can I help you?"

"Yes, you can. I am Mr. Ward, the owner of this building," the elderly, tall, stout man told him.

"I'm John Stone, your new tenant. Please do come in, Mr. Ward. I was expecting you," John said, smiling.

Mr. Ward entered the suite and went into the living room, then he looked down at Mary.

"This is my wife, Mary. This is Mr. Ward, our landlord," John told her.

"Pleasure meeting you, Mr. Ward. Please have a seat," Mary told him, and got up. "I'll make some tea," she added, as she left the living room.

"Mr. Ward likes his tea hot and sweet, hon," he told Mary.

Mr. Ward smiled at John. "You seem to have done your homework, John," Mr. Ward said, smiling as he sat down.

"Yes, sir. I know why you're here. You came to collect the rent."

"You're right. I like a man who knows his own mind. Your rent is $150 per month and it's due," he declared.

"That's what I want to talk to you about, sir. We can only afford about $100 per month," John told him softly.

"$100?" Mr. Ward asked, and shook his head.

"Well, Mr. Ward, we better get down to business. I want you to hear me out, please," John suggested.

"I'm all ears, young man. Spill it out!"

"I understand you have four of these buildings, and they all need upkeep. That's where I come in. As you can see this suite needs repairs and painting. I'm quite prepared to do all the work at a very little cost to you. The whole building needs lots of work. I'll do the passageways, the front and all the suites. This will improve your building considerably. And I'm quite sure when you sell this building, you can make a handsome profit. I can make this building beautiful again, also the other three buildings. Please give me a chance," John begged.

"You think you can make this old building beautiful again?" Mr. Ward asked.

"Yes, sir. And if the tenants are pleased with the work, I'm quite sure they'll agree to pay a little more on their rent, which can amount to hundreds of dollars."

"I must say, John, you're a good businessman. I like your ideas," Mr. Ward told him, smiling.

"Give me paint and plaster, sir, and I'll make this place like new again. But before I can start any work, I'll have to get rid of the rats, mice, and roaches in all the suites," John told him sternly.

"You can do that, also?" Mr. Ward asked eagerly.

"Yes, sir, I lived on a farm, and my father taught me how to get rid of those nasty rodents."

"I'm really impressed. I'll get you all the supplies you need to make a start on this building."

"I'll fix up Mrs. Big's suite first, and if you like what you see, I'll proceed to the other suites."

"Why Mrs. Big's suite?"

"She's like a mother to us, and we love her very much. That's why we're here," John told him.

"She told me something like that, also, and from the way she spoke, I thought you were related to her."

"In a way we are," John said, smiling.

Mary brought the tea into the living room. "Well, I waited until you guys got your business out of the way," Mary said, and poured a large cup of tea for Mr. Ward.

"Remember Mr. Ward likes it sweet," John told her.

Mary smiled and put three teaspoons of sugar into Mr. Ward's tea. Mr. Ward spent the next twenty minutes talking to John and Mary, while he drank his tea. "You're a smart young man. You'll go places. I wish my son were like you," Mr. Ward told John.

"Thank you, sir. That's a real compliment coming from you," John agreed. Mr. Ward got up and thanked the couple for their hospitality, then he left. Mary looked up at John. "He didn't take the rent."

"Maybe he forgot," John declared.

"No, I don't think he forgot. You just out-talked him," Mary said, and got up and kissed John. "Are you going to do some work for Mr. Ward?" she asked.

"Yes, but before I finish with him, he'll be owing us."

"You are so clever, John. That's why I married you."

"Well, it comes natural to me, hon."

"Well, since it comes natural to you, are you in for another session with me right now?" she asked, making faces.

"Certainly, ma'am," John said, and kissed her quickly, then he picked her up and took her into the bedroom.

Several weeks later, John had an unexpected visitor. He had just had his coffee break that morning, when he saw a young woman come into the store. He went to assist her. When he came face to face with her, he stopped. They both gazed steadily at each other. The woman pointed her finger at him, and he in turn pointed his finger at her. She was fairly tall, slim, attractive, and she wore a blue dress and white shoes. John was drawn to her immediately.

"Can I help you, ma'am?" he asked, looking at her.

"Yes, but first your face. You remind me of someone," she told him, shaking her head.

"And you are the split image of my sister," he said.

"And you are the split image of my father when he was younger."

"They always tell me I was the split image of Charles Stone," he told her, without thinking.

"Yes. How did you know that?" she asked.

"Well, Charles is my..." he said.

"Is your father?" she cut in quickly.

"No, my uncle," he said with a smile.

"You mean my father is your uncle?" she asked.

"Father?"

"Yes. I'm Linda Walters Stone."

"It's a pleasure meeting you, Cousin Linda. I'm John. James Stone is my father. Where's your father?" John asked.

"Five years ago, when mother died, we moved to New York City. Two years later, father met with an accident and he didn't make it. I came back here and got married to George, my sweetheart. My brother, Frank stayed in New York City. He's now a news reporter for a large television station," she explained.

"It's a real small world. I never thought we would meet here, Cousin Linda," he said, smiling. "And the mother you once knew died here in Philadelphia. My mother told me recently that Uncle Charles had an affair way back with a young woman here in the city, and the woman had a beautiful baby girl. When Uncle Charles got married to someone else, the woman gave him the little girl to raise," John explained to Linda.

"A little girl?" she asked.

"Yes," John answered with a half smile.

"There wasn't any other little girl in my family, only me. That means that I'm that little girl. If your story is true, my real mother may still be alive here in Philadelphia," she declared. Her mouth was wide open.

"Did you ever hear your father or mother speak of Sandra?" he asked suspiciously.

"Yes. He spoke several times of a Sandra Big. Can she be my natural mother?" Linda asked.

"Maybe," he said. "You can leave your phone number with me, and if I get any more information, I'll get in touch with you, or you're welcome to come any evening to suite 13, 502 Wall Street, Blackwater Apartments, just off Main Street," he added.

"John, you've really left me in suspense from what you told me," she said nervously.

"I didn't mean to. It just happened. Now, what can I get you from the store, Linda?" John asked.

"Well, after all this talk about my mother, I just can't remember what I came in here for. Oh, now I remember; I need a furnace filter," she said, and forced a smile.

"One furnace filter coming up, ma'am," he told her, smiling.

John got Linda Walters' phone number when she left the store. He now had a gut feeling that Mrs. Big was Linda's mother, but he wanted to be sure. He knew he'd have to wait for the right moment to confront Mrs. Big.

*

John came back to reality and started thinking about his present situation, a situation that was getting worse by the minute. He realized that there would be no escape from what was about to happen to him shortly.

Chapter Six

On that cold January morning, John felt uneasy. It was as though something was about to happen. But what? He felt, at that moment, he had to speak to someone who was close to him. He immediately went to the phone and dialed the number to the Stones' farm. He wanted to speak to his best friend, his mother. He hadn't spoken to her in months. Now, he needed her more than ever. His hand trembled as he waited for her to pick up the phone. He heard the phone on the other end ring twice.

"Hello, Sofie Stone speaking," she said softly.

"Hello, Mom. This is John, your son, John! He wanted to make a point to his mother. He wanted her to know that he was still her son, no matter what was about to happen to him.

"John! How are you? I was just thinking about you. I'm sorry to hear what happened to you and your family. I wasn't well for the last few months, otherwise, I would have come to visit you in hospital," she declared.

"I'm okay now, Mom. Don't worry. You were always there for me in the past. I love you, Mom," he told her sadly.

"And I love you too, son."

"Mom, I called you specially to let you know that I'm a suspect," he said grimly.

"Suspect for what, John?" she asked.

"I'm a suspect for murder. I wanted you to hear this from me first, and no one else," he blurted.

"Why, John?" she cried.

"No one saw the burglar who broke into our house, and my gun was used to kill my family. I had taken out some insurance policies on them just before it happened. All the evidence points to me," John explained frantically.

"You poor boy! If nothing happens, please come home. We love you and we're your family. Your home is still here," she cried.

"Mom, I'll let you know as soon as something happens."

"Yes, son, I'll pray for you. Call me again, soon," she said.

"Good-bye, Mom," John said, and hung up.

John went to Eagle Lumber that morning. He saw Mr. Johnson, the manager of the store.

"John, how are you?" Mr. Johnson asked. "I was sorry to hear about your family," Mr. Johnson told him sadly.

John smiled at him. "Thank you, sir. I wish I can say I'm fine, but I'm not," he told Mr. Johnson.

"When will you be coming back to work? All the customers are asking for you. You always had your way with them," Mr. Johnson said cheerfully.

"I can't say when, sir."

"Is there something I need to know?"

"The way how things are going, I may not be back for a very long time," John declared.

"Why is that, John? Aren't you well enough?"

"To tell you the truth, sir, I may be indicted for the murders of my family, but I didn't do it. All the evidence points to me. I don't know what to do," John said abruptly.

"John, that's terrible news! I can't believe the authorities will come after you for something you didn't do," Mr. Johnson said, looking at him from behind his desk.

"I thought I'd let you know this, so you can get someone else in my place," John told him sadly.

"You know, John, no one else can replace you. I must say this to your face. You're the best. I remember the first day you came in here for a job. I thought you were a green kid, and you proved me wrong in just a few minutes."

"I remember, sir. I took a fluke chance that day. I was desperate and I took a gamble and won," John said with a half smile on his face.

"Well, John, we'll have to keep our fingers crossed."

"Yes, sir, please do that," John said and left.

After supper that evening John and Karen walked to the park, then they sat on one of the empty benches. John just sat with her for a few seconds. He was silent as if he were collecting his immediate thoughts.

"John, what's wrong?" she asked.

"I want to remember this moment with you, and that's why I brought you here. Mary and I came here with the kids when we wanted to think," he told her delicately.

"Tell me, John, what's wrong?" she asked again.

John shook his head. "I may not get to do this again," he sighed.

"Are you going away?" she asked, touching his shoulder,

"In a way, yes," he replied softly.

"Where?"

"Maybe to prison for a long time," John told her. By tomorrow I'll be in jail."

"How do you know this?"

"Detective Lang told me that I'm now his prime suspect."

"John, I don't know what to say," she said and held his left hand.

"Thank you, Nurse Hill. You have done so much for me and I can never repay you. Thanks a million," he told her sadly.

"John, I wish that things could have been different."

"Maybe in another world it could have been different. I know the way you feel about me, Karen," he declared.

"Yes, I love you," she said softly, and held her head close to his.

"I can never return your love, and I can only be your friend, dear Karen," he said and kissed her on the cheek.

The following day was just as John predicted. He was picked up by Detective Lang and taken to police headquarters for further questioning, then he was read his rights. Then he was taken to the City Jail, and held there. John knew what the outcome was going to be, and kept a cool head. He lay back in his cell on a small bed. His thoughts started to go around and around.

*

In 1977, Mary, his wife, became pregnant with their first child. They both sat on the sofa that evening watching television.

"How is he or she, hon?" John asked.

"He kicked shortly. Feel my stomach and maybe he'd kick again," she said, smiling at John.

John felt Mary's stomach, then he felt the baby kicked.

"I felt him kick, hon," John said, smiling.

"I wrote, Mom, and told her we got married and I'm now pregnant."

"I wrote my mother also, but I never got a reply as yet," John told her. "Are you happy with the way things are going, hon?" John asked.

"I wouldn't have it any other way, John. We did the right thing, and I love you," she said, and bent over and kissed him.

"I'm working hard. We'll soon have enough money for a down payment on a house, so our family will have a nice place to live in. I'm going to find a house that I can fix up myself," John explained.

John held Mary in his arms and kissed her. "If the folks back home saw us now, what would they think?" John said, smiling.

Mary smiled. "They'd think we're still too young – too young for love. John, no matter what, I want you to promise that you'll always love me," she said cheerfully.

"I promise, hon, and I hope you'll do the same," John told her serenely.

"What are we going to call him or her?" Mary asked.

"We'll call him David or her Cindy," John replied.

"Fine with me, John."

The following weekend John had invited cousin Linda, her husband George and their son Ronald for supper.

"Well, it's nice of you to invite us for supper, John," Linda told him, smiling.

"My reason for inviting you is so you can meet a certain lady who lives in this building," John said abruptly with a half smile on his face.

"John, you're up to something? Does that lady happen to be Sandra Big?" Linda asked with a smile on her face.

John smiled back at her. "Cousin Linda, that would be telling."

"Oh, you're keeping me in suspense again, John. I haven't told George about what you told me, but I phoned my brother, Frank, and told him of your suspicion. He believes you," Linda declared.

A few minutes later there was a knock on the front door, and Linda went and opened it. She gazed steadily at the elderly lady who stood in front of her.

"I didn't know that John had visitors," Mrs. Big said, looking at Linda curiously.

"I suppose you're Mrs. Big. John told me all about you. Please come in!" Linda said and extended her hand to Mrs. Big. "I'm Linda Walters, John's cousin," she told her outright.

Mrs. Big entered the apartment. Then John came to meet them. "I see you ladies have met. Mrs. Big, this is Cousin Linda, Uncle Charles' daughter," John told her.

Mrs. Big stopped short and gazed at Linda. "So – you are little Linda? I used to see you in church when your father brought you there. You were such a beautiful little girl. Where's your father now?" Mrs. Big asked excitedly.

"Dad passed away six years ago in New York City. He had an accident and never recovered. And I came back here and got married. Come and meet my family," Linda told her anxiously.

"You have a family?" she asked excitedly.

"Yes, my husband, George, and my son, Ron," Linda told her quickly.

John saw how Mrs. Big's eyes lit up when she looked at Linda. Linda held her by the arm and took her into the living room and introduced her to George and Ron.

John saw the expression on Mrs. Big's face. She was so happy, because they were her real family. The family she had lost, and now they had found her. John knew that Mrs. Big couldn't bring herself to tell Linda that she was her real mother. It would have to remain a secret for the time being.

"You devil!" Linda told John when she got him alone.

"Well, you can't say you're not enjoying every moment of it also," he blurted.

"I never knew that my real mother was alive," Linda said sadly.

"Now what can I do?" she asked.

"Now you know, Linda. And in answer to your question, only you and Mrs. Big can answer it," he said bluntly.

"Look how she is admiring her grandson," Linda said, looking at Mrs. Big.

When Linda and her family left, Mrs. Big turned to John. "I hope she's going to let me baby-sit for her son."

"I'm quite sure Linda will let you baby-sit, and you'll have your hands full when we have our baby," John told her.

The following Sunday at noon, John and Mary sat on the sofa. They were looking at a show on the television, when they heard a knock on the door. "John can you get that," Mary told him. John got and went to the door and opened it.

"Who is it, John?" Mary shouted.

72

"Surprise!" John said behind her. Mary turned around quickly and saw what the surprise was. She jumped up and hurried over to her mother and father. She hugged her mother. "Oh, Mom, I never knew you'd come to visit us," she cried.

"That was John's idea. He thought if we came, we could cheer you up," Mrs. Young said.

"John, you devil!" Mary said and went to her Dad and hugged and kissed him on the cheek. "I don't know what to say; you guys came so far to see us. Where's my sister, Alice?" Mary asked cheerfully.

"She had to go out and she couldn't make it. She sends her regards," Mr. Young said.

Mary's parents stayed for the rest of the afternoon. They brought all of Mary's belongings that she had left behind. John and Mary waved to them as they drove off on their long journey back to Moorestown.

*

Later that year Mary had a baby boy. They named him David. Later, in 1978, Mary had a baby girl, and they named her Cindy. Mary stayed home with the children. John did all the work he could. He took on private jobs, repairing houses, but still he couldn't save enough money for a deposit on a house of their own.

It wasn't until one day he hinted to Mr. Johnson, his manager, his plight to buy a house for his family.

"John, I'm sorry for your plight," Mr. Johnson told him.

"Well, I'll just have to wait until I can find something up my street," John told him.

"My aunt told me a few weeks ago that she wants to sell her house to someone nice. The house is on 45 Blexley Avenue. As you said, it may be up your street. Take your family to see the house. I'll phone my aunt, Mrs. Miller, and tell her you'll drop by one evening. John, put your charm on her and she'll like you," Mr. Johnson said, jokingly.

"Thank you, sir. I'll look into it this evening."

"Don't mention. Go after your dream," Mr. Johnson told him, smiling.

That same evening, John loaded his family into his truck and drove to 45 Blexley Avenue. The building was a two-story house. It was made of bricks, stucco and wood trimming on the outside. The first floor consisted of a large living room, a small dining room, and a small kitchen, and the second floor consisted of a fairly large master bedroom, and two medium bedrooms. There was a small back yard, with a small vegetable garden. John and his family looked at the house carefully, and they liked what they saw. John knew that Mrs. Miller wanted them to have the house, and he was willing to buy it at a reasonable price.

"You are the right family for this house. I'll let you have it at a reasonable price," she said, smiling.

"I'm going to make this house beautiful again, Mrs. Miller, and you'll be welcome to visit us any time," John told her.

"That will be very nice of you young man, but the house will be yours to enjoy. The same as my family did all these years," Mrs. Miller told John consciously. "Now, we have that out of the way, let's have tea and some cookies," she added.

John bought the house with a very low down payment. Then he got his friend Hector to help him to work on the house for several weeks. On September 1979, John moved his family into their new residence on 45 Blexley Avenue.

Mrs. Big was sorry to see them go, and on certain weekends John would pick her up to visit them, and sometimes she would baby-sit for them.

*

In August of 1982, John received a phone call at his work place that Mrs. Big had taken ill, and was in the St. Margaret's Hospital, and she wanted to see him. John immediately went over to the hospital, and was shown to her room. Then he sat at her bedside, and felt sad.

"John, thank you for coming right away. I have made out my will. I'm leaving you and Mary everything. You're just like my real family. I'm glad you and your family will be there to give me a decent burial," Mrs. Big explained sadly.

"You mustn't say that. You're going to live for a very long time yet, Mrs. Big," John told her.

"No, John, my time is near. That's why I want you to bring Mary and Linda to see me before I depart," she cried. "You must go now and bring them to me. I can't hold on much longer. You all were my family for that short while and I really enjoyed myself. You even brought Linda back to me. You knew all along. Does she know that I'm her mother?" she asked.

"Yes, that's why she wanted you to baby-sit for her. She is a very proud person. She felt if you wanted to tell her that you are her real mother, you'd do so in due time," John declared.

"I want to tell her now before I go on my long journey to heaven. Please get Mary and Linda and bring them over right away," she told him sadly, gasping for breath.

I'll go and fetch them for you, Mrs. Big. So you be here when I get back," he said, smiling, and left.

Thirty minutes later, John returned with Mary and Linda. Then he took them into Mrs. Big's room. He thought it was best to leave them alone to say their final goodbyes to Mrs. Big. Mary came out of the room first, and Linda was left with Mrs. Big. Ten minutes later Linda came out of the room, with tears coming down her cheeks.

"She's gone. My mother. It's only these last few minutes we became mother and daughter," Linda cried, then fell into John's arms.

The next day John made all the arrangements for the funeral. Mrs. Big was buried two days later in the main cemetery, and a special headstone was affixed on her grave.

Two months later, John said goodbye to Linda and her family. Her husband was transferred to his new job in Pittsburgh.

"Please, John, put flowers on her grave, and I'll come from time to time to put some myself," Linda told him before leaving. John had lost his two best friends, and all he had to turn to was his own family.

*

It was September 1985, a bright Sunday. Mary's parents came to visit them. They brought gifts for their grandchildren, whom they hadn't seen for over two years. Mary hugged her mother, then her father.

"I'm so glad you guys came," she said softly.

John felt strange when the Youngs arrive. It was as if something was going to happen. He didn't know what. If it was good or bad. When the Youngs left, John went and looked at his handgun. He wanted to make sure it was there. He realized that he wouldn't hesitate to use it on any intruder to protect his precious family.

*

It was November 3, 1985. John had put his two children to bed, then he kissed them good-night and went back downstairs. He and Mary looked at television until 11.30, then they went to bed.

"John, I want you to make love to me," Mary told him, her hand on his chest.

"Why tonight? We always make love on weekends, hon," John told her softly.

"I really feel randy tonight, and I need you to take me," she said, and held herself close to him.

John felt tired, but he couldn't resist his beautiful wife when it came to having sex with her. When the lovemaking was over, they both went to sleep, then after an hour that morning, Mary woke John up.

"I hear someone downstairs in the house, John," she said softly, as she poked him in the side.

"What's up, hon?" he asked half awake.

"I hear someone downstairs," she whispered.

John shook his head, so as to make himself fully awake. He jumped out of bed and went for his handgun from out of the clothes closet, and tiptoed out of the room.

"Be careful, John," Mary said softly.

He went down the stairs slowly. When he got to the bottom of the stairs, he was hit swiftly on the head with a hard object. He then fell onto the floor unconscious. Shortly afterwards, he opened his eyes, and the bright lights on the stairs were on. Then he heard footsteps coming down the stairs. He didn't move. He waited until the intruder was near to him, then he got up quickly, and struggled with him. The intruder had a ski-mask in his left hand, and the handgun in his right hand. The two men struggled face to face. John kept looking at his hard, ugly face, a serious face with a scar on the right side. John was still gazing onto his face when the handgun went off twice. John fell to the floor and all he could see was the intruder gazing down at him. Then the handgun was thrown at his side. After a few seconds, he struggled and picked up the handgun. He slowly got up, holding his wounds with his left hand, and the gun in his right hand. He made his way through the front door, then he took a blind shot at the intruder, who was running down the street. Then he collapsed onto the sidewalk in front of his house. The gun fell to his side.

"What really happened? I want to know what really happened?" John said to himself as he sat in his cell.

"So you want to know what really happened?" a coarse voice said from the other cell.

"Yes. He killed my family and I am taking the rap," John told the guy in the other cell.

"That's what they all say. They didn't do it."

"But I didn't do it," he snapped.

"Well, tell it to the judge," the prisoner said, and started laughing at John.

"Yes, it is now a big laughing matter," John said to himself.

Later that evening the guard came to get John. He had a visitor. He was taken to the waiting area in front of the building. There he saw Karen Hill. He went over to the table and sat with her. He just looked at her, and didn't say any thing for a few seconds. It was as if he was trying to think what to say to her, then he forced a smile. "You are my first visitor," he said, partly looking at her and partly looking at the wall behind them. He felt dirty. He was in a government building where he never expected he'd be held as a prisoner.

"I went to your home and I saw the note you left me on the door. John, I'm sorry," Karen said frantically.

"Don't be Karen. I saw it coming," he said grimly.

"Do you have a lawyer as yet?" she asked.

"They are assigning me with one tomorrow. Not that I need one. I'm not guilty," John sighed. "I wish I had died with them, then I wouldn't be in this terrible situation," he blurted sadly.

"I'm sure this is a big mistake on their part. Your lawyer will be able to straighten out things for you, and you will be out of this place in no time," Karen told him.

"I hope so, Karen, but I doubt it. I know they'll throw me to the dogs," John said angrily.

John saw the guard wave to him that his time was up.

"I have to go now, Karen," he said and touched her hand.

"I'll be back to see you, John, so keep your fingers crossed," she told him as he left the room.

John went back to his tiny cell, and threw himself onto his small bed. He had all the comforts of home, a flush toilet and a small wash basin.

"So Brother, did you have a nice chat with your visitor?" the voice asked from the adjacent cell.

"Yes, I did. The lady in question is my nurse and friend. My name is John, since we weren't properly introduced," John said abruptly.

"You may call me Bill, but not William. So you have a nurse who's a friend?" Bill inquired.

"She took good care of me when I was ill in hospital. I was shot twice in the chest by the burglar who broke into our house," he told him sadly.

"You're lucky to have a personal nurse. I wish I had someone like that to take a personal interest in me," Bill said sternly.

"In a way I'm lucky; I really needed a good friend when I lost my family, whom I loved very much. Karen is the one who helped me back to my feet. I'm grateful to her, but I can never return the favor," John declared.

"You said you didn't do the crime?"

"Oh, no! I loved my family and I'd never harm them," he snapped.

"But John, they'll blame you, and you're going to be the one to pay. The first step is to get you in here, then the next step is to convict you, and send you to prison for life," the coarse voice in the next cell told him. John kept a steady gaze at the tall, black man in the next cell.

"I suppose you're speaking from experience," John said.

"Yes, I was convicted several times for burglary, and I served several years in prison," Bill admitted to John, who was a stranger to him. John felt the man was telling him the truth because he sensed he was going to be in real trouble very soon.

"Did you ever kill anyone in the process?" John asked.

"No. I only wanted to take some of their belongings, and not to harm anyone in the process," Bill told him.

"The burglar who broke into my house killed my family and shot me and left me for dead. I survived only to find myself here in jail," John blurted.

"He's not only a burglar, but also a killer," Bill declared.

"You're right at that, Bill," John snapped.

"I suppose they didn't catch that burglar, otherwise, you wouldn't be in this wretched place."

"Your guess is right, Bill. And the worst is yet to come," John admitted.

"I hope you have a good lawyer, Brother, otherwise they'll never let you out of this place," Bill advised.

"I really don't care a damn whether they keep me or let me go," John said loudly.

"That's the spirit, John. Keep it up and you'll be in prison forever," Bill told him and started laughing hysterically in his cell.

"I'm in deep trouble and he's laughing his head off. How funny!" John uttered to himself.

Chapter Seven

The following day a black lawyer was assigned to John. He arrived in John's cell just after 10.30 a.m. John was sitting on his bed, and he looked up at the lawyer, who was neatly dressed in a brown suit. He was tall, broad shouldered and in his thirties. John didn't get up to welcome him. He didn't think he needed a lawyer. He was bewildered, as his very life was on the line, and now he had to put his whole fate in the hands of a lawyer he hardly knew.

"Mr. Stone, I was asked to represent you. My name is Sam Anderson."

John kept a steady gaze at Mr. Anderson. "So – you are going to represent me?" John asked bluntly.

"Yes, Mr. Stone. Would that be a problem?" Mr. Anderson asked bluntly.

John got up from his bed and showed the lawyer to the table with two chairs. They both sat down.

"Well, Mr. Anderson, what do you need to know?"

"I want you to tell me everything you can remember, even the smallest details," Sam Anderson said, and took out his notebook and pencil from his briefcase, and got ready to take notes.

"You have to understand that the most crucial points of what happened that morning, I have no recollection of, and that is the murders of my family," John explained.

"I understand, Mr. Stone. We'll put all the pieces together as we go. It will be just like a puzzle."

"Call me, John," he said as he felt more at ease with his lawyer.

"And you can call me Sam," the lawyer said, smiling. "I feel by now you have got over the problem of my color and we can work together," he added.

John smiled at him. "You saw right through me. I'm sorry," John told him.

"Well, John, we have a lot of work to do, so I can clear you of these murder charges. You relate them to me now and I'll take notes."

For forty minutes John recounted all the information he could remember to his lawyer. Mr. Anderson studied the information for a few minutes, then he looked at John. The two men gazed at each other for a few seconds.

"Well, Sam?" John asked.

"I'll give it to you straight, John. All the evidence points to you, and we don't have a witness to corroborate your story. Your neighbor next door found you unconscious, and the gun was still in your right hand. This is going to be a very tough case on our part, unless we can come up with a witness to back up your story. I'll make some investigations immediately and get to the bottom of this," Mr. Anderson explained.

"I understand. You do your best to prove I am innocent, Sam," John said calmly.

"I'll see you on the day of your arraignment. They'll have to set a date so you can appear in front of a judge, and at that time you'll be free to go home or you'll be held over for trial," Mr. Anderson told him.

"Well, see you in court, Councilor," John said and followed Mr. Anderson to the cell door.

John was told on Monday that his preliminary hearing was set for Wednesday 12th of January. On that day he was taken to the court by two guards, and he met his lawyer, Sam Anderson. They sat a table and started to discuss what would be the outcome of the case.

"John, I spoke to your next-door neighbor, Mr. Roberts. He gave me a statement, and I got the impression from him that he saw more than he was willing to tell. If he tells what he really saw, you may be in the clear," Mr. Anderson explained to John.

"And if he doesn't say what he saw?" John asked.

Mr. Anderson smiled and shook his head. "Then you'll be in big trouble, I'm sorry to say. I'll do my best, but all the evidence now points to you, John," he stressed.

"I understand, and justice will be served one way or the other," John said with a grunt.

Judge Walter Blackman came from the back of the court and sat on the bench. John Stone's case was the first to be called. The judge read John's file, then looked at the three men in front of him.

"Your Honor, I am Sam Anderson, acting for the defendant, Mr. Stone."

"Your Honor, I am Donald Kemp, prosecution for the State."

"Thank you, gentlemen. Mr. Stone, I have read your file. Mr. John Stone, you are charged with the murders in the first degree of Mary Stone, David Stone and Cindy Stone. How do you plead?" Judge Blackman asked, looking at John.

"I didn't do it, Your Honor."

"Are you pleading not guilty, Mr. Stone?" the judge asked.

"Not guilty, sir," John said quickly.

"Your plea of not guilty will be noted on your file, Mr. Stone."

"Your Honor, in view of the serious nature of the crimes Mr. Stone is charged with, I would request that bail be denied," Mr. Kemp told the judge.

"Mr. Anderson, do you have anything to add?"

"Your Honor, Mr. Stone doesn't require any bail, and he is quite willing to stay in the City Jail until a date is set for his trial," Mr. Anderson told the judge.

"So noted Mr. Kemp and Mr. Anderson. Mr. Stone will be held in custody until a trial date is set, and you'll be notified. Thank you, gentlemen," the judge said and closed the file.

"Well, John, we'll be in touch," Mr. Anderson told him.

John didn't say anything, and was led away by a guard to the back entrance, and taken to his jail cell. He didn't know that his story would get so much attention because the press and the television had picked up on the story. He realized that the situation would get even worse. He had received many cards and letters from his friend and of the members of the Baptist church. The letters and cards were all addressed to the City Jail.

That evening John met Karen in the waiting room. They sat together at a table. He just looked at her for a few seconds, and he didn't say anything. His face was pulled together, and his eyes were red. He shook his head, and breathed in and out.

"John I'm sorry. I heard it on the news," she said softly, as she looked at him steadily.

John forced a smile, and clenched his right fist, and hit it lightly on the table as though he was beating a drum.

"The judge asked me if I were guilty or not? I wanted to know how could he ask me such a question? I loved my family. Why should I kill them?" John said bitterly. "Why is this happening to me?" he asked her.

"I can't answer your question. I'm more in the dark than you are! I think about you and I can't concentrate on my work. John, I think about what you are going through," she said, shaking her head from side to side, as the tears came down her cheeks.

"I can't let this happen to you, Karen. I never wanted you to get too involved with me, and now you are. It can't be, it can't be. You are too nice a person to get involved with me," John told her quickly.

"I became involved with you from the first moment you became my patient. I have no regrets, no matter what happens, John. You know the way I feel about you. I love you and I can't take back the hands of time," she said softly and touched his right hand that was on top of the table, then she gazed at him for a while. "John, you know I love you, and I want to help you in whatever way I can," she added.

"My dear Karen, you have helped me to see the light and more than I deserved. Now, I must face the music myself," John said with a smile on his face. "Now come on and smile for me now, and that's all I'll need to get me through each day," he added.

Karen gave John a big smile. "That should be big enough to last you for a few days, John. I wish there were more I can do for you," she said and squeezed his hand.

The guard hinted to John that his time was up. John got up and on his way back to his cell, he looked back at Karen. She waved at him and he read her lips, as they stated, "I love you."

On the 6th of March 1986, John Stone was finally put on trial. Judge George Sloan was presiding. The prosecution for the State was Donald Kemp. And Sam Anderson for the defense. The men and women of the jury were all in their seats. The courtroom was packed with spectators and the curious. The press and the television would carry the story.

John looked on carefully in front of the court, and he felt all eyes were on him. Everyone wanted to know what his fate would be.

"I can't believe all these people are here to see me go down the drain," John told Mr. Anderson.

"They're only here to see justice is done."

"My justice or the State's justice?"

"That's left to be seen, John. Be patient and don't be so serious. Smile now and then," he advised.

Judge Sloan arrived on the bench, and everyone stood up, then the first day of John Stone versus the State was about to begin.

This was the first time John was in a courtroom, and charged with a serious crime. He felt nervous and humiliated at the fact that he had become the center of attraction. He felt like a puppet on strings.

"Good morning ladies and gentlemen of the jury. My name is Donald Kemp, prosecution for the State. Mr. John Stone is going to be tried for the murders of his family, his wife, his son and his daughter. And after you have heard all the evidence, you must bring in a verdict of murder in the first degree. Thank you."

The lawyer for the defense stood up. "Good morning ladies and gentlemen of the jury. My name is Sam Anderson, defense for Mr. John Stone. Mr. Stone has been a very good citizen for over ten years since he came to live and work in the City of Philadelphia. Mr. Stone is a victim of an unfortunate situation, and that's why he's here charged with the murders of his family. And after you have heard all the evidence, you'll have no choice but to bring in a verdict of not guilty. Thank you."

The first witness was Sergeant Paul Lang who was called to the stand by the prosecution.

"Sergeant Lang, please tell the court why you arrested Mr. Stone for the murders of his family, Mary Stone, David Stone and Cindy Stone?" Mr. Kemp asked the witness.

"Yes, sir. After six weeks of investigation into the murders of Mr. Stone's family, three months before, Mr. Stone took out large life policies on his family and himself."

"How large were these life policies?"

"For $100,000 each, and this amount doubles in case of accidental death."

"What happened next, Sergeant?"

"Mr. Stone had bought a .38 handgun from a gun shop in the city. The owner will testify to that."

"What happened next, Sergeant Lang?"

"On the morning, the 3rd of November 1986, I was sent to the home of Mr. Stone, which was the crime scene. I collected a .38

handgun which was taken from the right hand of Mr. Stone by a paramedic, who was first on the scene. It was placed into a plastic bag for evidence. The gun was left with the policeman on duty at the crime scene that morning."

Mr. Kemp showed the gun in the plastic bag to Sergeant Lang. "Is this the gun you were given that morning?"

"Yes, sir."

"Is this the gun that shot Mary Stone, David Stone and Cindy Stone?"

"Yes, sir. The bullets came from that gun, and Mr. Stone's prints were on the gun."

"What did Mr. Stone tell you when you interviewed him the first time?"

"He told me he was hit in the head by an intruder who broke into his home. The intruder took his gun while he was unconscious. The next thing he knew when he became conscious, he struggled with the intruder, who came down the stairs. The two men struggled at the bottom of the stairs, then the intruder shot him twice in the chest. He fell to the floor. The intruder threw his gun back at him, then he picked up the gun and went after the intruder. He fired the gun outside the front door at the intruder, then he fell near the sidewalk unconscious. He still held the gun tightly in his right hand."

"Did you believe his story, Sergeant Lang?"

"Yes, at first I did, but after further investigation, his story didn't stand up."

"And why is that?" the prosecution asked, smiling.

"There was no forced entry into Mr. Stone's home. None of his neighbors saw anyone going in or out of the house. Mrs. Thomas, his next-door neighbor stated that the couple were always shouting and fighting over money, and she'll testify to the fact."

"Thank you, Sergeant Lang. Your witness Mr. Anderson," Mr. Kemp said and sat down at his table.

Mr. Anderson stood up and came out to question the witness. "Sergeant Lang, is it true that you're now on top of the list for promotion to lieutenant?"

Mr. Kemp stood up. "I object to the line of questioning, which has no bearing on the case."

Your Honor, I'm trying to bring to light why my client was charged," Mr. Anderson told the judge.

"Objection overruled. The witness may answer the question," the judge said.

"Yes," Sergeant Lang replied.

"Is it true that if my client is convicted of murder, you may stand a better chance of that promotion?"

"Yes. It may throw some light on it."

"The fact is that it may throw a lot of light on it. This case is the biggest case you have had in years. Can you tell me how many years?"

"My last big case was five years ago."

"So this case would put you in the limelight?"

"Maybe," Sergeant Lang said, smiling.

"Well, let's get back to the actual case at hand. So far Sergeant Lang, you have done a good job in your investigation. The life insurance policies and the .38 handgun are the two main items in this case. Do you agree, Sergeant Lang?"

"Yes."

"Do you know why Mr. Stone bought such large life insurance policies on his family and himself?"

"I don't know."

"Well, I'll put the question in a different way. Why do people take out life insurance policies?"

"The answer would be to protect themselves and their families."

"Is it possible that Mr. Stone bought those life policies to protect himself and his family?"

"Yes, it's possible."

"Now to the .38 caliber handgun. Sergeant Lang, if you were living in an area where there were lots of break-ins, would you buy a handgun to protect your family?"

"Yes. If you put it that way, sir."

"Isn't it possible that Mr. Stone bought the .38 caliber handgun to protect his family? And that's all?"

"Yes."

"You said in your statement that you interviewed several of Mr. Stone's neighbors. And they heard nothing on the morning of the 3rd of November 1986. Is that true?"

"Yes."

"Did those neighbors gave you the impression that they didn't want to get deeply involved in the Stones' murders?"

"Yes."

"They didn't want to get involved, therefore, the truth would never come out. Do you agree with that?"

"Yes."

"On the morning of the 3rd of November 1986, when Mr. Stone was found outside his home unconscious, the paramedic who was first on the scene had to pry the handgun out of Mr. Stone's hand. He said in his statement that Mr. Stone held the gun tightly, as though his very life depended it. Could it have been that he wanted to shoot someone other than himself or his family at that time?"

"It's possible."

"Maybe the intruder who was making a getaway?"

"It's possible," Sergeant Lang said.

"As you said, Sergeant, anything is possible. Thank you," Mr. Anderson told him.

John sat quietly in the courtroom and listened to all the questions put to the witnesses. He thought it was a waste of time, but it had to be done, so the truth would be open to anyone, especially the ladies and gentlemen of the jury.

Two weeks went by and John listened carefully to all the witnesses. He felt sick by all the questions asked by the prosecution and the defense. It was like a circus to him, with all the ranting and raving of the people in the court. One woman shouted in the court: "You should die for killing your family!" And she was removed from the court. He knew in a way she was right.

He listened to the doctor who saved his life, and the coroner who did the autopsy on his family, the insurance agent who sold him the life insurance policies, the gunsmith who sold him the gun. Then his next-door neighbor who held back some of what he saw, and his other neighbor who told the court that he was always fighting and screaming at his wife about money. She didn't like John because he told her not to tie the dog on his fence. Two weeks later the dog had died and she blamed him for it. The state was now blaming him for the deaths of his family.

John spent the weekend reading in his cell. When he wasn't reading, he would think how he'd face life if he were found guilty. His life would come to an end; he would be alive and yet dead to the world.

Karen Hill went to visit John that Sunday afternoon. She didn't say much. She picked each word carefully, and tried her best to cheer John up. John looked at Karen's beautiful face most of the time because he felt it would be the last time he'd see her close up.

"Well, the jury will finally make up their minds next week about me. I can't bear the waiting. I want to get it over with one way or the other," he told Karen sadly.

"John, you have to think positive and don't give up," Karen said softly and touched his hand.

"I'm sorry, but I can't help thinking that I deserve whatever I get. I let them die. I was responsible for them. I was the man of the house. I was too weak to save my family," he told her.

"You can't blame yourself, John."

"Who can I blame? No one but me," he said.

On Monday the prosecution and the defense would give their closing arguments. John didn't want to hear the closing arguments, but he was brought into court anyway.

Donald Kemp, the prosecution was first to address the jury. John realized that the prosecution was going to make the final dent on him, a dent that was going to put him away for a long time.

"Ladies and gentlemen of the jury, I must thank you for listening and gathering all of the evidence from all the witnesses who were put on the stand. Shortly, you'll have to take all the evidence in consideration, and deliberate on a verdict.

"You have heard the paramedic stated that Mr. Stone held the handgun tightly in his right hand after he had shot his family. Then he turned the gun on himself. He shot himself in such a way that he wouldn't die right away. Then he went outside his front door and fired another shot, so as to alert his next-door neighbor, Mr. Roberts. Fortunately, Mr. Roberts called 911, and Mr. Stone's life was saved.

"Mr. Stone took out large life insurance policies on his family and himself, then he bought the .38 caliber handgun.

"Mrs. Wilma Thomas stated Mr. Stone was always fighting with his wife, and this was over money. He was highly in debt, then he came up with a great plan, a plan to kill his family and collect the big bucks from their life insurance policies. But this great plan of his backfired on him, and he was only left holding a bone.

"No one in that area saw an intruder entering or leaving Mr. Stone's house on that sad morning of November the 3rd, 1986. Mr.

Stone was the only one there holding the handgun tightly in his right hand, and his prints were found on the gun, and most of all, the gun was his.

"So ladies and gentlemen of the jury, you must go through the evidence very carefully, and bring in a verdict of murder in the first degree. Thank you for your time and effort," Mr. Kemp said and sat down.

John knew it was now Mr. Anderson's turn to put forward his striking argument to the jury. He didn't think it would make much of a difference to them. He felt the jury had already made up their minds about him, but one had to go through the course of time in a court of law, no matter what.

Mr. Anderson got up from his comfortable seat and went over to where the jury were sitting. He looked at them for a few seconds before starting his closing speech.

"Ladies and gentlemen of the jury. You have heard the closing speech of the prosecution. You have also heard many witnesses who gave their testimony.

"Mr. Stone is a good citizen. He has been since he came to live in Philadelphia over ten years ago. He loved his family, and he has worked hard to take care of them. He went to church every Sunday. He would never do anything to harm anyone. He was always willing to help his fellow human beings.

"As I told you in my opening statement, Mr. Stone was a victim of an unfortunate situation. He was planning ahead for his family, so they could have had a better life in this modern society.

"He increased the life insurance on himself and his family. He wanted to provide for them in case anything happened to him and he'd be provided for in case anything happened to any one of them.

"There were many break-ins in that neighborhood, so Mr. Stone bought a handgun to protect himself and his family.

"That sad morning of the 3rd of November 1986, Mr. Stone heard a noise downstairs and went cautiously to investigate. He took no chances. He took his .38 handgun with him. He didn't turn on the light for the stairs. He went slowly down the stairway in the dark, and at the bottom of the stairs he was hit with a hard object on the head. Then he fell onto the floor unconscious. The intruder who hit him on the head took his handgun, then went upstairs to Mr. Stone's family. Mr. Stone didn't know what happened at that point. He was unconscious. When he became conscious, the lights were on in the stairs. His assailant came down the stairs, and they struggled together. His assailant had a ski-mask in his left hand and the handgun in his right hand. Mr. Stone saw his face, then the gun went off two times in his chest. Mr. Stone fell to the floor, and the gun was thrown at him by his assailant. The intruder made his way through the front door. Mr. Stone picked up the handgun and struggled after the intruder, then he fired the gun once at the intruder on the street, then he fell onto the sidewalk in front of his house. He held the gun tightly in his right hand. It was if his very life depended on that gun.

"But what really happened to Mr. Stone's wife, son and daughter? No one really knows. We can only assume what really happened that morning.

"Mrs. Stone heard the struggle downstairs. She turned on the lights on the stairs, and she came face to face with the intruder. He forced her into the bedroom. She fought him off like a wild cat, and pulled off his ski-mask. She saw his face and for that he shot her. The children heard their mother screaming and ran into the room. They found the intruder over her body, and they attacked him. He had no choice but to shoot them, also. Then he hurried down to the bottom of the stairs where he met Mr. Stone. You know the rest.

"I believe Mr. Stone's next-door neighbor heard the shots in the house. He also saw the intruder who came out of Mr. Stone's house. He saw him under the street lights. Mr. Roberts saw Mr. Stone took a shot at the intruder, then Mr. Stone fell to the ground. I believe that the intruder saw Mr. Roberts and threatened his very life. Mr. Roberts was afraid and didn't tell the whole truth in court. I hope that he'll come forward and tell the truth before it's too late.

"Ladies and gentlemen of the jury, Mr. Stone is a good citizen. Please don't punish him for something he didn't do. You'll have to bring in a verdict of not guilty. Thank you for your time."

The following day the jury came back with a verdict. John stood up with his lawyer as the foreman of the jury read the verdict.

"We, the jury, find the defendant, Mr. John Stone, guilty of murder in the first degree of his family."

"I'm sorry, John. I tried my best for you," Mr. Anderson told him.

John smiled at him. "Don't be, Sam. You did your best. Now it's time for me to pay. I don't want you to appeal against the verdict. I want this to end now," John told him bluntly, then he was taken away by a guard.

Three days later, John was taken to the court for sentencing. His last court appearance. He stood in front of Judge Sloan.

"Mr. Stone, do you have anything to say to this court before this court passes sentence on you?" the judge asked from the bench.

"Yes, Your Honor, I do. I have heard what all the witnesses had to say, and the jury listened carefully to them, and now it's my turn to speak. I wish I had died with my family, instead of having been tried for their deaths. I was a victim also, because I was shot by the same intruder. I didn't shoot myself or my family, as indicated by the prosecution. I want the whole world to know that I loved my family, and I would never have harmed them. If they were here, they would tell you that. I'm only guilty of letting my family die at the hands of the burglar. He murdered them with my gun. The gun I bought to protect them at all costs, but I failed to do so. Your Honor, I deserve the punishment you are about to pass on me for not protecting my beloved family," John said, with tears coming down his cheeks. Then John bowed his head in shame.

"Thank you, Mr. Stone, for a very gripping account, but all the evidence pointed to you, and you were found guilty of the murders of your family in the first degree. With the power vested in me by the State, I hereby sentence you, John Stone, to fifteen years in the state penitentiary. You were an outstanding citizen before this crime and you'll be considered for parole after six years."

"Thank you, Your Honor," John said humbly. Then he was led away by two guards. He looked sideways and saw Karen Hill in the courtroom, then he shook his head, and went with the guards through the back entrance. John realized that it was finally over, and now he'd have some peace and quiet.

Chapter Eight

John Stone was transported to the Pennsylvania State Penitentiary with four other prisoners. The black van stopped in front of the prison gate, then the steel gate opened automatically. The van then proceeded into the prison yard, and stopped by the side entry door.

The driver came out and opened the back door of the van with his pass key, then he smiled at his passengers, who were seated in the van.

"Well, you guys are here. Home sweet home. All out now," the driver said, and stood aside as the five prisoners came out of the van for inspection. Three guards came out of the building to sign for the prisoners, and took them in their charge. The chains from their legs were unlocked, and each prisoner was inspected.

John gazed around the area, and saw the large, gray building, which looked like a large rooming house from the outside. He knew in a short while he would be given lodging and board. He felt weak and his legs shook like a leaf. The good life he had cherished so much had now come to an abrupt end.

He remembered the booklet they had given him about his new home in the country.

The Pennsylvania State Prison was built in the early 18th century, and was one of the oldest prisons in the States. It stood on 75 acres of land. It had three levels, and it was built to house 3000 inmates, but in 1986 it housed over 4000. However, because of the overcrowding situation, prisoners only spent short sentences for petty crimes, also for crimes of a more severe nature.

The prison had a high electrified fence around it, and the exercise yard was big as two football fields.

John was taken to the second floor, where he had to strip, then he was searched. After, he had to taken a shower, he was given his quota of clothing, towels and sheets. Then he was taken to his cell on the third floor by one of the guards, who was tall, with broad shoulders. He wanted to be addressed as Mr. Whitman. John was taken to the northern side of the building and was shown to cell 1450. The cell door was opened, and John stood in front of it for a few second, and hesitated to go in.

"Well, don't be afraid to go in. Cell 1450 will be your home for several years," guard Whitman told him with a smile. John entered the cell, then turned around to the guard.

"Thank you, Mr. Whitman."

"I'm glad you remember my name. Most cellmates don't. The top bunk is yours. Mr. Lee will be your cellmate," the guard said and left.

John threw all his stuff on the small table in the corner, and sat down on one of the chairs, then he slowly viewed his cell. The cell was eight feet by ten feet, with two bunk beds, a small table and two chairs, a toilet and washbasin. He had all the comforts of home. The cell was painted in gray and he hated the color. He hoped some day he'd be able to paint it in a brighter color, off-white.

Lee sounded Chinese, John thought. They had put him into a cell with a Chinese cellmate. He didn't know how he'd deal with different nationalities in the prison. He would have to deal with Africans, Indians, Mexicans, and most of all, his own nationality. On the outside he had dealt with all sorts of people, but in the prison it was completely different. He'd have to play it by ear, and see how he'd be able to cope with the situation, a situation of bad guys of every nationality.

Later that afternoon, John met his cellmate, Mr. Lee, who was short, slim, with squint black eyes, and in his late fifties. He had a full head of hair, which was black and plastered down on his head. He looked at John for a few seconds and smiled at him in a friendly way.

"I'm Ling Lee," he said humbly.

"I'm John Stone," he said and shook hands with Ling Lee.

"I know all about you, John. I have read about you in the newspapers. I know you were treated unfairly, and you shouldn't be here," Ling told him.

John smiled at him. "There's nothing I can do about that now, Mr. Lee. What are you in here for?" John asked.

Mr. Lee sat at the table with John. "A long story, John. I found my beloved wife with another man. I was filled with rage, and she got the worst of me. The man escaped with his life, and I got a life sentence," Mr. Lee explained.

"I'm sorry, Mr. Lee."

"Don't be. I did what I had to do and I have no regrets for my action."

"I'm guilty for letting my family die by the hands of a burglar," John said and stopped short.

"You have to think of yourself now, John, and you'll have to live your life in a different way. You're in another world now, and there will be lots for you to learn," Mr. Lee explained.

"I don't know how I'm going to cope with all of this. Sometimes I wished that I had died with my family, and I wouldn't have to face all of this," John said sadly.

"You have to make the best of it, and there's nothing you can do, John. I only have five more months to do, and I'll be in another world again," Mr. Lee told him.

"What will you do on the outside?"

"I have a brother in Chinatown, New York. He owns a restaurant, and he'll find some work for me."

"I was lucky to get only fifteen years for my whole family," John told him.

"If you are lucky, you'll be out in less than half the time."

"What work do you do here?" John asked.

"I work in the laundry room. And most probably you'll be assigned to the stores."

"How do you know that?"

"My previous cellmate worked in the stores. So you'll be his replacement," Mr. Lee told him. "I have a feeling that we are going to become good friends."

John smiled at Mr. Lee. "I'm beginning to have the same feeling also, Mr. Lee."

The next morning after breakfast, John was assigned to the prison stores. His job was to separate the different sizes of clothing that came from the laundry room. He worked with five other prisoners, and Nick Wilson was the prisoner in charge of the stores. He was black, short, fat, and elderly. He assigned jobs to the other prisoners.

"John, I must warn you to keep away from Joe and Brian. They work on the other side of the store, and they'll try to bully you as you're new here," Nick told him.

"Thanks, Nick, but I'll mind my own business," John told him frankly.

Nick smiled at him. "If that's the case, you'll be in real trouble, Brother."

"What do you mean?" John asked.

"All I can tell you is to watch your backside, if you know what I mean?" Nick said quickly.

"I'm beginning to understand you, Nick. Now to work, and thanks for the information," John said, and begun to sort out the different clothing from the laundry baskets.

John realized what Nick had told him. He had read stuff like that in the newspapers about the men prisoners taking advantage and abusing the newcomers. Now he was in the same situation, and he didn't think that would happen to him. But maybe he was wrong and it could happen to him. Those bullies feed on the weak, and he was the weak, and there was nothing he could do about it. He wasn't a fighter; he was only a good talker.

The next day in the store, the two bullies, Joe and Brian, came over to him, and tried to introduce themselves. Joe was short, fat, his teeth were black from smoking, and he was partly bald. Brian was tall, slim, with long black hair, and some of his front teeth were missing. John remembered what Nick had told him and he didn't want to have any part of these men, but he didn't want to offend them.

"So you are new here? What's your name, Pretty Boy?" Joe asked with his mouth wide open.

"My name is none of your business. Now leave me alone," John told him bluntly.

"We're trying to be friendly, Pretty Boy, and you should take us up on our hospitality," Brian said, pointing his index finger at John. Then Joe put his right hand through John's hair. Joe and Brian stood close to John. He stopped breathing as he couldn't stand their bad breath.

"Nice hair you have, Pretty Boy," Joe told him.

"We'll be back again, Pretty Boy," Brian said.

"You men get back to work," Nick shouted from the other side of the building.

"And you have a nice day, Pretty Boy," Brian said, smiling. Then both men left. John stood there and gazed at them, and he realized the worst was yet to come.

Nick came over to John. "Those two are a bad lot. Keep away from them," Nick told him.

"I can certainly keep away from them, but can they keep away from me?" John said, pressing his lips together.

"That's something for you to decide, John. I know those two and they'll get you sooner or later."

"I would rather for them not to get me, but I know that's impossible," John said, and went back to sorting the shirts.

Nick turned back to John. "One more thing, if you need a shower, you can leave early before those two thugs get into the shower with you."

"Thank you again, Nick. I appreciate the advice."

John now had to worry about getting a shower, and also saving his backside. He didn't know who his real enemies were as yet, but he was sure that he was going to find out very soon.

That afternoon John left his workplace early as he was told to do, and went for a quick shower. There was no one in the showers when he arrived, so he could have a shower without any interruption. He stripped and got into the shower, then turned on the water, and soaped himself. When he washed away the soap from his eyes, he saw his two worst enemies in front of him. They had followed him to the showers. They were staring at him, and he realized what they wanted to do to him. He dropped the soap, and put his hands over his mouth.

"Pretty Boy, we got you now," Joe said teasingly.

John just stood in the shower, and he couldn't move. He was just waiting for them to attack him. He didn't have the strength to put up a fight with them. Then he realized that he had to do something to defend himself. He was a man, and he couldn't just stand there, and let the two bullies take advantage of him. He had to think fast and make his move. He bit his lower lip and breathed in and out.

"Well, Joe, we'll have to make friends with Pretty Boy. Look what soft, nice parts he has. We'll have to become friends with him, so we can all become friends," Brian said, smiling.

"We are wasting time. Get him, Brian, and we'll teach him a lesson that he'll never forget," Joe told his friend.

John knew he had to make his move immediately. He jumped out of the shower, hitting Joe to the floor. Brian then hit John several times in the chest until he fell to the floor, then the two men raped him several times on the floor. Then they left him bleeding from the mouth on the floor. He was weak and dazed, and his whole body was shivering.

"Why me? Why me?" he cried to himself. Then his strength slowly came back to him. He struggled up and went back into the shower. He felt dirty and he wanted to wash away all the dirt and germs that the two bullies had left on him. He cried, and tried his best to hold back his true feelings. He soaped his sore body over and over again to wash away the filth that was left on it.

Then he slowly dried himself and got dressed and made his way out of the shower area. He saw from a side glance that the other prisoners in the shower were looking at him curiously. He just walked past without glancing at his viewers.

John arrived back in his cell and climbed into his bunk bed. He needed to rest his painful body.

"John, are you all right?" Lee asked.

John groaned from his bunk, and didn't answer. Lee got up from his seat at the table and went to view John at a closer range. "What did they do to you?"

John turned to face Lee. "They raped me in the showers. Those two bastards. I hate them. The way I feel I could kill them. Those two no good..." John cried.

"I'm sorry, John, but you'll have to get tough with those two, otherwise, they'll do it again, if I'm right."

"They'll do it again?" John asked.

"Yes, I'm afraid so," Lee replied.

"This is really terrible. What can I do? I don't know how to fight."

"I can help you to defend yourself, John. You're my friend and I want to help you," Lee told him.

"You'll help me to fight?"

"Yes, I know Kung Fu, and I can train you in a short while to defend yourself against those two bullies."

"I don't know, Lee, I'm a peaceful person, and I don't want to make waves with anyone, especially in here."

"Well, it's your right to be a peaceful person, but you wouldn't survive in this place for very long. It's only the strongest who'd survive in this place," Lee told him sternly.

John came down from his bunk and both men faced each other.

"Look at me, Lee. Do I look strong enough to fight those two big thugs?" John asked.

"No, John, but your real strength is inside of you and all you have to do is to bring it out. That I can teach you," Lee explained.

John sat down at the table while Lee wiped the blood away from his face with a wet towel.

"I'll think about your offer, Lee, but I don't think it will be necessary."

"I'll be here if you need me, and I know that will be very soon," Lee told him sternly.

The next day John went to work in the stores, and the first thing he did was to march over to where the two bullies, Joe and Brian worked. He stood there face to face with the two men, and gazed at them steadily for a while.

"Pretty Boy came to see us, Joe," Brian said with a teasing smile on his face.

"Yes, he likes us now that he has had a taste of us," Joe said, smiling.

John didn't blink, and he just kept a steady gaze at the two thugs. "You try that again on me and I'll kill you both. I promise you that, and I'll face another life sentence," John told them sternly.

"Are you threatening us, Pretty Boy?" Joe asked him.

"Yes, and I mean it," John said quickly, and left for the other side of the store.

"We'll get you, Pretty Boy," Brian shouted after John.

John didn't look back or pay any attention to his attackers, and went back to his workplace. Nick came over quickly to him.

"I heard what happened to you, John. I'm sorry, but I warned you about those two. Some day someone is going to wipe them clean off the face of the earth," Nick told him.

"I hate those two bastards, and I'm afraid that someone maybe me," John said without thinking. "Maybe we can take out a contract on them," John added jokingly.

"That will be the day, but that's just a wish," Nick said with a smile, and went back to his side of the store.

John knew that the two bullies didn't scare easily, and he was sure they would come after him again. He didn't know when, but he knew it would be in the showers.

Three days later, John went for a shower. He had put off taking a shower for several days, and he felt he had to take a chance, but he never thought that fate was against him. Before he got his shirt off his back, the two bullies were all over him. They beat him and kicked him on the ground, then pulled off his pants and raped him several times. When they were finished with him, they kicked him again, repeatedly.

"Pretty Boy, that is for shooting off your big mouth that you were going to kill us if we did this to you again," Brian shouted at John.

"You can come any time to kill us, and we'll be waiting for you, sucker," Joe said. Then they both threw John into the shower and turned on the cold water. "Have a nice day, Pretty Boy," Joe said. Then they both left.

"I'll kill them. I'll kill them," John kept saying, as he lay in the shower, the water soaking his bare body. His body was sore and numb and he cried and sobbed. He didn't understand why this was happening to him, and what he'd done to deserve the torture and abuse of those two animals. He felt it was worse than being shot in the chest by the burglar who had entered his home in November 1985.

"John, let me help you."

John looked up, and he recognized the figure above him.

"Ling, they did it to me again," he said slowly, and he was so weak that he could hardly stand up. "I'll have to get tough with those bastards. You were right all along, I'm too soft," John said, sobbing.

"Don't talk, John," Ling said, and helped John out of the shower. He gave him a towel to dry off his skin, then John slowly put on his clothes. Ling helped him back to their cell. Once John was in the cell, he just lay on the floor. Ling simply looked at him, and made no attempt to help him up.

"Ling, you've got to help me. Now I'll do anything. Make me tough, make me strong. I'll do anything so I can fight those two bastards," John cried from the floor.

Three days later, John was transferred to the laundry room, and he knew that Ling was responsible for him been there. He couldn't understand why Ling was trying to help him. It was more likely that he was preparing him for something far greater than just protecting himself in prison, but maybe he was preparing him for life on the outside. He couldn't make sense from any of it, and he'd have to play it by ear.

At the end of each break, Ling would teach John a few easy karate and boxing moves, but most of all, he would teach him how to use and control his mind. Ling had weights for lifting, which were hidden away behind a large washing machine.

"We must do everything in secrecy. No one must know what we are doing, otherwise, we'll be in deep trouble, as this is against the prison rules," Ling told John softly.

"I understand. It will be our little secret. Where did you learn those moves, Ling?"

"When I was younger, I went to Kung Fu School for over three years, and I became a black belt. Then I was able to defend myself. I want to teach you all I know within a short while, so you'll be able to help others with your strength and agility. I have faith in you and I know you can do it," Ling explained to John.

"But how will I learn everything in that short time?"

"I have four or five months to teach, and that's a very long time for you to be my very best student. As I said before, John, I have faith in you, and you seem to pick up everything quickly."

"Thank you, Ling. And I am proud that I have you as my teacher."

"You are welcome, John."

"And after my training, I want to take care of those two thugs," John said eagerly.

"Yes, that will be your first priority, and maybe your starting point to self confidence," Ling told him.

John continued his training in the laundry room, and sometimes in his cell. He followed Ling's instructions carefully. It was something that was making him strong, and at the same time he was able to think more clearly.

After six weeks, John was ready to try out his movements, on no better persons than the two bullies, Brian and Joe.

"Well, John, you have done well, and you're now ready for your first assignment. You have a lot more to learn, but you're so fast in your movements that it makes up for what you don't know."

"All that hard work paid off, and thanks to you, Ling."

"I'm happy to be of assistance to you, John," Ling told him, smiling.

Ling had taught John how to use his mind, and he remembered what Ling had told him.

"It seems as though I have trained you well. You are not afraid of danger any more. I almost think that you like danger now, John," Ling told him.

"You may be right, Ling. I never had that much excitement in my life before, but now things are different. I'm looking forward to facing danger, and that's why I have to meet those two thugs very soon," John explained.

The next afternoon, in the laundry room, Ling gave John his final instructions.

"Well, best of luck, John. Those two animals got your message, and they'll show up in the showers to get you. They have no notion that you have matured since their last encounter with you," Ling told him.

"Yes, they'll be surprised," John said with a smile.

That afternoon John arrived at the back of the shower area. He stood sternly and waited for his two enemies to arrive. He smiled to himself and felt confident that he was now the pursuer, not the pursued. He saw the two bullies arrive in the shower area, then they continued slowly towards him. John felt like a hero in one of the old western movies. He stood straight and tall, and waited patiently for his opponents to come closer. Then they stood face to face. He didn't take his glance off the two men. He stood serious and firm on his own.

"Pretty Boy, where have you been hiding? We got your message to meet you here. We hurried over because we miss you. And here you are, giving yourself to us again. What should we do with you?" Brian said, looking steadily at John's face.

"Well guys, I'm happy to see both of you, especially after our last meeting," John said with a smug smile on his face.

"And I thought Pretty Boy couldn't speak," Joe said, starting to touch John's face. John quickly moved Joe's hand away from his face.

"I called you guys here to settle this conclusively, and to make sure you don't do what you twice did to me to anyone else," John said sternly.

"So, you came to fight us, Pretty Boy?" Joe asked, smiling, and making scornful faces at John.

"Yes," John answered quickly. Then his left and right fists went out swiftly to his opponents, knocking both of them to the ground.

Then he waited. Joe got up first and tried to punch him in the face. John ducked and kicked him in the chest, and he fell to the ground. Brian got up after that, and John kicked him in the face and sent him tumbling beside his partner, Joe. He waited for the two men to get up, but they didn't. John got hold of each man and threw him into a shower, turning the cold water on them. Then he left and made his way outside the shower area.

He knew he should have felt good about the whole situation, but instead he felt bad, so bad that he wished he hadn't beaten them up. But he'd had to prove to himself that he was man enough to fight his opponents, especially to fight and win fairly and squarely. He realized from that very moment that he would gain some respect from the other prisoners as well as from his two bullies. John met Ling Lee outside the shower area.

"Good job, John. I knew you could do it," Ling told him, smiling. "You fought well. They were no match for you."

"They were too hot for me, so I threw them into the shower to cool off," John said, laughing.

"All bets were on you, John. You're a winner," Ling told him, and clapped him on the shoulder. "Now, they'll have to respect you," he added.

Chapter Nine

It was Saturday afternoon when John was called to the waiting area. He had a visitor. When he arrived in the waiting area, he saw Karen. His heart shook instantly as he laid eyes on her. She looked so beautiful and for the first time he wanted to be near her, but he knew it was impossible. He sat down at the table, and gazed at her for a few seconds before speaking.

"Karen," he said softly. "This is a surprise. I thought of you a lot, but I never expected to see you here in person," he said, then forced a smile.

"How are you, John?" she asked. "I wanted to write you, but I thought it would be best to see you personally," she said quickly.

"I feel what you've to say is important that you had to come all this way," he said, still smiling.

"I met a nice young man, and we started going out together. He wants to marry me," she said, not looking at John.

"Well, good for you, Karen," John said cheerfully.

Karen looked up at him. "I thought you'd be mad with me after all we've been through," she said with tears coming down her cheeks.

"I didn't want it to be this way. You're a real gem. You're beautiful, thoughtful, and most of all, you'll make any man a good wife. If I were in a position, I'd ask you myself. It was so good while it lasted. I'm grateful to you for your friendship, and you've made me see the light," John explained. "Don't cry. Be happy," he added.

"I knew you'd understand. I'm sorry things couldn't work out differently for us. Maybe in another world," she said, sobbing.

"Don't be sorry. Be happy for us. I'll always remember you. You are the charming nurse who nursed me back to life, and you became my best friend. Thank you," he said, and touched her hand. Then he tried to hold back the tears.

"Are they treating you well, John?" she asked.

"Yes. I work in the laundry room. My cellmate is Ling Lee. He's like a father to me. He teaches me about life, and how to survive in this place."

"I think you have a real friend."

The guard waved at John that his time was up. John got up and touched Karen's hand.

"For luck, and goodbye, good luck," he said, and left. He didn't look back. He knew that Karen had her own life to live, and she was doing the right thing. She was going to get married to a nice young man, and face a good future together. He was in jail and he couldn't offer her anything but misery.

Two months later, on a Tuesday morning, John felt sad.

His good friend and cellmate, Ling Lee, was going to be released that morning. John wished he was the one to be released, but his time was yet far away. That morning John and Ling said their final goodbyes before going for breakfast in the prison cafeteria.

"Well, Ling, you've been a good friend. At first I didn't think we'd become friends, but you've invested a lot of time and energy on me when I was down and out," John said restlessly.

"And I'll miss you too, John. Please look me up when you get out of this place. I'll be at my brother's restaurant in Chinatown, New York."

"Take care of yourself, Ling."

"And you be good to yourself, John," Ling said. Then the two men hugged for the last time.

Two days later, John had a new cellmate. His name was Mike Williams, who was tall, slim, black and in his late twenties, and he came from Brooklyn, New York. John didn't say too much to him at first. He really missed his old friend, Ling Lee. Then he realized that Ling had trained him to take charge, and that was what he should be doing, instead of feeling sorry for himself. It was only after a few days later that John became friends with Mike. He noticed that Mike looked up to him as a model prisoner, so it was up to him to teach Mike the right ways of life. They sat at the table that evening, and then the discussion begun, and the two men were curious to know about each other. One prisoner was white and the other was black.

"Why are you here, John?" Mike asked.

"Well, it's a long story. They said I killed my family for the insurance money. A big mistake. Someone else did it and I was left to pay. The system isn't always right," John explained seriously.

"Sad story, John," Mike said without taking his eyes off John.

"Why are you here, Mike?" John asked.

"I couldn't find work in Brooklyn, and I had to sell some drugs to survive. I was caught and ended up here."

"Tell me about New York and the people who live there," John asked cheerfully.

Mike told John all about New York, the city that never sleeps. John was excited, and felt that he should go to New York City when he was released from prison.

"Well, John, if we weren't prisoners in this cell, we wouldn't become friends. Prison brings us closer together. I'm black and you're white. If we were on the outside, we would be enemies," Mike explained.

"You're right, Mike. It would only happen like this; we as cellmates. You are white and I am black."

"Since you're the first white guy I have ever got this close to, I want you to tell me about yourself and your family. Where did your forefathers come from. Maybe we can learn a lot from each other," Mike said, tapping his index finger on the table.

"My forefathers came from Ireland in 1850, when there was a famine over there. They came to the new land by boat. They were dead poor and started farming in Moorestown from a small piece of land, and as the years went by they obtained more and more land to carry out their farming. When they passed away, my father inherited the farm. My father wanted to leave me the farm, but I didn't want to be a farmer. I eloped with my girlfriend; we got married and had two children," John said.

"Then they were taken away from you?"

"Yes. Now, tell me about yourself."

"Well, my forefathers came from Africa, and they became farmers also, on the white man's plantation. The only difference is that they were slaves. So you see the only difference was, you white people from overseas came here of your own free will, and you were free people. We were brought here against our will as slaves," Mike explained sadly.

"I guess we've come a long way, Mike. We are both free, yet now we are both prisoners of the State."

Mike smiled at John. "You're right, John. We became free just to land in jail. How dreadful!"

"Mike, as you said we can learn a lot from each other, but a little at a time," John told him.

Six months later, John met the new warden, Bill Jackson. That morning most of the prisoners were lined up in the yard to meet the new warden. A speaker was set up for the warden to speak to them. Most of the prisoners knew John and respected him. He had become a leading figure all over the prison.

When Warden Jackson tried to speak to the prisoners, some of the prisoners were chatting, and the warden couldn't be heard over the speaker. Then a tall, white, stout prisoner shouted, "Nigger, go home. We don't want you here."

The warden was black, tall, with broad shoulders, and he had a coarse voice, and he was in his early forties.

John quickly went over to the prisoner who shouted that dirty word, and held him tightly by the arm.

"I think you owe the warden an apology," John told the prisoner, and squeezed a little harder on his arm.

"Okay," the prisoner said. "Warden, I apologize. I'm sorry, sir, for what I said."

John released the prisoner. "Now, you men be quiet, and let the warden speak his peace. Thank you. Please continue, Warden. They won't bother you again," John told the warden.

Warden Jackson shook his head, and smiled at John.

"Thank you, whoever you are," Warden Jackson said to John. Then he spoke for the next five minutes without any interruption.

When all the prisoners went back to work, John was left behind. He knew the warden would want to talk to him for what he had done. The warden came to him.

"That was a very nice gesture, what you did for me," Warden Jackson said.

"Well, sir, I thought they should hear what you had to say, even though they didn't want to."

"And what about you?"

"John Stone is the name, sir. I wanted to get to know the man behind the words," John said, smiling.

"I think you know what you want, John Stone. I have a great feeling we're going to meet again soon. We better get back to work. Where do you work?" the warden asked.

"In the laundry room, sir."

John knew because the warden was black, he'd have very little co-operation from his workers or prisoners, and sooner or later he'd have his hands full. And for some strange reason, John felt sorry for him, and wanted to help him in whatever way he could. But that would only happen if the warden asked for his help.

Two days later, John entered the warden's office. The warden had sent for him.

"Have a seat, John," the warden said, then got up and poured him a cup of coffee. John took the cup and sat down in front of the warden's desk.

"I suppose you know why I sent for you, John?"

John took a sip of his coffee, and shook his head up and down, then smiled at the warden.

"You need some help, and I'm the right man for the job."

"You're not only smart, John, but you are also clever," the warden hinted.

"Thank you, sir. How can I help you?"

"I was looking through your file, and I'm sure you're the right person to assist me. You see, John, I'm new here, and I want to make a good impression."

"What can I do to help, sir?"

"You see the last warden was white, and I'm black. I want to make a success of this job. It seems as if I'm drowning after my first week on the job."

"As I said before, sir. What can I do to help?"

"I need someone like you who knows how to get things done. You're an accountant and you know how to work with figures, and you know how to plan."

"I'm listening, Warden."

"You see my job is a big one, and I'm allotted a certain amount of money to run this prison, and it's not enough. I have to make certain cuts, and that's where you come in," the Warden explained.

"I'll do my best to help you, Warden."

"If you can help me, I'll make it worth your while. All you have to do is to go through each department, and see where we can cut expenses."

"Well, for a start, you use contractors to do nearly all the jobs in the prison. If we can do those jobs ourselves, we can save a lot of money, sir. In the clothing store, if we can make some of those same clothing ourselves, we'll save a lot of money," John explained.

"I like that. You're not on the job as yet and you're making cuts already. I was right about you, John," the warden said, smiling.

"Glad to help, sir."

"John, you've some great ideas, and I hope we can work on them further. I'll give you special permission to do this job. You'll report to me direct."

"Yes, sir. When do I start?"

"You've already started, John. At a later date, I'll take you to my home. My wife hates the color of the paint in the rooms, especially in my son's room."

"Say no more, sir. I can sort that out. I can give your house sparkling new colors, providing I can go out."

"That's what I was hoping you'd say, and you can go out. I trust you."

"Well, I'm at your disposal."

The warden issued John with special instructions, and he and Mike Wilson were assigned to their special jobs, visiting the different departments, and making notes of what had to be done to cut expenses.

One evening three weeks later, John got a weird dream. He dreamt about Ling Lee. He saw his former cellmate's face in his dream. He saw him cross a busy main street, then suddenly a large truck came up from behind him and hit him from the side. Then John woke up; he had sweat running down his forehead, and he was breathing in and out quickly.

"Oh, no. It couldn't be. You didn't have to go that way," John said to himself from his upper bunk.

The next evening, John received the sad news that his friend Ling Lee was hit by a truck and died on the spot. That night John got a weird dream. He saw Ling Lee in his dream.

"Follow your dreams, John. They'll all come true," Ling told him softly with a smiling face.

Then every night after that John received a new dream, a dream that might become reality some time in the future. He'd make notes of each dream the following day. He took his dreams seriously. He believed his dead friend was trying to send him a message for when he was released from prison. He believed that his dreams might become part of his life once he got on the outside. But he didn't know how all of that would devolve in the future. He'd just have to wait and see, and would play it by ear.

One week later, the warden sent for John in his office.

"I've read all your reports, John, and I've taken action as you requested. We'll save a lot of money from what I've read. Good work," the warden said, smiling.

"I'm glad you're pleased with the reports, sir."

"I'm trying to sort out the problems here, and I've some problems at home. We've had an estimate to do some work on the house, and it would cost $15,000. I don't have that sort of money at hand," the warden explained.

"Can I help? I'm good at that sort of work as I told you before," John said, smiling.

"Is there anything you can't do, John?"

"If you buy the materials, I can do the work and Mike can be my assistant."

"My wife really wants to get the work started, especially in my son's room."

"How old is he?"

"Ten."

"Well, let's give your wife what she wants. You swing it so we can get out, and I promise you we won't escape."

"I can take you to my home tomorrow, and I'll be responsible for you."

Two days later, the warden took John and Mike to his house to do some renovations and painting. John and Mike were very polite to Mrs. Jackson. She was tall, slim, attractive, light brown complexion, and she was neatly dressed, and she smiled when she spoke. She took to John and Mike, even though she knew they were prisoners. She wasn't afraid of them. She offered them coffee and cookies before they started work on her son's room.

"If you and Mike can transform my son's room, I'd supply both of you with all the coffee and sandwiches you can drink and eat," she said with a smile.

"Well, you're in charge of us, ma'am," John said. Then both men went to work on her son's room on the second floor. Everything went on smoothly on the first day. Then on the second day John and Mike were working on the same room, and for some strange reason, John kept looking out of the window every now and then.

"Are you expecting someone?" Mike asked.

"I suddenly got this strange feeling as though something is about to happen. I can feel it in my stomach," John replied. Then he went to the side window, and saw a black man. The man headed to the front door and rang the doorbell. John listened closely, then he suddenly had the impulse that something bad was about to happen. But what? He went to the door of the room, and listened closely.

Mrs. Jackson opened the door as though she knew the man, then she was caught in the arms by the man with a knife. The door closed behind them. John listened carefully, then his mind snapped into place. He now knew what was taking place. It was a burglary.

"I want your money, lady, or I'll take your life," the thief said loudly.

"Don't hurt me. I'm here all alone," Mrs. Jackson said nervously.

"Where do you keep the money?" the burglar asked, looking upstairs. "Up those stairs, isn't it?" he added.

"Yes, we keep the valuables up in the master bedroom," she said, shaking.

"Let's go, Missus," he said and pushed her in front of him. She went up nervously, stair after stair.

John told Mike to keep quiet, then he slipped into the master bedroom and hid behind the door, waiting for the thief to come in. He held his breath, and waited patiently. Mrs. Jackson entered the room first and she saw him. When the thief was in sight, John slammed the door hard on the man's arm, hitting the knife to the floor. The man was taken by surprise at the sudden impact. John closed the door behind them.

"Now, whoever you are, it's you and me," John said, looking steadily at his opponent, who was black, tall and slim, in his thirties. The man tried to get the knife on the floor, then John made his move and kicked him in the chest. The man fell to the floor and tried again to get the knife. John slammed his foot hard on the man's hand, and kicked the knife away. The man tried to get up and John hit him hard on the face, knocking him to the floor. Mike entered the room and they both held and took the intruder downstairs. Mrs. Jackson called the police, then called her husband at his office. She came down the stairs half way, and stared at the three men below.

"I've called the police, and they'll be here shortly," she shouted.

"If you turn a muscle, I'll break every bone in your body," John told the intruder. "You're a bad guy and you'll have to pay for this, scaring Mrs. Jackson with a knife like that," John added.

The warden arrived ten minutes later. The police had already arrived. He went over to John and Mike.

"Good work, John and Mike," the warden said, going to his wife, who was in the room, and giving her a big hug.

"Are you all right, Polly?" he asked.

"I'm a bit shook up, but I'll be all right," she said. "It was a good thing John and Mike were here. John really gave that thief a walloping, otherwise I don't know what he would have done to me. I'm lucky this time."

Warden Jackson went over to the sergeant in charge. His assistant had already taken the prisoner out to the police car. The warden explained the whole situation to him, and that he didn't want to make it public.

"This is going to sound funny when I make my report, sir," the sergeant said, smiling.

"What's going to sound funny, Sergeant?"

"Your two prisoners catching a burglar in your house."

"Sergeant, you must understand that these prisoners are here only on a project, and they're highly trustworthy. I really don't want you to make too much out of this story."

"I understand, sir. I've taken a statement from your wife and the two prisoners, and they may have to testify in court at a later date."

"We'll cross that bridge when we come to it, Sergeant, and thank you for understanding the whole situation."

After two weeks, John and Mike finished the work on the warden's house and went back to work in the prison. Two days later, Mrs. Jackson sent John and Mike a home-made fruitcake, and thanked them for the work they'd carried out. Specially her thanks went to John for saving her life from the thief who broke into her home.

John was able to concentrate on the work at hand in the prison. He was able to view a long list of prisoners and pick out all of those who would be of help, carpenters, plumbers, cooks, painters, tailors, and most of all, farmers. He'd train each of them to do a required job in the prison, so as to cut the prison's budget. The farmers would cultivate the 250 acres of land behind the prison, and grow vegetables for the prison's consumption. The warden was really pleased with the way John was running the whole show, and he gave John and Mike their own office on the ground floor.

One evening John was writing in his notebook, and Mike was sitting on his bunk. He turned to John and smiled.

"John, are you writing about me in that notebook?" Mike asked.

"No. Well, to tell you the truth, I started making notes of everything I did. I've been getting these weird dreams lately. These dreams started when my friend Ling Lee died in an accident in New York City. It's very strange," John said, tapping his index finger on the table.

"What sort of weird dreams?" Mike asked.

"A few weeks ago, I dreamt that I was out of prison and I headed for New York City. That's when it all started to happen. An old woman was robbed as soon as she got off the bus in New York City, and I went to her assistance. It started that way," John said.

"But that's good."

"Yes. I went on to rescue a woman from a high bridge, and a policeman in a subway station."

"That's even better. You're a hero by this time," Mike teased.

"Then," John said, and hesitated.

"Then what, John?" Mike asked.

"The weirdest of them all was when I went to save a blind woman on a busy main street. There was a billboard over the street of a beautiful girl smiling down at me. This blind woman was about to be hit by a truck coming around the curved road. I went to save the woman, but I was too late, and we were both..." John said, and stopped abruptly.

"You were both what?" Mike asked quickly.

"Sadly, we were both killed by the truck. After that I never got any more weird dreams."

"No more dreams? What does it all mean, John?"

"I really don't know, Mike. If my life is to end like that, I'd rather die that way, trying to save someone nice."

"John, that billboard you saw in your dream is just like the one on Main Street, Brooklyn, New York, where I live. I'm beginning to think that those dreams of yours are not so weird after all. Let's hope that last dream doesn't come true," Mike said.

"But I have to take these dreams seriously. I'm sure that dream has something to do with my very life existence. I can't explain, but I feel that I'll eventually meet this woman in real life. I'll also meet the people in my other dreams," John explained.

"I hope this woman of yours will be beautiful when you meet her," Mike said, smiling. "In a way I'll hate to lose you that way, John," Mike said sadly.

"Why is that, Mike?"

"To tell you the truth, I never expected it to happen, but you have become my best friend."

"Thank you, Mike. And what do you think of my dreams?"

"I don't think too much of dreams, but I'll tell you all you need to know about New York City if you're going to meet that beautiful woman on Main Street."

John smiled at him. "I'll take you up on that, Mike. I'll need to know my way around the city that never sleeps, as you said before."

Chapter Ten

That weekend John had a very special visitor. He was summoned to the waiting area. When he arrived there, he saw who it was. "Mom," he shouted, and ran to her. They embraced and he kissed her on the cheek. "I never expected you to come to see me," he said. Then they both sat down.

The tall, slim, pale woman sat at the table opposite John and gazed at him for a few seconds. John couldn't believe that his stout mother was thin and bony.

"I came specially to see my favorite son," she said sadly. "Your brother Harold drove me all the way here. I had to see you, son."

"Why, Mom?"

She shook her head. "It may be my last time to see you, son."

"Tell me what's going on, Mom."

"I'm dying, son. The doctor gave me just a few more weeks to live," she said and forced a smile behind her tears.

"Don't say that, Mom, you'll live for a long time to come. You can't leave me at this point in my life," he cried.

"You'll have to be strong, son. You have your whole life in front of you," she said with the tears in her eyes.

"What a life," he said and touched her hand. "So Harold is outside? Why doesn't he come in and face me?"

"He didn't want to see you. He thinks you did it."

"Poor Harold. He always had a chip on his shoulder. I feel sorry for him."

"Your father still blames you for running away with Mary."

"My life had been good with my family until that horrible morning," he blurted.

"I brought you some of your favorite cake, and it will be the last time you'll be able to eat my cooking," Mrs. Stone said with the tears running down her cheeks.

"Mom, don't cry."

"Son, I am crying for both of us, your downfall and my demise. I can't help it. I can't keep Harold waiting. It's a long way back to Moorestown," she said and stood up. "I had to come to see you because I knew you wouldn't be able to attend my funeral. They wouldn't be able to let you out to my funeral," she told him softly.

"Don't say that, Mom. You'll live for a long time," John said and got up, and stood face to face with his mother.

Mrs. Stone shook her head. "Any time for me is a long time, son," she said, and bent over and kissed John on the cheek.

"Good-bye, Mom," he whispered.

"John, for God's sake, when you're out of this place, come back to the farm where you belong with your family."

"I'll come back, Mom, but just for a visit and not to stay. My place is somewhere else where I can find myself," he told her.

"Good-bye, my son," she said and left.

"Good-bye, Mom, I love you," he whispered to himself.

John took the home-made cake and went back to his cell. He didn't know what to think. He had lost his family and now he was losing his beloved mother. All those whom he loved were been taken away from him. He felt that life was surely no bed of roses, and he'd have to cope with whatever came his way, bad or good.

"John, do you still get those visions?" Mike asked.

"Now, that you ask, yes. A few nights ago, I had this strange dream, I saw my old cellmate, Ling Lee. He was showing me the way to New York. The lights were bright and the buildings were tall. He was smiling as he waved me on," John explained.

"From what you told me about Ling Lee, he was a strange dude. He got into your head and you can never get rid of him. He worked his strange magic on you," Mike told him.

"You may call it magic, but it is something greater than magic that I feel," John commented.

"Well, whatever works best for you, John," Mike said with a smile. "I'm learning a lot from you, John, and some of those events are really strange."

"Mom, happy trip home," John whispered to himself.

"Delicious cake, John," Mike said. "Pity about your mother."

"Yes, a pity. My mother told me I wouldn't be able to go to her funeral," John said sadly.

"Sad, sad, John!"

Two months later, John was summoned into the warden's office. "John, I have some bad news for you," the warden told him.

"Bad news?"

"Yes. Your brother, Harold Stone called me on the phone, your mother passed away," he told him.

"Well, my mother was sick, and I expected this any day. Poor Mom. I hope she didn't have to feel pain before she died," John said sadly.

"I'm sorry, John. Your brother said your mother will be buried in the next two days."

"My mother said to me when she came to see me that I wouldn't be able to attend her funeral, and she was right."

The warden smiled at John. "I don't think that she was all that right."

"What do you mean, sir?" John asked.

"It means that I'm going to allow you to go to your mother's funeral," the warden said, smiling.

"Excuse me, sir, but are you going to put your ass on the line for me?" John asked.

"Yes, John. You put your ass on the line for my wife that time. I can't forget that."

"Do you trust me that much?" John asked.

"Yes. I'll give you a pass for two days to attend the funeral. So get to the stores and get your suit out."

"Thank you, sir."

"You're welcome, John."

John arrived in Moorestown at 6.30 that afternoon. He jumped off the bus at the Moorestown stop, then he looked right and left, then he crossed the road with his small holdall. Then he stood in front of Harold, his brother, who was fairly tall, broad shoulders, and dressed like a farmer. It was still bright and Harold looked at John up and down for a few seconds, sizing him up. The two men were like strangers, and John knew he would have to break the ice with his brother. He knew the way his brother felt about him. He wanted so much to mend their bad friendship there and then.

"Hi, Harold. How did you know what time to meet me?"

"Well, your warden was very precise in giving me your time of arrival here, so here I am."

"You don't seem very pleased to see me."

"I never expected to see you again. After what you..."

"You mean after what I did my family?"

"Something like that," Harold said with a smug smile on his face.

"And here I am in person," John told him boldly.

"It was mother's wish that you attend her funeral, and say a few words. You were always her favorite, and you are a person of words. And I was the farm boy," Harold blurted.

"I see, if it weren't for mother, I wouldn't be here."

"You were always the favorite, even to the last," Harold told him.

"You're the same old Harold, always jealous of me."

Harold cut John short. "It's getting late. Let's get going," Harold said and went into the cab of the truck. John followed into the passenger side and off they went, on their way to the farm. They were both silent.

When they arrived at the farm, Harold got out of the truck first, then John got out. John stood there for a few seconds and looked around the farm. Harold gazed at John, and waited for him to say something.

"It hasn't changed in all these years I was away," John said, not looking at Harold.

"The farm is still the same. You're the one that has changed," Harold told him.

"And changed for the worse," John admitted.

"Let's go in and see the folks, John."

John followed Harold into the large farmhouse and into the living room. He saw all eyes were on him. Rose was the first one to get up and go to him. She was fairly tall and she had put on much weight since John had last seen her. She looked at him for a few seconds, then gave him a hug. Then she took him over to their father. John looked down at his father, who was now old and gray. His father looked up at him, and studied him for a while.

"Sir, I'm sorry for your loss, and my loss also." His father looked at him sadly and didn't respond to him. Then John turned away from his father.

"Son, I love you and I missed you," his father said behind him. John turned around quickly. His father stood up and opened his arms, and John went into his arms.

"I love you too, Dad, and I am glad we have finally become friends again, just like before," John told him softly.

"I always thought of you as master of the farm, even though you were away, and I prayed that you'd come back some day," his father said with tears in his eyes.

"All those days I wanted to come back, but my pride prevented me from doing so. But you were always in my memory, Dad."

Harold looked on for a few seconds at his father and John as they became friends again. He shook his head, and quickly went out of the room.

Rose then introduced John to her husband and her two children, then to Harold's wife and two children. Then she took him into the kitchen and served him supper. She sat at the table with him. "I'm glad you made up with Dad. You were his favorite, and when you left, it broke his heart. He wanted you badly to be the master of this farm, and when you went away, he had no choice but to make Harold the master of the farm," Rose told John.

"It's really strange coming back here after all these years, and seeing everyone with their family."

"I'm sorry, John. You lost your family. It was a great loss, and we were all sorry."

"Yes. I still miss them after all these years. They live on in my memory. They said I killed them for the insurance money, but I didn't. I loved them," he said softly.

"When you were younger, you always told me your problems, so if you'd like to talk, I'm here to listen," Rose told him.

"I only wish that I could tell you my problems, but it's so hard. The things I have been through. My life has become a complete failure. I don't deserve to live. If only I can give my life to mother, and she can have my life to live again," John told her sadly.

"John, what are you saying? Have you gone completely mad?" she said, gazing at him steadily.

"Maybe I am, Rose," he replied without looking at her.

"Mom spoke of you all the time, and she kept those pictures of your children, and she'd look at them nearly every day. Those were her first grandchildren, and she was proud of them. I know from the bottom of my heart that you didn't kill your family. It was a mistake."

"It was a big mistake, Rose. I'm only guilty for not protecting my family, but not guilty for killing them. I'm paying for only that guilt which I am guilty of," John said sadly.

118

"What are your plans when you get out, John?"

"When I get out, it will not be good. I keep getting these weird dreams."

"What dreams?" she asked.

"They're dreams of me saving certain people that I have never met. I don't know what to make of them. In one dream I died trying to save a blind woman on a busy main road in New York City," he explained.

"I'm sure there's nothing to your dreams, so don't let them get you down, John."

The next day at the graveside, John was among the family members and close friends of the family. When the pastor gave his eulogy and prayer, John got his chance to say his final goodbye to his beloved mother.

"Sofie Stone was the wife of James Stone, the mother of myself, John, Harold, my brother and Rose, my sister. We all loved her to the last. Mother didn't think I would have been able to make it here, but the warden was good enough to give me a two day pass to attend her funeral. It was mother's wish that I send her off on her last journey to heaven because she loved me. She always told me I was her favorite son, but I feel that all her children were her favorites. We all love you mother and we'll always remember you for what you meant to us. May God bless your soul wherever you are," John said with the tears coming down his cheeks.

The casket was lowered into the grave. John looked on . He picked up some of the earth, and held it in his hand for a few seconds, and closed his eyes as if he were praying, then he opened his eyes, and threw the earth on the casket.

"Earth to earth, dust to dust," he said softly. Then he went over to his father and went into his arms.

"I love you, Dad," John told him.

"I miss you, John," his father said. "I was a fool to let you go, and you had such bad luck."

"It was my decision, Dad, and my luck, and no one could have prevented what happened."

John went over to Mr. and Mrs. Young and stood in front of them. "Mr. and Mrs. Young, thank you for coming, and I'm really sorry how everything has turned out. I hope you can forgive me as I am paying dearly for all that has happened."

"We forgive you, John," Mrs. Young said.

"Thank you. Now I must get back to my home in the city." John saw everyone looking at the narrow road to the cemetery. He looked and saw two policemen heading his way. He knew at once he was going to be escorted back to the bus station in a police car. He went to meet them half way. "Are you here to escort me back, officers?"

"Are you John Stone?" the tall officer asked.

"I am."

"We're only here to escort you back to the bus station. Your warden notified us you were here on a two day pass, so if you're through, we'll drive you to the bus station."

John said goodbye to his family and friends, and left with the two officers for the bus station. He caught the 2.30 bus for Pennsylvania, and arrived several hours later at the State Prison. His cellmate Mike was glad to see him back.

"Well, I wasn't sure you'd be coming back. You could have gone your own way," Mike told him.

"I couldn't let down the warden. He was good enough to let me go, so I had to be good enough to come back," John told Mike. "My, Mom, I'll miss her. She was all I had left, and now I have no one to turn to."

"You can turn to me, John."

"I know, but it isn't the same. You're just a friend, but thanks anyway," John told him, and forced a smile.

The following day the warden sent for John in his office. John sat in front of his desk.

"John, I'm sorry about your mother. I hope everything went well," the warden said from behind his desk.

"Thank you, sir. Everything went as planned," John said with his head down.

"I would like your opinion on what I'm about to tell you. I have had two estimates to renovate the whole outside of the prison, but I don't even have half of the money to do the job. I really need your expertise again," the warden explained.

"Well, sir, I'm here and I'll do my best to help you. You have put your butt on the line for me, so as to let me go to my mother's funeral, and I'm grateful to you," John said, shaking his head.

"How can we go about this, John?"

"Give me a pass to go outside, and I'll make notes of what we'll need to do the job, men, material, and equipment," John told him with some seriousness.

"I wish you were on my staff permanently."

"That's just a wish, sir, but I'm here at your service," John said with a smile.

"Okay, I'll make all the arrangements to get you on the outside. I want this done as soon as possible."

When John got back to his cell, his cellmate was curious to know why the warden sent for him.

"So what did the warden have to say?" Mike asked.

"I was given an assignment and you'll be my assistant," John told him from his bed.

"I have learnt a lot from you for the last four years, John. We're doing a lot to help the warden, and I strongly feel that he should help us to legally get out from this hell-hole," Mike told him from the table at which he was sitting.

"All in good time, Mike. Then you'll be able to go on the outside again, and you'll be able do an honest day's work."

"You're right, John. Good things come to those who wait," Mike said.

"And my motto is that good things come to those who go to get them," John said, smiling.

Mike smiled at John's remark. "Smart move, John. No wonder you're so successful," Mike said and started writing his letter to his aunt. "I'm going to tell my Aunt Mildred all about you," Mike said, then he started laughing.

"What's so funny, Mike?" John asked.

"I think if you were given the chance you'd be able to run this prison better than the warden, and that's a fact," Mike told him.

John just lay back, and he knew that Mike was right. He always tried to do his best at any job he was given. He remembered how happy he was when he was made assistant manager at Eagle Lumber five years ago.

*

Mr. Johnson, the manager, always took an interest in the way John handled all the customers. John always treated the customers as friends as well as customers, and he always gave them his personal treatment. He sold them merchandise that they would have never bought on their own. He took the trouble most times to find out what they wanted, and how to go about solving their problems, and from each transaction he was gaining more experience.

At mid-day one day, Mrs. Johnson came into the store, and John went to meet her. He had never met her, and he thought she was a prospective customer.

"Good morning, ma'am, can I help you?" he said, looking at her with a smile.

"So you are the young man my husband is always telling me about?" she told him.

"Your husband?"

"Yes, I am Mrs. Johnson. I'm searching for my husband."

"Oh, Mrs. Johnson, I am John, your husband's assistant. Mr. Johnson speaks of you very much, ma'am."

"Nice things I hope."

"Yes, ma'am. The way he speaks of you, I always thought of you as a housewife, but if I may say this ma'am, you're so young and sophisticated. I'm sorry for thinking the way I did about you before," John said with a smile.

"Why, thank you, John. I can say for a fact that you are going to go very far," she told him.

"I suppose you are here so Mr. Johnson can take you out for lunch."

"Lunch?"

"I'll tell Mr. Johnson you're here, ma'am," he said, and left. John found his boss and told him very quickly.

"Sir, your beautiful wife is here. I think she expects you to take her out for lunch. I am sorry, sir, but I opened my big mouth. So please take her for lunch, and I'll hold the fort for you. Be nice to her."

"John, I'm happy to say that you don't miss a trick in the book," Mr. Johnson told him.

"Well, it's just my natural self, sir."

"Well, hold the fort, and I'll be back soon. And don't sell the fort while I'm away," Mr. Johnson said jokingly.

Four weeks later, Mr. Johnson took ill and he was admitted into hospital. John had to fill in and had become manager for that period of time. He knew he was in charge and he had to make some changes to the place. His first priority was to have the front of the store clean and painted in a different color. That weekend he had the two offices and the whole store painted. He ordered new supplies, and all merchandise was placed differently on shelves. The old merchandise was sold at reduced prices.

Mr. Johnson came back to work after four weeks, and he couldn't believe what a wonderful job John had done during his absence. "John, if I didn't know better, I'd say you were working hard to get my job," Mr. Johnson told him jokingly.

"Well, sir, I always try my best at everything I do," John told him shyly. John knew that Mr. Johnson was right. He wanted badly to be the boss, but he realized that would never happen.

He realized he was in prison, and he'd have to work hard to improve the building over his head, and at the same time he'd help to cut the cost of running the prison. He really took his work very seriously, even though he was only paid a small amount for his time.

For the past two years John was given several assignments, and completed each successfully. He felt it was time for him to get out of prison, and he wanted to ask the warden to help him, but after careful thought he came to the conclusion that the warden was only there to run the prison the best way he knew how, and not to help prisoners to get out of there earlier than they should.

John's best break came when he received a letter from his next-door neighbor, Mr. Roberts. The letter read:

Dear John,

How are you? I hope you won't be bitter with me when you have read this letter. I have fought with my conscience all these years, and now I must ask you to forgive me for not telling the truth in court. I am sorry that I made you spend all those years in prison, when my true evidence could have set you free. But I was afraid of the burglar who killed your family, and I didn't want him to come after me, and do the same to me.

You see the very same day I found a note in my mail box, and it read:

If you ever tell the police about me, I'll come after you, and shoot you like your next door neighbors.
Signed: The B.

I was afraid for my life at that time, but now it doesn't matter, I'm dying. I don't have long to live.

I hope this letter will help you to be released from that dreadful place you are held.

I am writing this letter from St. Mary's Hospital.

Forgive me, John, and goodbye.

Yours truly,

Sid Roberts.

PS. Show this letter to your warden and maybe he can help you to get an early release from prison.

"I can never be bitter with you, Mr. Roberts. You saved my poor life, but this news is better late than never," John whispered to himself.

John immediately went to the warden's office and showed him the letter. The warden took the letter and read it with interest.

"John, this letter is very interesting. I'm going to send this letter to the Chief of Police in Philadelphia, and we'll get some action. I'll also talk to him on the phone, so he can interview Mr. Roberts before he dies."

"You think this letter will get me out of here, sir?" John asked the warden, clenching his fingers together.

"It may do the trick, John. We'll just have to wait and see," the warden told him.

John got up from his seat, and he had a big smile on his face. "Thank you, sir."

"We'll keep our fingers crossed."

John went back to work and left the warden to do whatever he had to do. "Thank you, Mr. Roberts," John said to himself.

Two weeks later John was summoned to the warden's office. "John, I got a reply back from that letter you had given me. I have some good news for you. 'Mr. Sid Roberts was interviewed by two

124

investigators from the police department. Mr. Roberts stated that he
saw Mr. Stone come out of his house that morning and fired after the
burglar, then he collapsed in front of the sidewalk. He heard several
shots fired before that, and he went to his front window to investigate.
Then he saw the burglar in front of his house, and under the street
light. The burglar looked up and saw him. He was threatened by the
burglar, and was afraid for his life. But he was able to tell the truth.
Mr. Roberts died two days after making this statement. Arrangements
are being made by the District Attorneys' Office for an early release
of Mr. Stone.' So John, there you are," the warden told him.

"That's the best news for me in a long time," John said, clapping
his hands together.

One month later John stood in his cell that morning, and his friend,
Mike stood in front of him.

"Well, John, this is goodbye. You'll be free today. I phoned
Aunt Mildred last night that you'd be coming today," Mike told him
sadly.

"I hope your aunt will like me."

"At first she may not like you, but you're a person that everyone
looks up to, especially me. You know that?" Mike told him.

"Yes, Mike I know that, and I'll miss you too."

"A word of warning, John. The neighborhood in Brooklyn is
black and the people in that area are dangerous, so be on your guard
at all times."

"Thank you, Mike, but you know where I have been for the last
six years. All the really bad people are here, Mike," John said with a
smile. "And most of all, you taught me how to be black, so don't
worry about me. You take care of yourself and get out of this place."

"Well, I'll miss you good friend," Mike said and gave John a hug,
then he left for work. He looked back and shouted, "Don't forget to
save that beautiful girl on Main Street."

Later that morning, John went to the warden's office to collect his
release documents.

"Well, John this is where we say goodbye. These are your release
documents, and in the envelope is some money for your bus ticket and
for your room in New York. If you need any more money, let me
know. You have done a lot for me and I thank you, and I'll miss
having you around," the warden said sadly.

"I'll have to find myself a job and earn myself some real money, sir."

"Well, be careful out there, John, and thanks again for all the help you've given me throughout the years."

"Well, if you need any help in a hurry again, I'll come back to help you, not as a prisoner, but as a free person."

"Thank you, John, but it's time for you to help yourself on the outside," the warden said, and shook John's hand. John was now free to leave and take up his new life on the outside.

Chapter Eleven

It was a bright and sunny Monday afternoon, 29th of June, 1992, when John Stone was released from the state penitentiary in Pennsylvania. He had served just over six years of his fifteen years, until his sentence was overturned by the District Attorney's Office, on the new evidence they had received.

John heard the steel gate click behind him. He felt at ease as he was now on the outside looking in. He was now six years older, taller and wiser. He was John Stone when he went into prison, but at that moment he didn't know whom he had turned into. He felt he was a new person, a strong and powerful person with magical powers, and he'd use his strength for the sake of helping other unfortunate people. He knew he was now on a very special mission, a mission of life and death.

"I'm free as a bird," John said with a big smile on his face. "I can fly wherever I want to," he grinned. He looked up at the tower, and without thinking, he waved goodbye to the prison guard. He knew he was waving goodbye to everything behind him, and to his surprise, the prison guard waved back to him.

He looked right and left, and when there was no traffic, he crossed the main street to the sidewalk. He headed for the bus stop, which was four blocks down the street. As he walked down the sidewalk, he breathed the fresh air in and out. "What will I do with myself?" he whispered. "You'll go to New York City, and there you'll find what you are looking for," he said with a smile. He felt the refreshing breeze blowing on his face. He looked up at the skies, and shook his head, then he looked in front of him. He passed several factories and business places on his right hand, and some of the workers who were outside looked at him suspiciously. Then one worker pointed at him and smiled. It was the first time he had seen those buildings up close. He realized his viewers knew that he was an ex-convict from the nearby prison.

John carried a small holdall with all his belongings, and he had over $600 in his pocket. It was all the money he had earned in prison, and it wasn't much for nearly six years of his life in the hell-hole.

John was tall, dark, slim, and he had large muscles on his chest and arms. He had lifted weights to develop his strong and muscular body. He was handsome, with long black hair and brown eyes. He had a small scar on his right cheek. He received it from the two prisoners who had punched him in the face. He wore a black leather jacket that the warden had given him as a going away present. He wore a brown shirt, tight blue jeans, and a pair of black runners on his feet.

He hurried to the bus stop when he saw the bus approaching from behind him. The bus would take him to the main bus station in Pennsylvania, and there he would board another bus for New York City.

He arrived at the main bus station twenty minutes later, then he bought a bus ticket to New York. He looked around the bus station, and took a seat on a bench in the middle of the building. He knew he would have to wait for some time before he would be able to board his bus for New York City.

John summed up his life in just a few minutes. He wasn't a hardened criminal. He was just a victim of a very bad situation. While in prison, the system had made him into a fighting machine. Now he couldn't resist the tone of a good fight, or the tone to rescue someone from danger or harm. He would jump to the possibilities, as if he were an automatic machine set to do a job.

In the meanwhile, he gazed steadily around the building. The building had changed a little since he had last taken the bus to attend his mother's funeral a few years ago. He couldn't help noticing all the happy faces that went past him. He also saw many passengers coming, going and waiting around the building for their bus. He felt for the first time in years that he was among real people, who were free to do what they wanted.

The bus station was brightly lit with fluorescent lights in the ceiling. There was a coffee and sandwich bar on the northern side of the building, and different food machines at the side of the main wall. The ticket and information office was at the back of the station. The buses picked up passengers from the eastern side of the building, and took them to their destination.

John gazed shyly at the family opposite him. The woman was attractive, and she kept her small son and daughter close to her. They reminded him so much of his family, whom he had lost nearly seven years ago now.

The little girl smiled at him when she saw him glancing in her direction. He saw her and couldn't bear to look at the happy expression on her face. He knew she was real, and his dead daughter, Cindy, was just a figment of his imagination. He really didn't know what was real any more. He shook his head without thinking, so as to bring himself back to reality. Then he saw the little girl laughing at him because he had shaken his head. He realized at that moment she thought he was funny, and was shaking his head to make her laugh.

The little girl pulled her mother's hand and pointed to John. He saw what was going on and put his head down. He didn't want the woman to think he was spying on them. When he looked up again, the family were looking in the opposite direction. John felt embarrassed and went to sit on another bench. He looked at his watch, and it stated 1.45, and he knew they'd call very soon for passengers to board the bus for New York, and in the meanwhile he'd make himself scarce.

After a few more minutes, it came over the intercom. "Bus number 20 for New York City is now in lane 2, and is now ready for boarding," said the announcer in a deep voice.

John heard the call for his bus, and he waited for the rest of the passengers to board the bus first. When he saw just a few passengers outside, he hurried over and lodged his holdall into the cargo compartment of the bus. Then he entered the bus and gave the driver his ticket. He went behind the bus to take his seat then he sat next to an elderly lady, who had a window seat. She looked up at him and smiled, and he forced a smile back at her.

The bus slowly pulled out of the bus station, and John was on his way to his new destination, a destination he thought would eventually kill him or make him, and it would be in New York City; the city that never sleeps.

The lady next to John looked up at him.

"Are you going to New York City on vacation?" she asked.

"No, ma'am, I'm going to find work. I already had a long vacation, and now it's time for me to get busy," he replied, looking at her steadily.

"I'm going to visit my daughter who lives in New York, but from what I've seen on television, I wouldn't like to live there. It's a jungle," she said, shaking her head.

"Tell me about it, ma'am," John said, and eased back his head on the top of the head rest, and closed his eyes. He suddenly dozed off and all the faces of his family came back to him. The sweat poured down his face after a few minutes, and his head moved slowly from side to side.

"Mary, where are you?" he said softly several times to himself. The lady next to him looked up and saw what was happening, then she shook his shoulder.

"Sir, are you okay?" she asked.

John slowly came to his senses, and looked at her for a few seconds. "Yes, I'm okay, ma'am," John replied, looking at the elderly lady. "Just a bad dream," he added.

"My name is Emily."

"Pleased to meet you, Emily. I am John."

"You were saying Mary. You'll think I'm nosy," she said with a smile.

"Mary was my wife."

"You said 'was'?"

"Yes, Emily. Seven years ago all my family were killed by a burglar, and I couldn't save them," John told her.

"You poor man," she said and touched his hand.

"I'll be poor until the end," John told her and eased himself back into his seat.

Several hours later the bus arrived at the bus station in New York City. John and Emily got off the bus and went to collect their belongings from the baggage compartment. Then John said goodbye to Emily, and he went to the gents' washroom to freshen up, then he made his way out of the bus station. It was still light. He looked right, and saw a white youth pull Emily's small bag away from her, and was running toward him. As soon as the youth came upon him, he hit him with his holdall, knocking him down to the sidewalk, then taking the small bag away from him.

"Naughty boy. Stealing from a nice lady like Miss Emily," he said softly to the youth. "Get going before I turn you over to the police."

The youth got up and ran away. Emily came quickly to John, and he gave her the bag. "Thank you, John," she said and gave him a hug. "You're a real life-saver. I had all my money in that bag," she added with a smile.

John thought of what she said. He couldn't save his own family, and Emily was now telling him he was a life-saver. "You're welcome, Emily. Now let me walk you to your cab," he said, taking her arm.

"You're a real gentleman," she said, looking up at him. "I hope we meet again," she added with a smile.

"I'm sure that you'll see me again sooner or later," John said, smiling. Emily, for some reason, reminded him of his own departed mother. John saw Emily into her cab and waved goodbye at her as it pulled away. Then he became confused, as he didn't know which way he was going. He knew his destination was somewhere in the Brooklyn area.

John arrived at his destination an hour later, after taking two taxis. He paid the driver and made his way to the rooming house on 2286 Atlantic Avenue. He observed that the buildings in that area were run-down, and he realized it might be a bad area to live in, but he had two choices, take it or leave it. The best possibility was for him to take it and make the best out of a bad situation. There was a small light just above the front door of the rooming house. John knocked hard on the door, and a few seconds later it opened. Then he came face to face with an elderly black woman, stout and tall, standing in the doorway. She looked at John carefully under the dimmed light.

"Aunt Mildred?" John asked, looking at her.

"Yes. Who are you?" she asked bluntly.

"I'm Mike's friend, John."

"But you are...?" She stopped short.

"Yes. I'm a white brother. Mike taught me how to be black, so take no notice of my white face, Aunt Mildred," he said with a smile.

Aunt Mildred giggled a little, and waved him to come in. "I like you already, John. You make me laugh," she said and closed the door behind him. "The rent is fifty dollars per week in advance."

"Yes, ma'am," John said and dropped his holdall, and took out some banknotes from his pocket, and gave her fifty dollars. She took the money, then gave him two keys from a bunch which she took out of her pocket. "Your room is upstairs on the second floor, room 8."

John took his bag and went up the stairs to his room.

"If you want food, you'll have to go to Main Street," she shouted after him.

"Thank you," he shouted back.

John, after resting for an hour in his room, decided to go for a bite to eat. He walked four blocks on Atlantic Avenue, then on Main Street until he came upon a small hamburger joint. He ordered two burgers and fries and a large coffee. After the meal, he made his way slowly back from the way he came. He looked carefully at all the buildings on Main Street, until he came to Atlantic Avenue. He only passed a few people on the way, and they were all black youths. They looked at him suspiciously as they passed him. He felt if he had darkened his face, they wouldn't look at him so suspiciously.

The air was mild and the skies were dark. He couldn't believe he was in a new world, and it was the world of his visions and dreams. He had a strong feeling that one of his dreams was about to become reality very soon. He crossed Main Street to Atlantic Avenue. It was quiet for a while, and after walking two blocks, he suddenly heard the screams of a woman. They were coming from behind a building in a back alley. He listened carefully, then he ran to where the screams were coming from. It was as if the screams were drawing him closer to the woman in trouble. He came upon a side entrance, then he advanced closer. He approached cautiously behind the building, and under the dimmed light he saw three people against the brick wall. He went closer and saw two men and a woman. The two men were trying to rape a young black woman.

"What's going on here?" John shouted at the two black men. They both turned around in surprise to face their intruder. The woman quickly pulled up her panties, then pulled down her dress, and ran quickly past the men.

"You put your nose in our business, Brother. Now, we'll rape you," one youth told John. Then they both pulled their knives and came slowly toward him.

"No need to get rough, lads. I'm sorry I made your date run away. I said I'm sorry, let's call it a night," John told the two youths.

"No way, Brother. When we're finished raping you, we'll cut you up into little pieces. You'll pay with your blood for poking your big nose in our business," the other youth told John.

132

"You speak very well, Brother. You should join a political party of your choice, make speeches like that and you'll be elected," John told the youth.

"You're making fun of me. I'm real mad now. You'll pay," the youth shouted.

John waited until they were near enough to him, then he dived for their legs, and kicked both of his opponents in the groin. Then he came from behind them, kicking them hard on their asses. They were no match for him and ran quickly out of the back alley.

"We'll get you again, White Brother. We'll get you," the other youth shouted.

"Yes, we'll meet again, Brothers, and thank you for the workout. Now it's my bedtime. I must get to bed," John said to himself. He slowly headed to his room on Atlantic Avenue.

John got back to his room and took off his jacket, shirt, and pants. He left on his underpants. He put his clothes neatly on the nearby chair, then he threw himself onto the small bed. The bed springs rang out a soft song. He just lay there and listened until there was no more melody to the bed springs. There was a dim light in the ceiling; the room reminded him of his cell in the prison, and he realized that the room was worse than his cell. Now he was out of prison, he deserved better, but he knew he had to live out the spell that was cast onto him.

He looked up at the ceiling and saw a big spider making its way across the room. He didn't want to kill it, as that was bad luck. Then he thought, how bad could his luck get? It was bad as it was, and nothing was going to change it in a hurry. The mice ran up and down his room, and the roaches came out of their hiding places, then the mice would make supper out of the roaches.

His heart started beating faster as he remembered how his life had changed in just a few minutes. And to be honest with himself, he didn't have a life any more. Now all he could think about was bad things that would only lead him into trouble. Now trouble was his name and his game. If that made sense to someone else, it didn't make any sense to him.

The next morning, John went for a run, and when he came back to the rooming house, he met Aunt Mildred. She was cleaning the passageway at the bottom of the stairs.

"Good morning, Aunt Mildred," John said to her with a smile.

"And good morning to you too, John," she replied, not taking her eyes off of him. "So you went out for an early morning walk?"

"Actually a run." John looked around the place, then at Aunt Mildred. "I'm handy, and I can make this place beautiful for you," he told her.

"And how much will all this cost me?"

"Nothing. You provide the materials, and I'll do the work. In that way you can increase your rents."

"Mike told me about you and I didn't believe him. He said you rearranged the whole prison. You helped the warden, so he could keep his job. Now I suppose it is my turn," she said, smiling.

"I'll be able to start next week, ma'am."

"I like you, John, you're so polite."

"I can't help it. It's my nature."

"I'll have some breakfast for you when you come down," she shouted after him.

"Thank you, I'll be down in a minute," he shouted back.

After breakfast, John went around the town, then across the Brooklyn Bridge, then onto the subway at Hoboken, and he traveled up and down the subway. He came up at 14th Street and looked at all the tall buildings in the surrounding areas. It was as if he was in another dimension. When he was out of breath from walking around, he found the nearest fast food shop to have a bite and a drink. Then he went up and down the main roads again, looking at the business places, and at the faces of the different people whom he had never seen before. Then finally he went back to the subway, and made his way back to his rooming house. He knew that the following day he'd roam all over the city again. Everything he saw excited him, and he wanted to see more and more.

The following day was Friday, and John set out after breakfast. He walked around and around the Brooklyn area. It was as if he was searching for something that would give him a clue why he was there in that area. Then he came upon a spot on Main Street, and he stopped abruptly, and looked up at the billboard over the road. He had seen it before, but he couldn't remember where. He knew sooner or later it would come back to him. He turned away, then suddenly he remembered where he had seen the billboard. He had seen it in his dream. It was that horrible dream where he died trying to save a blind woman on the busy main street. The sweat started to pour down his forehead. It suddenly dawned on him that sooner or later he would have to face this inevitable reality. He felt sure that he would have to face the event and he'd have to be prepared for the occasion when it arrived. John smiled to himself, then he was drawn to Hoboken subway. He went down and joined one of the trains. He didn't know its destination, but wherever it was going, he'd go also. He sat down and was able to think. He felt the whole situation was becoming a game of cat and mouse. He knew he was the cat, but he didn't know who was the mouse, and that was what made the situation so intriguing and dangerous.

Then he came up on 14th Street, and he went around the same area as the previous day. On the main street he came upon a beautiful girl. She was standing against a building. John couldn't help himself from looking at her steadily. Her dress was short, showing her long smooth legs, and the top of her dress was low, and most of her large breasts were showing on top. John smiled as he approached her. He came in front of her and stopped abruptly. He eyed her up and down, as if he hadn't seen anyone like her for a long time. He felt thrilled by her presence, and it was as if she was just there to please him. She smiled at him as if she knew him for a long time.

"Hi, handsome," she said, smiling.

"Are you speaking to me, ma'am?" he asked politely.

"Yes, handsome," she replied.

"So what can I do for you, Miss?"

"No, it's what I can do for you, handsome," she said, as she slowly chewed the chewing gum in her mouth. "I can take you home and we can have a good time," she told him.

"Thank you, Miss, but I'll have to decline your invitation. I'm not home and I'm having a good time. So you have a nice day," John said, smiling, and went on his way, leaving behind the beautiful hooker. "Such a pretty young lady. She should find herself a real job," John said to himself.

After that, John had something to eat that afternoon, then he headed back to the subway on 14th street, and jumped onto one of the trains. He had a strong feeling that something was about to happen. But what? He knew he was going to find out the outcome of his encounter very soon, and he had to be on the alert.

John sat at the end of one carriage. He felt uneasy and gazed at everyone that came in and out of that compartment. Then he saw a white, tall, stout man came into the compartment. He wore an overcoat, and John saw a shotgun poking under his coat. The man went to the far end of the carriage where an elderly woman was sitting. She held her purse close to her. The man stood over her, and pointed part of the shotgun under his coat at her. John got up quickly and went towards the woman. John saw the woman take the money out of her purse, and give it to the robber.

"Sir."

The robber turned around quickly to face John. "What do you want?" the robber asked.

"Please give that kind lady back her money!" John told him sternly.

The woman looked up in surprise. The robber poked the money into his coat pocket, and pointed the gun at John.

"Are you going to shoot me?" John asked.

"As soon as you give me all your money. You're a stupid lad. You should have minded your own business," the robber told John with a grin.

"Well, if you put it like that, you can have all my money, but please don't shoot me. Do you promise?" John said politely.

"The money and quick about it," the robber told John bluntly.

"Yes, the money," John said and pushed his right hand into his pocket and pulled out a handful of notes. John conveniently let the notes fall to the ground, then he took a step backward, looking steadily at the robber.

"Sorry. There's your money," John told the robber, and pointed to the ground.

"You think that's funny?" the robber asked bluntly,

"No. I'm sorry, sir, but it just slipped out of my nervous hand."

The robber looked at John, then down at the money. Then the robber decided to bend down to get the money, which was in one roll. His gun pointing to the ground. Then it was time for John to act. John took one step forward and kicked the robber under the throat. The robber fell to the ground, gasping for breath. John kicked the gun away. The robber tried to get up and John punched him in the face several times. The robber fell to the ground. John picked up his money from the ground, then he got the money from the robber's coat pocket and gave it back to the elderly woman. The woman took her money from John. She was nervous at the whole situation, and went quickly to the other side of the carriage.

When the train stopped, John threw the robber and his empty gun out on the platform, and went back to his seat at the end of the train. When the train got to Hoboken Station, he got out and made his way up the escalator, then up ahead he suddenly saw a familiar face. He was sure it was the face of the burglar who killed his family. He ran quickly up the escalator, but the face of the man that had haunted him all those years had disappeared into the crowd. He looked and looked, but he couldn't see the ugly face that he despised with all his heart. John now knew that the killer lived somewhere in New York City, and he was sure they'd meet again very soon.

John went to bed early that evening because he knew he had to be up early the next morning, so he could make the trip to his home town. He wanted to recapture some of his memories of the past, and most of all, he wanted to see Karen Hill again. She was once his dearest friend.

He hadn't seen or heard from her in all those years he was in prison. He knew she was married, and maybe by now she had several kids. He certainly didn't want to interrupt her married life, but he just wanted to see her again. She was his best friend once and he couldn't forget it.

Chapter Twelve

John arrived at 2.45 at the Moorestown bus stop. His brother, Harold was there to meet him. He had called him the night before to inform him of his time of arrival.

"John, I'm glad you're here. As I told you on the phone, Dad isn't very well. He's been looked after in an old people's home. He wanted to see you and I'm going to take you there right now," Harold told him.

"Yes, if that's the case I'd like to see Dad," John said and jumped into the cab of the truck. Harold drove John to Moorestown Old Peoples' Home, and parked his truck in the visitors' parking lot. Then he took John to their father's room. Harold stood by the door and John went to his father's bedside. He looked down at his father sadly. His father was resting, then he opened his eyes, looked up at John and smiled.

"John, you've come," his father said softly. "I knew you would. Come and sit down, and talk to me," he added.

John pulled up a chair and sat next to his father. "Dad, it has been a long time. I miss you. I always remember what you had told me on the farm. You wanted me to be master of the farm, and I turned you down. I'm sorry Dad," John told his father sadly.

"You didn't want to be master of the farm. You wanted your brother to be master of the farm. But in my heart you were the master of the farm. I realized you were deprived of your rightful inheritance, and that's why I wanted to see you."

"You wanted to see me?" John asked.

"Yes. I took out an insurance policy for $250,000 a few years ago, and I have named you as my beneficiary. You have had a hard life, and I want to leave a little something for you," his father explained.

"Thank you, Dad, but I don't need any money. I'm in good health and I can work on any job," he told his father quickly.

"No matter what you say, son, the money will be yours. It's my gift to you, and you deserve it. You'll have a little something to spend on yourself, and when you have a family again. It was dreadful the way you lost your family, but life goes on."

"Don't speak like that, Dad, you'll live for a long time," John told his father, touching his shoulder.

"I'll be here only as long as life permits. Well, son, thanks for coming."

"Goodbye, Dad. I love you," John said softly.

"I hope you visit me soon again, son. I must have my rest," his father said and closed his eyes.

John got up and slowly went out of the room. Harold was waiting for him in the waiting room. He came face to face with Harold.

Harold got up to face John. "Dad wanted so much to see you. It was as if his whole life depended upon seeing you. He is trying to be strong, but he doesn't have long to live. You'll have to let me know where to find you, just in case it comes to the worst," Harold told him boldly.

"I understand, Harold. Did Dad tell you he was going to leave me his life insurance money?"

"Yes. I helped him to set it up for you. I got everything, and you got nothing. I felt guilty because of this. The money will come in handy for you to make a new start," Harold told him.

"You're getting really soft hearted in your old age, Harold," John said with a smile.

"I know we never saw eye to eye, but I've always admired you. You were the strongest, and you always knew where you were going. I'm weak and I only wanted to be a farmer like Dad. I wanted to be like you, but I am me," Harold said.

"I know the way you feel, and it doesn't get any better. Now that we have that all out into the open, I'd like you to take me to the Youngs' residence."

"They wanted to see you. They have moved into a new area. I'll take you to them."

Ten minutes later Harold arrived at the Youngs' residence. He rang the doorbell, and a few seconds later, Mrs. Young opened the front door. She saw Harold first.

"Harold, how nice to see you," she said, then she saw John. She looked at him for a few seconds.

"Hi, Mrs. Young," John said with a smile.

"John, how are you? I'm so glad to see you," she said quickly.

"I'm fine, ma'am," he told her shyly.

"Please, do come in!" she said and moved away from the doorway, and led the two brothers into the living room. Mr. Young sprung up from where he was sitting when he saw his two visitors.

"John, Harold so good to see you both," Mr. Young said and shook both of the brothers' hands.

"I wasn't sure you good folks would be pleased see me after all that has happened," John said, facing Mrs. Young.

"John, to be honest with you, we thought you were responsible for the deaths of our daughter and grandchildren at first, but we were dead wrong to think that way. We realized after that you were the fall guy, and the person who killed your family went scot-free. We're truly sorry," Mrs. Young said and gave John a hug.

"We heard of all the good work you've been doing, and we're proud of you. Your next-door neighbor saw the burglar, who came running out of your house. He didn't give this evidence in court, otherwise, you wouldn't have been convicted," Mr. Young told John.

"Mr. Roberts was my next-door neighbor, and I'm not bitter at him for holding back that evidence. I'm grateful to him for saving my life. He died several weeks ago, and he wanted me to be free before he went to heaven," John told them sadly.

"What are your plans now, John?" Mrs. Young asked.

"I really don't know. My life will never be the same again, and I'm taking one day at a time," John replied, shaking his head.

"Well, enough talk, gentlemen. It's time for supper. John always liked my supper."

"Those were the good old days," John told her. "Your cooking was always delicious. Thank you for the invitation, ma'am. It would make a great change after eating the State's food for over six years," John said as they were led into the dining room.

"But you look so healthy, John," Mr. Young said.

"The food was bad, so I had to exercise night and day."

The three men sat at the dining room table while Mrs. Young put the plates, knives, forks, spoons and the supper on the table.

"Well, John, we wanted to talk to you about the insurance money, which was put into a trust account, and that's after all the expenses were paid. We wanted to know what you want to do with the money," Mr. Young explained to John.

"I do not need that money. We'll have to find a good purpose for it, so hold it a bit longer," John replied with a smile.

"Now, you gents please dig in. Supper is in front of you," Mrs. Young told the men, then she joined them.

John said a small prayer, then they started to eat.

"John, it's so good you still have the same old touch, and it's so good to have you here again," Mrs. Young told John.

"Thank you, ma'am."

John and Harold arrived at the farm at 8.30 that evening. John met his sister, Rose, and her family, and Harold's wife and family. He was the only one who didn't have a family, and he felt left out.

Early next morning Harold took John to the bus stop, and he gave his younger brother some money for his journey to Philadelphia, then back to New York.

"Well, John, have a safe trip back to New York. And you'll have to call me to find out about Dad. I have the phone number you gave me, so I'll call you if anything happens," Harold said, then he gave John a hug.

"Thank you, Harold. I'll be in touch," John said and jumped on the bus to Philadelphia.

John arrived at 10.30 that morning. John felt somewhat strange, coming back to the same place in which he was once so happy with his family. The sad memories started coming back. He tried his best to block them out, but they were so great that he had no choice but to relive some of the happy memories he'd once felt in the past.

John thought of Karen Hill. He didn't know where she lived, and he was aching to see her once more. When he was in prison, he felt guilty because he saw Karen's beautiful face constantly. He felt guilty because he should have been thinking about Mary, his wife, but instead he thought about Karen. Now he wanted to see her in person, so he went to the St. Mary's Hospital to find her.

He arrived at the hospital just after 11.00, and went to the receptionist at the desk. She was tall, slim, and attractive. She looked up at John and smiled.

"Can I help you?" she asked politely.

"I don't know if you can, Nurse, but here I go. I'm from out of town, and I came to visit a friend of mine. Nurse Karen Hill," John told her, smiling.

The receptionist looked at John for a few seconds.

"Nurse Hill is off duty and her married name is Williamson."

"Williamson?"

"Yes. And you want to see her?"

"Yes, I really want to see her."

The receptionist looked up a card, and started dialing on the phone, and after a few seconds: "Karen, this is May the receptionist. I'm sorry to bother you on your day off, but I have a gentleman here, who said he is a friend of yours, and he wants to see you."

"Well, please ask him his name."

"She wants to know your name."

"Tell Karen it is her friend John Stone."

"I heard that. Give John my address and send him over. And thank you for calling me, May."

The receptionist put down the phone and wrote the address down on a piece of paper for John, and gave it to him. "I heard so much about you, Mr. Stone, and good luck to you," she said, smiling.

"Thank you. And you have a nice day too," John said to her and left. He arrived at Karen's apartment ten minutes later. He went up to the second floor and rang the doorbell, and a few seconds later the front door swung open. John stood there gazing at reality. It was the beautiful face he had not seen in years. He felt that if he had tried a little harder, he could have fallen in love with Karen, but at that time he was still in love with his deceased wife, Mary.

"John!" Karen shouted. "It's been such a long time," she added and held out her arms. John went into her arms. "Oh, Karen, I longed for the moment that I could hold you in my arms again, even though you're married. It's so good. And you haven't changed a bit. You're still as beautiful as ever. It was you who kept me from going crazy all those years. I never stopped thinking about you, and at sometime or other I fell in love with you, but you were no more to be. I had sent you away, away to love someone else," John told her as he embraced her in his arms inside the apartment. He closed the door.

"John, I have always loved you, even though you were unable to give me your love, for reasons I knew," Karen confessed. Then the little boy came and tugged at Karen's dress.

"Mommy, who is this?" he asked with some curiosity.

Karen looked down at Ted. "This is Uncle John, Ted," his mother told him.

"Hi, Ted," John bent down and shook his little hand.

"He's five years old and will be going to school very soon," Karen told John.

John stood up face to face with Karen. "Where is his dad?" John asked softly.

Karen shook her head. "He left two years ago and we are now divorced," she told John sadly. "Ted has no father now, and he needs a father." John took Karen in his arms.

"I'm sorry, Karen. You had to deal with me first, and now this. I never wanted to see you like this, but I guess we all have to lie in our beds, then make it up after," John said, trying to comfort her.

Ted went back to the living room to look at his favorite television program. John and Karen went into the kitchen to exchange their thoughts.

"I was released last week, and I have a room in New York City. My destiny lies somewhere out there. A lot has happened to me and I need to put myself together again," John told her in the kitchen.

"I heard about Mr. Roberts. One of the nurses who knew you from the Baptist Church helped Mr. Roberts to write that letter. That was a good break for you, John."

"Yes, a good break," John said and sat at the kitchen table. Karen poured him a large cup of coffee, and sat down beside him.

"But the real killer is still out there, and I have a feeling we're going to meet again," John said, sipping his coffee.

"Why don't you leave it alone, John?" Karen said, gazing at him steadily.

"I wish I could, but my whole life is going in a different direction and I can't control what happens. My whole life depends on the outcome. It's a long story and I don't want to get into it at this stage," John said, tapping his left index finger on the table.

"Be careful, John. It's a jungle out there."

"What are your plans, Karen?"

Karen smiled. "Well, I'm seeing someone and he likes Ted. Ted needs a father. Someone he can look up to."

"I'm glad. Because my life is too complicated for any relationship with a woman at the present moment," John confessed, and drank his coffee. John suddenly had a funny feeling. Ted's face. He had seen that face before, and it was the same face on an old photograph of himself. The time frame and the face. It all made sense. He thought it was a dream, a dream he had years ago, making love to Karen. He shook his head.

"It can't be. It was just a dream," he whispered to himself.

"Did you say something, John?" Karen asked.

"I was thinking about Ted. His face reminds me of..."

"Yes, of you," Karen said. "He reminds you of you because he is you," she added softly.

"I guess you're going to tell me what really happened that night when you stayed with me."

"Yes. I think I owe you that much, John," she told him, not looking at him. John paid careful attention as Karen was about to speak.

"Do you remember our last night together?" she asked, looking at him.

"Vaguely. And you're about to tell me."

"Yes," she said and hesitated. "That night I stayed with you because you were depressed. You were afraid that you were going to be arrested for the murders of your family. I had a funny feeling, if that happened I'd never see you again. I put you to bed, and I told you I'd leave shortly, but I couldn't bear to leave you alone. I needed you in my life even if it was for just a few hours, but most of all I wanted to be close to you," she explained.

"So you stayed with me?"

"Yes. It was my chance to get closer to you, but I didn't know how close. When you were asleep I got this mad idea to strip and get into bed with you. I hesitated. I knew it was wrong, but I still took off my clothes and went into bed with you. Your body was warm and soft, and I touched you between the legs and you started to get a hard-on."

"And what really happened, Karen?" John asked with his face pulled together.

"It's hard for me to tell you what happened next, but you have to know the truth, the whole truth, John."

"Go on."

"I got close to you, and suddenly you put your right hand around my shoulders. Then you came closer to me and said, 'Mary, I love

144

you.' I said, 'I love you too, John.' You then kissed me hard on the lips. You thought I was Mary, and you were making love to her, but in fact you were making love to me. After several kisses, you took your clothes off, then you went on top of me, and I felt your warm body on mine. It felt heavenly, then I felt your hard penis between my legs, and it tickled me. I pushed my right hand under your body, and held your penis tightly in my right hand. It felt stiff and smooth in my hand. I played with the head for a few seconds, then I inserted it slowly into my vagina. It was painful at first as your stiff penis went deeper inside my vagina. I held more closely onto you, as you made your up and down movements on top of me. After a few minutes your movements accelerated, then I knew you were about to eject your sperm into the passageway of my vagina. I knew if I was going to make it work, I had to work with you, then after a while we both came to a climax together," Karen explained. She shook her head. "I'm ashamed of myself," she said with her head down.

"There's nothing to be ashamed of, Karen. You did what you thought was right. I never thought what had happened was real. I thought it was a very sexy dream I had that night," John told her, touching her hand.

"A few weeks later I found out that I was pregnant with your child."

"Then what happened, Karen?"

"Ron Williamson was always kind and friendly to me. We started going out and I told him what my plight was. He told me he loved me and he'd take the responsibility of the child, so we got married three months afterwards. I wasn't in love with him. After Ted was born, Ron and I made love several times, but I was just pretending. Then, after a while, I just couldn't make love with him any more. I was still in love with you, and I couldn't get you out of my mind. Ron and I got a mutual divorce two years later. I'm seeing someone now, as I told you, and he likes Ted. I don't know if it will work out," Karen explained.

"You can't give up. You'll have to try and try again," John told her with his right fist clenched. "I'm sorry everything turned out that way, Karen."

Karen smiled at John. "Don't be, John. You gave me something beautiful. You gave me Ted. I want this to remain between us, John. No one must ever know," Karen cried.

"I understand. What can I do to help?"

"Just being here helps. John, I know you have your own life to catch up on. We'll be here and you'll be welcome to visit us. We'll always be good friends, no matter what," Karen told John softly.

"I'll always be your friend, no matter what," John said sadly, and he touched her hand in a gesture of friendship. John got up and looked at Karen for a few seconds.

"Are you leaving now, John?" Karen asked, looking at him.

"Yes. I have to visit the Baptist Church, then I'm going to the cemetery. I'm glad I came. I thought I was all alone, but now I'm not," John said and went into the living room. Karen followed behind him. John stood there looking at Ted, who was looking at a kid's television program.

"Well, Ted, Uncle John wants to say goodbye," John said to him, smiling. Karen looked on carefully.

"Bye, Uncle John," Ted said to John, looking at him, then back to his television program.

Karen followed John to the front door. "What are your plans now, John?" she asked.

"I'm taking one day at a time," he told her.

"That's good and I wish you all the luck," she said and went into his arms. Then she looked at him steadily.

"Kiss me goodbye, John. Give me something to remember you," she said and placed her lips close to his. John kissed her hard on the lips. "Good-bye, John. We'll keep in touch," Karen said, trying to hold back the tears.

"Yes, Karen. You take good care of yourself and Ted," John said and left.

When John was outside on the street, he looked back, then kept on his way. He couldn't believe what had happened. He had gone to see Karen only to find out he had a son, a son he could never, for the moment, call son.

John headed quickly on Main Street. He wanted to get to the Baptist Church before the morning service ended. He arrived there ten minutes later, and entered the church. Pastor Boyd was making his final remarks on his sermon. John stopped halfway down the passageway. Pastor Boyd saw him and stopped speaking, and the whole congregation started to look at John.

"Brother John has come to join us this Sunday," Pastor Boyd said to the congregation.

John went to the front of the pulpit. "I'm sorry, Pastor Boyd, Brothers and Sisters, for stopping your service, but the Good One above sent me here today." John turned to the congregation. "I'm here to thank each one of you for praying for me in my days of sorrow, and sending me all those beautiful cards while I was in prison for a crime I didn't commit. I hope you'll continue to pray for me, so I'll become stronger to face life again. Thank you, Pastor Boyd, Brothers and Sisters. Good-bye," John said, then walked slowly out of the church. He stopped outside and heard the singing of a hymn by the members.

John hurried around to 45 Blexley Avenue, and he stood in front of his former residence. The house looked the same to him, but the owner had changed the color of the paint in front. Then he looked up at Mr. Roberts' house.

"Wherever you are, Mr. Roberts, thank you," John whispered to himself. Then he headed for High Street, and caught a no. 2 bus to the cemetery. Then he got off and walked slowly inside the cemetery until he came to the graves of his family, Mary, David and Cindy. He stood in front of their graves. He felt sad and numb. He turned to Mary's grave. "Mary, please tell me what to do. I need your help and I need your strength. Please, help me, so I can go on with my life," he cried, then he took two steps back when he saw Mary appear in front of him. He stopped dead in his tracks and gazed at her. He couldn't tell whether his memory was playing him tricks, or whether the vision of Mary was real.

"John, we were your family once. We're happy here, David, Cindy and I. John, you have to get on with your life. Before you had a wish to die and be with us because you loved us so much, but now you have to have a will to live for us. Be happy!" the vision of Mary said and disappeared.

"Thank you, Mary. No matter what you say, I'll always love you, David and Cindy, always," John said with tears in his eyes.

"Is that you, John?" a woman's voice asked behind him. John turned around quickly.

The woman ran into his arms, then he realized who she was. "Alice?" he said softly.

"Yes, I'm little Alice, Mary's sister," she answered.

"You're not little any more. Let me look at you; you're a beautiful young lady. I only wish that Mary were here to see you," John told her, smiling.

"John, I always loved you; you were like a big brother to me. You were the brother I never had," she told him, holding a bunch of flowers in her right hand.

"And you were like my younger sister," he told her.

Alice drew herself away from John. She gazed at him and saw the tears running down his cheeks. "At first I thought you did it, but I knew in my heart that you couldn't harm anyone, especially Mary. You loved her so much," Alice said with the tears coming down her cheeks. "I cry too for her, John, and I loved her too. She was my one and only sister. I bring flowers every time I can spare and I talk to her, the same way you were talking to her," she said quickly. John took her in his arms. "We both loved her," he said. Then Alice went and separated the flowers on the three graves, then she returned to John.

"Mary spoke to me. She told me to get on with my life," he said.

"That's what you have to do, John. You're alive. Get on with your life."

"Your mother told me you work in Philadelphia now."

"Yes. I work in a computer factory. I work on the invoices. The pay is good, and I am able to go to college in the evening," she told him as they walked out of the cemetery.

"Are you planning to come back here, John?"

"No. I'm staying in New York. I hope to obtain work very soon. I had to come here to pay my respects."

"I understand, John. Can I take you anywhere, John?"

"You drive now?"

"Yes. I got myself some wheels, so I can get around."

"Take me to the bus station, and maybe I can get an early bus back to the big apple," he told her.

Alice drove John to the main bus station and all he could think about was to get back to his room in Brooklyn. She kissed him goodbye at the bus station. He was just in time to catch the next bus out. And on the bus to New York, he still felt sad and numb, but as the bus traveled further away from Philadelphia, his sadness and numbness gradually disappeared.

"I want to be strong," John whispered to himself, then he started to hum Mary's favorite song to himself, *Danny Boy*.

Chapter Thirteen

John needed to work out, so as to increase his body strength. He joined Wong Fu's Karate School, which was situated on Main Street. His instructor was Mr. Fu. He told Mr. Fu what Ling Lee had taught him. Mr. Fu told him that he'd do his best to help him to advance in the training of karate. John realized that he needed to work hard to bring the best out of him, and he also needed to feel pain on his body, so that he'd know that he was alive, alive to face any danger that he may encounter.

After John finished his lesson with Mr. Fu, he confided in him.

"The late Mr. Lee, my old instructor, died in an accident a few years ago, and his spirit seems to be guiding me. I started getting visions and dreams of incidents in the future. Can you tell me what to make of that?" John said.

"Mr. Lee was your close friend, and his spirit will guide you and protect you from danger," Mr. Fu told John.

"Then this is all true?"

"Yes."

"In one of my dreams I died trying to save a blind woman. What does it mean?"

"Mr. Lee's spirit will guide you and you'll see the light to overcome the situation."

"I hope so."

"I may as well tell you now. I felt the vibration from the moment you came through the door that there was something special about you. I can predict that you're going to do great things in our small city," Mr. Fu told him.

"Like what?"

"You're going to encounter some very dangerous situations and you life will be in great danger. You'll have to train very hard to overcome these situations. Why do you fight as if you life depended on it?"

"That's because my family were all killed by an intruder who broke into our house. I couldn't save them, and I paid dearly for it in prison."

"One day the danger will bring you back to your natural self, Mr. Stone."

"Thank you, Mr. Fu. I'll be here tomorrow morning for further training," John said and the two men bowed to each other.

John went to the hardware store on Main Street and ordered some building supplies, so he could carry out some work on the rooming house. He paid for the stuff and asked them to deliver it there.

When John arrived at the rooming house, he went into the kitchen to see Aunt Mildred. He saw her sitting at the table, and she was sad. She looked up at him, and he knew that something was wrong. "Sit down, John," she said. She poured him a cup of coffee.

"Drink it while it's hot," she told him. "Mike told me you're a good person, and that if I ever needed help, you'd be the one for me to turn to," she explained.

John took a sip of his coffee. "Now tell me, what's on your mind, Aunt Mildred?" John asked.

Aunt Mildred gave John the letter that was in front of her. John read it, and looked at her for a few seconds. "You're three months behind with your mortgage payments. You owe the bank over $2000. How did you get so far behind?"

"It's a long story. And if Mike were here, I wouldn't be in this trouble," she told him, shaking her head.

"Is there something you are holding back from me?" he asked with directness.

"Two of my roomers haven't paid me rent in months, and lately they have threatened me. I now have to give them money. I'm a woman and I can't protect myself from those thugs," she told John, without looking at him.

"Give me their names and I'll handle it in my own way," he told her, his right hand clenched on the table.

"Peter and Rick. They're in rooms 6 and 7. They're a bad lot, especially Peter. He carries a sharp knife in his back pocket."

"I'll speak to the manager about this letter. I have ordered some supplies, so I can start work on this place, and I'll make it beautiful again."

Aunt Mildred smiled at John. "I feel safe with you around. Are you really serious about working on this place?" she asked.

"Yes. I'm going to clean and paint, and at the same time I'm going sweep out those dirty rats who are not paying you rent," John told her, smiling.

"Mike was right about you, John. You're a good person."

"Well, someone has to look after you, Aunt Mildred. First, I have to take care of that little matter of your back mortgage," John told her quickly.

"Thank you, John. And bless you!"

John had put all of Peter's and Rick's stuff into two garbage bags, and placed them downstairs. When the two men came in through the front door, John was waiting for them.

"I'm sorry gentlemen, but your stuff is all packed, and you need to leave peacefully," he told the two men.

Then one of the men came over to John. "Who do you think you are?" he asked rudely.

"My name is John Stone, the new manager."

"Well, my name is Peter, the bad guy, and you'll have to deal with me. And for this I'm going to hurt you," he said, smiling.

John went face to face with Peter. "Now I'm not going to say this twice. I need your keys, gentlemen," John said with a clenched fist. "Don't make me mad, otherwise I'll have to use this on both of you."

The two men backed down. They threw the keys on the floor and took their respective garbage bags.

"Thank you, gentlemen. And you have a nice night," John told them.

"We'll get you, white manager. We'll get you," Peter said as they left the building. John closed the front door, then he picked up the keys on the floor.

"So far so good, but they'll be back, and I have to be prepared. I have to be one step ahead." John whispered to himself. He went to his room and made plans. He knew he had to deal with two dangerous enemies now, and at some point or other he'd have to face them. Most probably he'd meet them in the dark, and Peter would be the one with the knife. John realized that he'd have to use caution in the matter.

That night John left the door of his room opened. He made his bed up as if he was sleeping in it, and he turned off the lights in the room, and he sat at the side of the door. He couldn't afford to go to sleep, otherwise, he'd be dead, with a knife stuck in his back. He got up and turned on the light in the room. Then he remembered the stick in the clothes closet. He took the stick and it was just what he needed for protection. He turned the light off, and sat down at the side of the door. Now all he had to do was wait for his attackers to arrive. He was sure they would come to even up the score.

Several hours after, he suddenly dozed off. When he came to himself, he shook his head to bring himself back to reality. He held the stick tightly in his right hand, then he heard the footsteps coming up the squeaking stairs, then the footsteps got closer to his room. Then his door opened slowly. Then a lone figure headed slowly toward his bed. John knew at once that the figure was bad Peter. John heard a muffled sound from the bed. Then he got up quickly and slammed the door hard on the other figure who was standing in the doorway. Then he lunged at the person standing at his bed, hitting him hard with the stick on his back, then on the knees to bring him down. He saw the shining knife and he hit the knife out of Peter's hand, then he hit hard on the knees again. The person fell onto the floor, then John turned on the light, and picked up the knife. He bent down over Peter, and held the knife close to his throat.

"Now, who do we have here?" John asked with a smile. "Big, bad Peter has come back to do me in. I'm so sorry that your backup man ran away. Now it's you and me, but I don't want to wake up the other roomers, so I'll ask you to leave quietly. Now get up and make your way out," John told Peter. Peter got up slowly and tried to attack John, John pulled back and hit him hard on his hand with the stick. "Now get out, and don't make me mad," John said and pushed him out of the room, down the stairs and outside.

"Now I can get some sleep. I have a busy day tomorrow," John whispered to himself and went back to his room.

The following morning John went to the bank after his karate lessons, and presented himself to the manager.

"I'm here on behalf of Mildred Williams. You sent her this letter," John told him and gave him the letter.

"Yes. She is three months behind, and we'll start foreclosure proceedings if we don't receive any money within the next few days," the manager told him.

"I'll take care of the amount owing. I'd like you to get in touch with my bank in Moorestown, and the money will be transferred to you, sir."

"And your name, sir?"

"John Stone."

"Are you the John Stone from Philadelphia?" the manager asked.

"The one and only."

"We've heard a lot about you here in New York."

"All good I hope, sir."

"Ted Martin is the name, Mr. Stone. I'll get this done right away, Mr. Stone. And thank you for coming in. Tell Miss Williams we'll be in touch with her," the manager said and led John out of his office.

John arrived just after midday at the rooming house. He saw Aunt Mildred.

"I saw the bank manager, and I was able to sort out everything for you. So don't you worry about a thing. I also got rid of your two bad roomers, so I'm going to start working on their rooms," John told her.

"Your supplies came this morning. You'll have to have a snack before you start any work," she said and led him to the kitchen table. "I'm curious. How did you get rid of those two bad roomers?"

"Well, it took a little persuasion for them to leave, but they went quietly."

"Will wonders never cease?" she told him, smiling.

The following evening John went for a run. He had to practice because he knew it would come in handy one day. On his route he saw some people gathered outside a building, then he saw the smoke coming from the building. He knew there was a fire in the building, and he stopped and looked at the smoke coming from the building, and a strange feeling came over him. Then he saw a black woman running down the sidewalk and she was screaming. "My baby is inside the house," she kept saying. She turned to go into the building and the neighbors held her back. "Someone help me to get my baby out," she said loudly. John knew at that moment that was his clue to get into the building in one piece, and get the kid. He made his way inside. He heard the voice behind him, "He's upstairs in the back bedroom." John got into the building from the front and held his breath. The smoke was intense. He kept low and hurried upstairs, then he got into the passageway. He wiped the water away from his eyes, and opened the back bedroom.

"Where are you, son? Uncle John is here to get you out. Your mom sent me," John said loudly. There was no answer. The room was full of smoke, and John knew he had to work fast, if he were going to get the boy out in time. He looked under the bed, and no one was there. Then he looked into the clothes closet, and that was when he saw the little creature hiding in the closet. "There you are," John said and picked up the kid. "What's your name?" John asked.

"Roy."

"Well, Roy, my name is John. I want you to hold tight onto me. We'll have to get out of here quickly because your mom is waiting for you outside."

"Yes, John. I want my mom. Take me to her," the boy cried. John came out of the room and studied the situation very carefully, and he knew the back was the only way out. He opened the window in the bedroom and went out onto the roof. The boy held tightly onto his shoulder. He went toward a drainpipe, and started to climbed down. "Hold tight, Roy."

"This is fun, John. I never did this before," Roy told John.

"I'm glad you like it, Roy, but I wouldn't like to do this in a hurry again," John told the little boy with a smile. Then they landed on the ground. John pulled out two of the next-door neighbor's fence boards, and went over to the yard next door. He then ran in front with the child on his shoulders. He put the boy down onto the sidewalk. When the child spotted his mother, he ran to meet her. John stood there and watched as the child embraced his mother. It was a happy reunion. John smiled, then he turned away and continued running. Then he heard the boy's mother shouting behind him. "Thank you, Mister." John continued on his run as if nothing had happened. He knew in time to come the public would get to know him better, but at that moment he wanted to keep a low profile in the public eye.

"Well, it seems as if my dreams are coming true," he whispered to himself. He knew if everything kept up like that, his next encounter would be the young woman on a bridge.

The following day, John finished his karate lesson and jumped on the bus. That morning was a bit foggy. He felt a sudden chill run through his body as the bus reached the Brooklyn Bridge, and proceeded slowly across it, then it came to a sudden halt in the middle of the bridge. There were cars and people on the bridge and they were looking at a woman on the second rail of the bridge. John knew that was his cue to get going. He headed for the door and the driver let him out. He pushed through the crowds and saw the woman, then he started to climb up to the second rail to meet her. Then he heard a voice below shouting, "Don't let her jump. Save her, sir." John edged closer to the slim, black young woman on the ledge. The attractive woman wore a short blue dress, white flat heel shoes, brown stockings, and her hair was tied in a pony tail. She was nervous and looked straight in front of her. She didn't see John edging closer toward her, then she suddenly turned and saw him. "Don't you come any closer to me. I'm going to jump," she said softly. John saw the tears coming down her cheeks. "Who are you?" she asked.

"I'm just a friend. I was just passing by when I saw you. I figured out that you needed a friend, a good friend to get you out of this mess in one piece," John told her kindly. I forgot. My name is John Stone. What's your name, Miss?"

"I'm Rachel."

"Why are you here, Rachel?"

"My boyfriend left me. I love him so much. It hurts," she cried. "He doesn't want me any more," she added, shaking her head in the wind.

"I know it hurts, Rachel, but you can't just end your precious life like this. I know that you're a beautiful person inside and out, and any man will love you for who you are. So please, Rachel, let's get down from here and talk about this over a cup of tea," he told her frankly.

"You don't know what it's like to be loved by someone," she said, not looking at John.

"Yes, I do, Rachel. I'll tell you a little story. Seven years ago an intruder broke into my house, and killed my wife, my son and my daughter. I was shot twice in the chest. The doctor saved my life, but when I found out my family that I loved so much had died, I wanted to die also, until someone became my friend, and taught me to live again. You have to live for those people who love you, your family and friends," he told her sadly.

"Are you telling me the truth?" she cried. "Your family were all killed and you have no one to love you any more?" she asked.

"Yes, Rachel. Now give me your hand and let's get down from here," he told her, then he stretched his right hand out to the dark stranger on the ledge. He wanted her to have a good grip on his hand. He wanted to take her to safety.

"Before you came, I wasn't afraid of killing myself, but now I'm so afraid, afraid of losing the people I love most of all. Help me to get down, John," she said and tried to reach John's hand, but suddenly she slipped from the railing. John closed his eyes as she fell from the bridge and into the water below. "I can't let you die, Rachel. You have a lot to live for, so here goes my swimming lessons," John said, then he jumped after her into the cold water of the river to save the young woman he hardly knew. He hit the water hard, and he saw Rachel go under the current. He dived under, but missed her. He came up quickly, then he dived again, and missed her. He dived again and this time he felt her soft body, and it felt good. He held her tightly around the waist. He felt happy as he brought her up from under the current. "I couldn't let you die, Rachel," he told her. Then he swam slowly on his back to the boat that was coming to rescue them. The boat came to their side, and John held onto it while the two men in it pulled Rachel into the boat, then they helped him on board.

"Well, if someone had told me I was going to go for a swim this morning in the cold river, I would have brought my bathing suit with me," he told one of the men, jokingly. They put Rachel flat on her belly, and pressed the water out of her stomach. Then they turned her around, and she started to breathe on her own. She opened her eyes and looked up at the two men over her and said. "I'm alive. I'm alive," she said slowly, and raised her hand to John. He had already bent over her. He held her hand. "You're safe now, Rachel. We'll get you to a hospital," John said, as the boat docked. The ambulance was waiting on shore. John picked Rachel up and took her to the waiting stretcher, and the two attendants took her inside the ambulance, then drove her away. John took off his shirt and wrung it out, and put it back on. Then he started to trot on the sidewalk until he came to Main Street, then to Atlantic Avenue. He knew the run would bring his body temperature back to normal.

He entered the rooming house and Aunt Mildred was waiting for him, as if she was expecting him to arrive at that moment. "So, what happened to you?" she asked, looking him up and down.

"I just had a slight accident," he told her politely.

"Well, get those wet clothes off and I'll dry them for you. And after I'll have something hot for you, John," she shouted after him.

John changed into his dry clothes and went into the kitchen. Aunt Mildred had toast and hot coffee ready for him.

"Sit down and eat and drink while it's hot," she told him. John sat down and started to drink his coffee.

"Well, why are you looking at me like that?" he asked her.

"You could have been killed," she told him frankly.

"What do you mean?" he asked, looking at her.

"I saw it all on television, John. The television cameras were on the bridge, so I was able to see the whole thing live," she explained.

"I didn't know that," he said casually.

"I know you don't want any publicity, but sooner or later they'll find out that you are some hero," she told him.

"I'll be more careful next time, Aunt Mildred, so don't worry," he told her, smiling. John knew he couldn't tell her that he was on a mission, or a test for his very own life.

A few days later, John came up the escalator at Hoboken subway station after he went sightseeing in New York City. It was pass 7.30 that evening, and he came to the top of the subway, then suddenly he felt a chill run through his body, and he knew at that moment what that meant. Trouble was just around the corner. But where? He looked around the area, then he saw the problem that was about to happen. He edged closer and saw the two black youths were fighting on the northern side of the building, then he saw the black policeman going toward the youths. He started shouting at them. "Break it up, fellows." John knew he had to get over to the policeman and fast, so he took off as fast as he could, then lunging on the policeman just in time, as the handgun in the youth's hand went off, missing the policeman by an inch. John then rolled over several times and kicking the youth in the stomach. The youth fell to the ground. John got up and kicked the gun away from his hand, then slowly pulled him up from the ground.

"You're a bad boy, shooting at a policeman." The other youth ran away. The policeman got up and handcuffed the youth, then he turned to John. "Thank you, Mister."

"John, at your service, officer," he told him and went on his way.

"Thank you again, John," the policeman shouted behind him. Everyone was looking at John as he made his way out, but he just kept on going. Then he jumped onto the bus, which took him all the way to Atlantic Avenue. He realized as he walked the rest of the way to the rooming house that everything was happening so fast, and at that point he didn't have time to think. His mission of rescue had now become a matter of life and death to him.

Chapter Fourteen

It was a warm evening, and John felt uneasy in his room, then he decided to go out for a walk on Main Street. He went to his usual hamburger joint for something to eat and drink. It was just after 10.30 when he made his way slowly back on Main Street. His main thoughts were far away. He was thinking of Ted, the son he couldn't call son, and Karen, the mother of his child. She could never be his woman. They could never be anything else but good friends. He couldn't butt in because of his reputation, and now his life had taken a different turn. He really didn't want her to get involved with him, because he was now living a dangerous life.

He walked several blocks on Main Street. The street was quiet and no one was around. John stopped suddenly in front a large building. He didn't know why he stopped. He put all his thoughts behind him and tried to concentrate on what was about happen to him. It was as if someone was trying to warn him that he was going to shortly meet several tall and dark strangers. The way he felt, he knew it spelled trouble. He walked slowly and cautiously away from the building, then he suddenly stopped again. He realized at that moment he would encounter danger shortly. He stood there waiting. But for whom? He smiled and clenched both of his fists, and he was ready for anyone who tried to harm him. Then he saw the four figures come out from the side of the building. They were two black youths, and the other two youths looked like Indians. It was now a showdown between him and them. He knew the odds were against him because there were four of them and one powerful one of him, so he'd have to use his head to overcome the four tough youths in front of him. He knew they'd soon tell him what they wanted. They came up and stood several feet away from him, sizing him up for their kill.

"Good evening, gentlemen. Nice night," John told them politely, looking at them steadily.

"What's nice about it, Brother?" one youth said and came closer to him, then a second youth came closer to him.

"So this is the brother who drove me and you from our date a few nights ago. I told you, Brother, we was going to meet you again. Now here we are," the big youth told John bluntly.

"Well, guys, I told you I was sorry. I'll tell you again, I'm sorry. And I don't want you to hold this against me. Let's let bygones be," John told them politely, then he moved his toes from side to side. "What do you say, guys?" he asked.

The first youth, who seemed to be the leader of the four, came closer to John. "I'll accept your apology, Brother, for that time only."

"Now thank you, guys. Does that mean I can go now?" John asked softly. He could smell the rank liquor on the youths' breath. Then he knew they were drinking.

"You can go when we finish with you, Brother."

"Don't tell me you're going to hurt me?" John asked the big youth in front of him.

"We want your money, then we'll hurt you. We won't hurt you very much, just a few broken ribs and smash your head in. You're too smart for us. Now let's have your money, Brother," the head youth told John. The other two youths went behind John. Two behind him and two in front of him. The odds were now in his favor. He pulled out all the money he had in his pants pocket, and showed it to the head youth. "If this isn't enough, I can go to the bank and get you some more money," John told him. He then purposely dropped all the banknotes to the ground.

"You think you're smart, Brother," the head youth told him, pulling out his sharp knife.

"No need for a knife, Brother. The money is yours. Can I leave now? I need my sleep," John told him eagerly.

"The only sleep you'll get is in a wooden box. Now pick up that money and hand it to me like a gentleman, Brother," he said, pointing the knife at John's throat. John had to think fast because this was his chance to take them down. He knew they would never let him leave in one piece. He lunged swiftly through the opening of the two youths in front of him, then came up swiftly on his feet from behind them. He chopped the first youth from behind, then kicked the head youth to the ground. Then he knocked the knife from the head youth's hand,

and kicked it away. John saw the two other youths coming at him. He lunged at them, throwing both of them to the ground. He chopped one quickly, then the other. They didn't move. John knew they were dazed. He went over, picked up his money and put it back into his pants pocket. Then he turned to the youths.

"You guys should find yourself some real jobs," he told them. Then before he knew it, a police car pulled up at the side of him. He saw the two policemen coming towards him with their guns in their hands.

"This is the police. Put your hands up," the policeman told John. John quickly put his hands in the air, and waited for them to approach him.

"Good evening, officers. You're just in time," he told them.

"What's happening here?" the first officer asked.

"Well, these four young men wanted my money, then when I gave them my money, they wanted my life. That made me mad. I don't want to part with my life just yet, officer," John said. The other officer shone his flashlight in the faces of the four youths, then he turned to his partner. "All these men are wanted for burglary and rape. We have been after these criminals for a long time, and in a few seconds you have them flat on their backs."

"What's your name? And you can take your hands down," the officer said.

"My name is John Stone, and I live at 2286 Atlantic Avenue. In case you want to get hold of me, officer," he said softly.

John watched both of the officers cuff the four youths and put them into the police car.

"We'll be in touch with you, Mr. Stone," the officer told him. Then they drove off.

"Now I'm free to go to my room in one peace," John whispered to himself. Then he took a slow trot back to the rooming house.

The following week John did all the scraping and painting to the outside of the rooming house. The next-door neighbor had lent him a long ladder. He painted the front of the building in a light gray and brown trimming on the windows and the eaves. Everyone around was taking notice of what John was doing. He was really making the front of the rooming house beautiful.

"Please do mine when you are finished," his next-door neighbor, Mr. Brown told him.

162

John smiled at him. "Why not?" John replied.

John made sure after he finished all the rooms inside the building, so that Aunt Mildred could get two new decent roomers for the two vacant rooms.

That day John went to his karate lesson, then he went sightseeing in the city. He then headed back to the rooming house after several hours. That afternoon he jumped off the bus on Main Street. It was just after 2.30, and the day was gloomy as if it was going to rain. John walked slowly on the sidewalk toward Atlantic Avenue. Suddenly his whole body shivered and he stopped abruptly. He didn't know why he stopped. It was as if someone was trying to give him a clue. He turned around and looked across the road. He stood there and gazed at the large billboard with the beautiful woman on it, who was smiling down at him. He had seen the billboard before and he was sure it had something to do with his worst dream. He stood there and stared. "No, it can't be. Why is this happening to me?" he said to himself. He saw the passers-by gazing at him curiously, but he took no notice of them. His main focus was over the road. "Destiny is putting me through a challenge for my very life," he said to himself. Then he took a few steps forward on the sidewalk, then he stopped abruptly, and he turned back. Then he stood in front of the billboard, and gazed at it again. This time it seemed as if the beautiful girl on the billboard was not smiling at him. She was serious and now she was pointing at him, as if she was trying to clue him in on something that was about to happen. John closed his eyes and tried his best to visualize his worst dream. Then he opened his eyes after a few seconds.

He saw the bus stopping at the bus stop, then it pulled away, leaving the way clear for him to see a woman on the other side of the road. She held a stick in her hand. He knew at that moment she was the woman in his dream. He was now looking at the reality of his dream, and it was so clear in his mind, yet he couldn't make up his mind what to do. He stood there spellbound. He noticed the passers-by looking at him, but again he took no notice of them. His attention was in front of him. He saw the woman waiting on the sidewalk, and she was facing him. He realized that she was waiting for an opening to cross the road alone. He looked right and left to see if any vehicles were coming or going, and there was nothing in sight, then he heard a loud sound of a large truck. It was just coming around the bend to his right. Then he glanced at the woman, and she had already stepped off the sidewalk and onto the road. She was crossing on her own with her stick. He knew at that moment what it meant. He had to do something and quick. He felt as if he were glued to the sidewalk. "You have to do something, John. Do it now, if you're going to save the woman and yourself," the voice inside of him said. Then he heard an imaginary gun fire, as if it were the starting of a race. He pushed himself hard from the sidewalk, then he glanced over and saw the large truck. He realized the driver couldn't see the blind woman from around that bend. John pushed as hard as he could. "I can't be late. I must save her and myself," he kept saying to himself. The woman was now in his pathway and all he had to do was to push her back toward the sidewalk. He knew she was light and he would have to pick her up bodily with his right hand, which was extended for that purpose. He got to her in the nick of time. His hand clung around her waist. He knew the blow would have knocked the wind out of her, but it was the only way to get her out of the way of the truck. The truck passed, blowing its horn loudly. John held the woman tightly in his arms because it was a matter of life and death. His death and hers. His worst dream had now come to an abrupt end. The woman was shivering in his arms. "You are safe now, Miss," he told her. Some of the passers-by looked on strangely. "Just an accident," John told them. Then an elderly man went on the road and picked up the woman's stick and gave it to John. "Thank you, sir," John told him. "It's nice of you to look after her. You're a good person," the man told him and went on his way.

"Miss, are you all right?" John asked, still holding her in his arms.

She moved slowly away from John. She was shivering and didn't speak right away.

"I'm all right now. Thank you. You saved my life," she said, looking at him through her dark glasses.

"And thank you. You saved my life also," he told her.

"What do you mean?" she asked.

"In my dream I died trying to save you."

"I dreamt that too. You're the man in the cell. It's all real. I can't believe it. You're here in person," she said excitedly. "My name is Meg Smith. At last we meet. I had that dream four years ago. It was just after I had my accident and lost my sight," she told him quickly.

"My name is John Stone," he told her softly. He looked at her closely. She was slim, fairly tall, pretty in an unusual way. Her face was round and she didn't wear any make up. Her long brown hair was tied with a black ribbon. She wore a brown pullover and tight jeans, and black sandals. Her blue jeans were wet in front. John then realized the woman had peed her pants. When John had held her in his arms, he felt something he had never felt in a long time, a woman's touch, a woman's soft breasts against his body. It was as if he was falling in love with a strange woman he hardly knew. He realized that she was maybe ten years younger than he was, and it was destiny that had brought them together in this strange and unusual way.

"Why are you gazing at me like that?" she asked.

"How do you know I'm looking at you?" he asked.

"I can't see, but I can feel your gaze on me," she told him, smiling. "And by the way, my eyes are brown," she added. "You seem to know everything else about me," she said with a giggle. "Now it's my turn," she said.

"What do you need to know?" he asked.

"I'm really curious to know you better. I have seen you in my dreams. You were behind bars and fighting to get out. We're linked to each other in a strange way, a way that we can never be apart," she told him.

'It's strange you should say that. I feel the same way also. I feel that we're about to become one," John said, without thinking, then held her left hand with his right hand.

"Let me take you safely over the road."

"I thought you'd never ask, my hero," she said with a giggle. "I live at 45 Foster Road."

"I have your walking stick," he said and looked left and right on the main road then, when it was safe, he led her over the road to the sidewalk. They didn't say anything.

"I feel so funny, hand in hand as if we are on a date," she said, smiling. John looked at her as she smiled and he smiled back at her, even though she couldn't see him. He noticed that her lips were thin and her breasts were small, and not fully developed as with other women. He felt, as he walked with this strange woman he hardly knew, that all of his dreadful feelings were washed away. This woman was giving him a transfusion of life, a feeling that he had lost several years ago. They entered Foster Road, and he wished the road was longer so he could hold her hand for a longer time. "You're very quiet, John. Tell me about your dream," she said.

"Which one?"

"The one where he tries to kill you."

"You get that dream also?"

"Yes."

"Who is going to try to kill me?"

"The man with the mask. He is going to shoot you again," she said sadly. "And he's not going to do that if I can help it," she said bluntly.

"What can you do? You can't see," he told her politely.

"You may be amazed at what I can do. I know for sure that something good will happen. That's why you're here. You see I'm here to help you, and that's why we have come together," she explained.

"I understand. It's like destiny."

"Yes. We both will revive each other in a strange way that we would never expect," she told him.

"It's so strange – it's just like a dream, a dream with your eyes wide open," he said, without thinking.

"John, you must understand that this is not just an ordinary dream, but a real dream – a dream of life itself," she said softly.

John looked at her as she spoke and her thin lips moved up and down, and he could see her white teeth in her mouth. Then he had the funny notion that some day he would kiss those same tantalizing lips of hers.

"You're thinking of me in a most unusual way, and maybe some day it will become real for both of us," she told him.

And as she spoke, he knew for sure what she meant. They would have a love of their own some day, but he was falling in love with her on the spot, and for some strange reason she knew it and felt it, as they held hands. She could feel his very thoughts and maybe his very soul. She now had the power over him, and he was under her control for better or for worse.

"I believe you have passed my home," she told him with a smile.

"So I did," he told her, smiling.

"You did that purposely."

"I know," he said and they turned back.

"You really want to be with me?"

"Does it show?" he asked.

"Yes, it does," she said and squeezed his hand. "I'm late and my father must be waiting for me," she told him quickly.

"Now here we are," he told her as they came to 45 Foster Road. They stood in the gateway and they didn't say anything for a few seconds.

"Am I going to see you again?" she asked.

"You know the answer to that better than I do," he told her.

"You're right. I do. Thank you for the company," she told him softly.

He still held her hand. "You have such a smooth and soft hand, Meg."

Meg smiled. "I love the way you say my name, John. I must go in now," she said.

Then the front door of the house opened. "Meg, you are here. I was worried about you," the elderly gentleman said. He was tall, broad shoulders, and partly bald.

"Papa, this is John. I nearly had an accident and John was able to help me across the main street," she said, looking at her father."

"Why don't you invite Mr. John in for coffee," Mr. Smith said, looking at John.

"John, would you?" she asked, looking at him.

"Okay. If you insist," he said, taking her hand, and helping her up the stairs.

"You're a real gentleman," Mr. Smith said, as they approached him, and they went inside the house. Meg led John into the living room.

"Please sit down, John, and make yourself comfortable," she said, then she went toward the kitchen. John sat down and Mr. Smith sat opposite him.

"You live around here, John?" he asked.

"I live in a room on Atlantic Avenue, sir."

"Meg is a good girl, but since the accident she always says crazy things. I don't really understand her," Mr. Smith told him.

"Meg doesn't have her sight, but she can feel things, things you and I can't feel or see," John explained.

"You just met her and yet you seem to understand her better than I do," Mr. Smith said. "I wish you'd be her friend. At times she's so lonely. She needs someone young to be her sight, someone like you, John. You understand her," Mr. Smith said, smiling.

"I'll do my best, Mr. Smith," John said.

Meg came into the room with a pot of coffee, sugar, milk, three cups, and some cookies on a tray. She then placed it on the small table in the middle of the room. John looked at her carefully. He observed that she had changed her blue jeans. She did everything as a person who could see. She poured coffee in all three cups, and her father made no attempt to help her. She gave one cup to her father, then the other to John.

"Help yourself to sugar or milk," she told John, then she took the third cup and sat next to John. John took a sip, then he looked at her father, then at Meg.

"Papa, John is the one I was telling you about. You remember I told you he was in my dream. I saw him in jail. He was wrongly accused. I saw him trying to save me from that truck, and we both died," she told her father.

"What is she saying, John? Tell me," Mr. Smith asked.

"It means that your daughter can see into the future. She sees things that are about to happen. We were about to die by a truck, but for some strange reason I changed the event of time, and rescued Meg without any incident. We're here and alive," John explained.

"You mean this really happened on the Main Street?"

"Yes, Papa. John really rescued me from a passing truck, otherwise, I wouldn't be here," she said softly.

"What did you have to do that was different?" Mr. Smith asked.

"I trained for weeks. I had to run faster than usual to meet Meg on the other side of the road. That was the only way I was able to save your daughter, sir."

"I can't believe what I'm hearing. It's incredible what I'm hearing," he said to John.

John had seen the two-story house from the outside. It was an old house that needed a lot of repairs. He knew before long he would be volunteering to do the work on the house. He looked around the living room, and there were cracks and the paint was peeling. This was just one room, and the other rooms would be the same way. John always wanted to see things in a beautiful fashion, even though his

very life was in ruins. He spent nearly an hour with Meg and her
father. He found them to be poor, but decent people, and he felt
comfortable with them. John then thanked Mr. Smith and Meg for
inviting him into their house, and he left. He couldn't believe his
worst dream was over, and now he had Meg Smith to think about. He
knew he wanted to see her again, but for the time being he'd have to
keep a low profile on the whole situation.

John arrived at the rooming house at 4.30 that afternoon, and went
straight to his room. He threw himself onto his bed. Then he started
to think. Everything was happening so fast and he had no idea where
he was heading. He found himself thinking about Meg Smith. She
wasn't beautiful, yet when he held her in his arms, he felt the warmth
of her body going through his. It excited him and it felt good. He
had forgotten how good it was to hold a woman of your dreams in
your arms.

Later that afternoon, John went into the kitchen and had something
to eat. Aunt Mildred served him and noticed the change in him.

"You seem to be in a good mood, John," she said to him, as she
poured coffee in his cup.

"Well, to tell you the truth, I met a pretty lady today. She invited
me into her house for coffee. I also met her father," he explained.

"She must have seen you as a handsome guy."

"No such luck," John told her.

"Why is that?"

"She couldn't see me because she's blind."

"I'm sorry."

"Don't be. She's an amazing young lady. She's blind, yet she
sees into the future."

"That's amazing. I thought I was the only woman in your life,
and now you tell me there is another woman," Aunt Mildred told him.
"But I'm glad for you, John."

"I want you to know you'll always be my first lady," John told
her, smiling.

"I suppose you'll be leaving me very soon?"

"I don't know, but maybe sooner or later I'll have to move on."

"Well, later is better for me," Aunt Mildred said, smiling.

"I forgot to tell you that I rang the warden of the prison. He told
me that Mike may be out soon."

"That's good news to me. By the way, I heard over the news that the father of the girl you saved on the bridge is offering a reward to the man who saved his daughter's life. That reward will come in handy for you, John," she said, and gave him the address on a piece of paper. He took it and put it in his shirt pocket.

"Thank you, Aunt Mildred. I'll get to it as soon as possible," he said, and started to think.

"It seems as though you're in love," she said, smiling. John didn't respond to her comment.

John had to get out and think. He found himself on a bus, then on the subway, and there he could think. Then after several rides up and down the main subway lines, he decided to get off at Hoboken Station. He took the escalator up, and made his way out. Then someone touched him on the shoulder. He stopped abruptly and turned around quickly, and he came face to face with the black policeman whom he had saved from the youth's bullet a few days earlier.

"John, I was hoping to see you again," the officer told him.

"You were?"

"I'm the guy you saved from that passing bullet. I was lucky you were passing the same time. I'm Billie Moore," he said.

"John Stone."

"Yes, I remember. I told my wife about you, and she told me if I ever saw you again, I should invite you for supper."

"That would be fine."

"Say on Sunday afternoon. I would pick you up."

"I'm at 2286 Atlantic Avenue. Aunt Mildred's rooming house. You can't miss it. What time?"

"Say about 4.00 p.m."

"Well, see you then, Billie," John said and left.

John knew somehow that Billie Moore would fill in a little more of the blank puzzle that was forming in his memory. He would soon find out on Sunday afternoon.

Chapter Fifteen

Billie Moore picked John up at the rooming house, and drove him to his residence eight miles away in the suburbs.

"So you are new here, John?" Billie Moore asked.

"Yes, I came from Philadelphia."

"I can't remember your last name, John."

"The last name is Stone. John Stone," John told him, not looking at him.

Billie Moore kept on driving and kept his eyes on the road, then he turned slightly towards John. "I thought your face was familiar. I followed your case some time ago. I really thought you got a bum rap. The true evidence never came out," he said. His eyes on the road again.

"I'm glad you know my story, saving me the time of telling you," John told him.

"I heard many stories. The killer was never caught, and he struck many times after that in Philadelphia."

"I was sure that I saw him at the Hoboken Station one afternoon. I went after him, but lost him in the crowd. I'd really like to get my hands on him," John said bluntly.

"You said you saw his face and that's why you knew him?"

"Yes, I'd know that ugly face anywhere, and I'd like to get my hands around his neck. If you know what I mean."

"Yes, I know the way you feel. You'd like to kill him," Billie Moore said, and pulled into his driveway. "I have an idea and I'll put it over to you when we get into the house," Billie added.

They entered the house and Billie introduced John to his wife, Wilma, who was tall, slim and attractive, then to his son, Roy, who was eight and his daughter, Silvie, who was ten. Then John was led to the dining room table. Billie opened a bottle of white wine and poured for himself and his friend. John took the glass and they clinked glasses.

"To you, John."

"And to you and your beautiful family. And thank you for inviting me here this afternoon. I'm really grateful to you and your wife," John told them politely.

"I should be grateful to you, John. I don't get it, how did you know I was in danger that evening?" Billie asked.

"I really can't explain, but some time ago I started getting these dreams and visions, and I was guided here. When I arrived here everything started happening, and I couldn't believe that these dreams would become reality," John explained.

"Did you get a dream or vision about me been shot?"

"Yes, and that's why I was around there that evening. I knew beforehand what was going to happen."

"That's amazing. Well, John, I'm glad you were a guiding angel in my corner," Billie said and took another sip of wine.

John watched Wilma Moore as she displayed all the food on the table, then they all sat down to have a delicious meal.

"Well, John, the food is all on the table, so you can dig in," Billie told John. His two children watched on carefully.

"Well, just one moment. Please let me say a few words," John said, then clasped his hands and closed his eyes. The family realized that their guest wanted to say grace. "Great One above, please bless this family and this house, especially this delicious meal Mrs. Moore has slaved over a hot stove to prepare. And bless their hearts for being so kind, and invited a stranger into their home to partake in this meal on the table. Amen," John said and opened his eyes. "I'm sorry to have held you up, but I had to thank the Great One above," John said with a smile, then everyone smiled with him. John looked at all the food on the table, roast beef and potatoes, fried sweet potatoes, black-eyed peas and rice. John was shy to start first, so Billie put some of the food on John's plate.

"And you'll have to try some of my hot sauce on your food," Wilma told him.

"You're too kind, Wilma. I can't believe I'm here and eating supper with you nice people."

"Don't you have a family, John?" Wilma asked.

"John lost his family in an accident, Wilma," Billie told his wife.

"I'm sorry. Well, we must consider ourselves fortunate," she told John.

"Yes," John said, smiling. "I lost them so long ago, but yet they're always with me. Their love and everything we shared. You see family is forever, no matter what," John explained. After that, John just enjoyed his meal, and he didn't say any more about his family. He told them about his life on the farm when he was a boy. The two children listened to him carefully, and they also had questions for him that he answered.

After supper Billie took John into the living room, and they had coffee.

"This is a beautiful house you have, Billie," John told him.

"Well, if it wasn't for Wilma, we would still be in the dumps. She pushed me to buy this place, and it was a good investment for our family."

"And good for you."

Billie wrote something on a piece of paper and gave it to John. "I want you to contact this lady. She is a friend of mine and she may be able to help you. Her name is Norma Stewart, and she's a television news reporter. If no one else will, she'll be able to get your message across to the public."

"I'll give her a call tomorrow, and see what she can do for me," John said and stood up. He was ready to leave. He said goodbye to Wilma and the kids, and he thanked them for their hospitality, then Billie drove him as far as Main Street. John thanked him and got out of the car. He headed up Main Street, and all he could think of was Meg. Her face was drawing him to her house. He crossed Main Street and headed slowly along Foster Street. He passed number 45, then he headed back and stopped in front of the house, then the front door opened.

"Mr. John, please do come in!" Mr. Smith shouted from above the stairs. John looked at him in surprise for a few seconds before going up the stairs.

"Hello, Mr. Smith," John said to him shyly.

"I'm okay, John. Meg sent me to get you."

"How did she know I was outside?" John asked.

"She feels. She feels things. She knew you were outside. I don't know how," he told John, and led him into the living room where Meg was sitting on the sofa. John looked at her with a smile.

"John, how are you? I felt your presence outside, and I sent father to get you," she said anxiously. John sat down next to her on the sofa. Mr. Smith smiled at the couple.

"I'll make some coffee," he said and left the room.

"So where did you go to?" she asked.

"I went to a friend for supper. He dropped me off on Main Street, and I wanted to come and see you," he said softly. John saw Meg's hands in her lap, and he couldn't resist. He took her right hand in his.

"What took you so long, John. I wanted you to come and touch my hand as you're doing now. From that first moment you held me in your arms, I felt we belong together. I can't stop thinking about you," she explained.

"I feel the same way too," he said softly. Then she swung her head close to his face. He saw her thin lips just looking at him, then he kissed her lightly.

"I'm in love with you, Meg, and I can't help myself," he told her, holding her close.

"Let me help you, John. Let me be the love that you lost long ago. Let me be something in your life. I told Papa the way I feel about you and he understands. I'm sure he likes you too," she said, smiling.

When Mr. Smith arrived with the coffee, he poured for John and Meg, then he left the room. "You see – Papa understands, he left us alone," she said. Then John held her in his arms. Meg wore an old dress, and it had holes in it. John saw her breast from one of the holes on top of her dress, and her panties from the other hole on her leg. But most of all, he saw her as a warm and gentle person, and he wanted to be near her.

"How did you lose your sight, Meg?"

"I was just sixteen at the time. Terry took me that evening to his friend's birthday party. He was my boyfriend. He borrowed his father's car that night. When the party was over, we headed back on High Street, and that was when this car came straight at us. We didn't know what hit us. They said the driver was drunk. Terry didn't make it, and I lost my sight," Meg cried.

"Don't cry, Meg," John said, and patted her head.

"I feel bad because I can't see you. The eye doctor told me that I would be able to get my sight back if I had an eye operation. But it cost lots of money. We don't have any money. I have a disability pension and my father an old age pension. My brother Malcolm is in the army, and stationed in West Germany, and he sends us money sometimes. I only wish I could see, and then I could go to work and help Papa. Since Mama died, me and Papa are very close. And if anything should happen to him I don't know what I'll do," she said sadly.

"You'll have me to take care of you," he told her frankly.

"And if anything should happen to you? Your life will be in danger very soon. He'll want to kill you as soon as you try to expose him."

"How do you know that?"

"That's what you have to do to bring him out into the open. You saw his face and you must make it known to the whole world. You'll be sending a message to the murderer who killed your family. And for that he'll have to kill you," she explained.

"You seem to know what will happen better than I do," he said and got up.

"Are you leaving now?" she asked.

"I must get to my rooming house," he told her.

"We have a spare room here. You'll be welcome to stay with us. Papa wouldn't mind. He likes you," she said, then she got up and led John to the front door. "Good night, John," she said and held her face close to his. He kissed her lightly.

"I'll be back again, Meg," he said and left.

John made his way onto Main Street and all he could think about was when he kissed Meg. He knew he had to do something to help her and her father. He wasn't going to help them because he loved Meg. He was going to do it because they really needed someone there for them, and that would make a great difference. He didn't have any money and he needed some if he were going to help the family. Then he remembered the piece of paper Aunt Mildred had given him. The reward money from the woman's father. The woman he saved on the bridge. He didn't know how much it would be, but anything would be better than nothing. If not he'd have to ask for some of his trust fund. And he didn't want to touch that money. Meg told him that if she had an eye operation she might be able to see again. He realized that was a very big maybe, but it was worth a try if he could raise that much money for an eye operation. Then she'd be able to see him, and maybe the first thing she would say, "You're an ugly son of a gun,

John." He smiled to himself and he realized that he was wishing for too much to happen. He looked at himself from head to toe, and he knew he had become a bum. He breathed in and out and knew he had to do something to bring himself back to a natural gentleman. He felt it was easier said than done, and it would be a challenge for him to make it come true.

The following day, John called Norma Stewart, the news reporter, at her office. "Norma Stewart speaking."

"Miss Stewart, I was given your number by Mr. Billie Moore. He said you may be able to help me," John told her over the phone.

"How can I help you, sir?" she asked.

"This is sort of personal and I'll have to see you in person to discuss it, and what I'll have to say will be very interesting to you."

"How interesting?"

"Well, it will become front page news," he told her quickly.

"I don't have any time today. Maybe you can call me tomorrow," she said bluntly.

"Miss Stewart, you don't understand. This is very important," he told her sternly.

"My time is very important, sir. What is your name?"

"John Stone."

"Did you say John Stone?"

"Yes. Does my name mean anything to you, Miss Stewart?"

"It certainly does, Mr. Stone."

"Well, are you going to see me?"

"Yes. I'll meet you at 2.00 p.m. at Dave's Cafe. It's just across from our station. See you then Mr. Stone," she said.

"See you at 2.00 p.m. Miss Stewart," he said and hung up.

John arrived at Dave's Cafe just before 2.00 p.m. The cafe was situated in a side street from the television station, which was on 5th Avenue. John took a window seat, then he ordered coffee, and shortly afterward Miss Stewart walked inside. John had not seen her before, but yet he knew it was her. She was of African descent, tall, attractive and well dressed. John got up and waved at her, then she headed his way and stood in front of him.

"Miss Stewart, so nice of you to come," John said and shook her hand. "You're so much nicer in person," he added. She looked at John for a few seconds before she sat down.

"You look so familiar. I have seen you somewhere," she told him. "Yes, now I remember. You were the man on the Brooklyn Bridge. You saved that woman from drowning in the river," she said with a smile.

"I thought that was my little secret, but now you know. I ordered coffee for us," he told her.

"That's fine. Something to drink while you tell me your mystery story, Mr. Stone."

"Call me John."

"Norma," she said and took out her notebook and pen from her bag, and she was ready to take notes.

Thirty minute later and two cups of coffee, John told Norma Stewart about the killer who murdered his family. He told her he saw the same man going up the Hoboken Subway Station. He wanted to bring this killer out into the open.

"What you told me is very interesting. What I'm going to suggest is that you come down to the station after 10.00 a.m. tomorrow. As you stated you can still remember the face of this killer. You can give all the details to our artist and he'll be able to bring him to life," she explained.

"That's a good idea, Miss Stewart," John said, smiling.

"Call me Norma."

"John for short."

"How did you get to know Billie?"

"We met by accident at the Hoboken Station when a youth tried to shoot him. Luckily, I was able to push him out of the way."

Miss Stewart shook her head. "It seems to me you're a man of action. I'm quite sure that this is going to be a great story," she said and got up. They shook hands.

"I'll be there tomorrow, Norma," he told her as she left. He went out behind her and saw her cross the road to the television station. He stood on the sidewalk, then he saw a man coming up from behind. The man hit her in the back and grabbed her bag. John made his way quickly over the road, meeting the man on the sidewalk. John lunged behind him, knocking him to the sidewalk. Then when the pickpocket raised up to face him, John hit him several times on the face, then took the bag away from him.

"You better beat it, you low-down drifter," John said to him. The man got up and ran away. John walked back to Norma. She was still standing in front of the building and he noticed she was shaking. He helped her into the building and into her office. She sat down at her desk, and he gave her the bag.

"Thank you, John, for retrieving my bag," she said softly.

"I'm sorry I didn't escort you over to this building."

"That would have been nice, but I don't need an escort every time I go outside. And I'm not afraid of those thugs out there," she told him quickly.

"You're a brave lady," John said and left.

"Thank you again," she shouted behind him.

When John got outside, he took the piece of paper out of his pocket, and looked at it. He wanted to get that reward. He had enough time so he headed for that address that was along the water front in Brooklyn. He took the subway, then he took a bus to the nearest point, and walked the rest of the way to M&G Manufacturing. He went straight up to the office and saw the receptionist. She looked up at him curiously.

"Can I help you, sir?" she asked.

"I came to see Mr. Mitchell, the owner," he told her politely.

"Do you have an appointment with him?"

"No. But he would like to see me."

"Would he?" the receptionist asked.

"My name is John Stone. I'm the guy who saved his daughter from drowning in the river," he told her bluntly.

"You came to collect the reward?"

"Yes."

"A word of warning. He's very cheap. Don't let him cheat you," she said, smiling.

"Thank you. Now may I see your boss?"

The receptionist got up from behind her desk, and led John into her boss's office.

"Mr. Stone to see you, sir. He's the guy who saved your daughter's life," she said quickly and left the office. Mr. Mitchell came from behind his desk and shook John's hand.

"Please have a seat, Mr. Stone," he said and went back behind his desk. "Mr. Stone, I must thank you for helping my daughter. I think I am partly at fault. I forbade her seeing that young man. I didn't approve of him. That's why she went on that bridge. She wanted to get my attention," Mr. Mitchell explained.

"I understand, sir. How is Rachel?"

'She's fine. She's back with the same guy. She spoke of you, Mr. Stone. She said that you lost your family and you had nothing to live for, also. Is that true?"

"Yes, sir. I lost my family and everything I owned. I just got out of jail, and I'm trying to pick up my life," John told him sadly.

"Mr. Stone, I offered this reward two weeks ago, but no one came forward to collect it."

"I didn't know of any reward. What I did, I did because your daughter needed help at that moment, real help. I became her friend in deed and not in need. When I climbed up on the rail of the bridge, I became responsible for your daughter's safety. I tried to take her hand, and that's when she slipped into the river. I risked my own life and went after her. I couldn't let her die in that river," John said sadly. "Your daughter needs lots of love. Give it to her. A family is forever," John added.

"Thank you, Mr. Stone. That was very brave of you," Mr. Mitchell said, and took out his check book from his drawer, then wrote John a personal check. He passed the check to John. John took it, looked at it and put it on the desk, then he looked at Mr. Mitchell.

"Is something wrong, Mr. Stone?" he asked.

John smiled at Mr. Mitchell. "You're a businessman, sir, so I hope you don't get upset for what I'm about to tell you. I know for sure that my life is worth very little, but what value do you place on your daughter's life?" John asked sternly.

"What are you getting at, Mr. Stone?" Mr. Mitchell asked bluntly.

"Your check, sir, is for $500.00 dollars. Is your daughter's life worth that small amount?"

"I now see your point. I'm sorry, Mr. Stone. I'm a shrewd businessman, otherwise, I wouldn't be sitting here," Mr. Mitchell said with a smile. "I see I'm not the only one who is shrewd. I'll remedy the situation," he added and made out a new check, then gave it to John. John looked at it and smiled.

"I hope that will be sufficient for your services, Mr. Stone."

"Thank you, Mr. Mitchell. This token is very much appreciated, and it will help a friend in need," John said and shook Mr. Mitchell's hand. "Please give my regards to Rachel."

"I'll do that, Mr. Stone. Good-bye and good luck."

John headed out of the office, and he placed the check in his shirt pocket. He went up to the receptionist.

"You were right about him, Miss. Thank you for the tip," he told her and left.

John walked slowly on the sidewalk until he came to Main Street. He smiled to himself and clapped his chest where the check was in his shirt pocket. He knew he had some money now to help Meg Smith and her father. He couldn't let the black businessman cheat him out of his rightful reward. He had earned that money with his very own life.

John felt very pleased with himself, and without thinking he started humming his late wife's favorite song, *Danny Boy*. He headed on Main Street, then he looked over the road and saw the billboard. "You're a beautiful lady and I love you," he said to the beautiful and smiling face on the billboard. He looked right and left, then crossed the road quickly, and headed up Foster Street, then he made his way up to 46 Foster Street. He knocked at the front door and waited patiently for the door to open. He waited for a few seconds and he hoped that Meg would be the one to open the door.

"Come on, Meg. Where are you? I'm here waiting for you," John whispered to himself. Then the front door opened quickly, and Meg stood in front of him.

"John, how nice to see you," Meg told him.

"I thought those were my lines," he told her with a smile.

"I knew you were going to come today," she said, and pushed her right hand out. John took her hand and went inside, closed the door, then he held her in his arms and kissed her. "I dreamt of this every night since we last met," she told him softly.

"Me, too. I held you in my arms every night, but it wasn't real. It's now real. You're here in my arms, and I'll never let you go. You mean the whole world to me, Meg," John told her softly. He saw she was wearing cut-off blue jeans and a tight pink shirt. Her feet were bare and her hair was tied with a white ribbon. He thought of her as a little girl playing around the house, but she was no girl. She was a mature woman, and ready for the right man's love.

"John, you have changed my whole life. I feel alive again, and I want you to feel alive again, also," she said, her thin lips close to his.

John led Meg into the living room and they sat on the sofa. He kept a careful eye on her smooth legs. It was as if he was seeing a woman's bare legs for the first time. He couldn't help himself. He wanted to touch her bare legs, and also her body, but somehow he held back.

"Papa is away. He's buying some groceries. So we're all alone. You can do what you want with me, John. I'm yours to take, and no one has touched me before. I want you to be the first one," she told him softly.

John realized that he was attached to Meg, but he wasn't ready for any heavy stuff such as sex.

"Meg, I love you, but we're not ready for an act of sex as yet. We'll have lots of time later," he told her frankly.

"I understand, John. But I want you to kiss me and hold me tight, and I'll wait until we're ready for a more serious relationship," she said, placing her lips close to his. John kissed her hard on the lips.

After he'd kissed her, he knew for sure that he wanted her, but for some strange reason he held himself back. Then he got up.

"This is a good time for you to show me the house," he told Meg.

"I know what you're trying to do," she said with a smile, and got up from the sofa. She took him upstairs and showed him her bedroom.

"Here's where I do all my thinking of you, John," she said and went into his arms, then he kissed her. "We'll do it when you're ready, John. I'll wait," she said, then led him into her father's room, then into what used to be her brother's room. "This is now a spare room, and your room when you're ready," she told him and squeezed his hand. Then she took him into the kitchen. "This is where I do all my cooking, and some day I'll be cooking for you. Well, what do you think?"

"Well, I need to put in some elbow grease and paint into each room," John told her.

"Is it that bad? I haven't seen this place in years," she said, smiling.

"It's nothing I can't fix, Meg. I'm handy."

"Papa will be back from shopping soon, so please stay for supper. My treat."

"I accept, ma'am."

Chapter Sixteen

John arrived on Tuesday morning just after 10.00 a.m. at Channel 8 Television station in New York City. He met Norma Stewart, and she took him into a room at the back of the building. Then she introduced him to Philip Watkins, who was the artist.

"Give Philip all the information about the burglar, and he'll create that face for you. I'll see you when you are through," she told John and left the room.

John sat with Philip in front of his desk. Philip got out his sketch pad and pencil.

"Well, John, we'll start with the shape of his face. Tell me everything you can remember."

"His face was somewhat long, with a pointed chin, a scar on the left side of his cheek," John explained slowly to the artist.

After forty minutes of changing and inserting to the face, the final composite sketch of the killer's face was completed. John gazed at the completed sketch of the killer's face. "That's the face! I can never forget it. Our next move is to put a name to that ugly face. Thank you, Philip," John said excitedly.

"I'm glad I can help, John, and good luck. I'll get Miss Stewart for you," he said and left the room. Shortly afterward Norma Stewart came into the room. John gave her the sketch, and she sat in front of the desk with him. She looked at the sketch for a few seconds, then she turned to John. "Are you sure of this face, John?"

"Yes. When I saw him a few weeks ago at the Hoboken Subway Station, his face was still the same. I'm sure, Norma," he told her frankly.

"John, I spoke to my director and he gave me the go ahead. Then he said with a big smile that I'm going to have my hands filled with you. I didn't really understand what he meant at that time, but now I figured it out. His name is Frank Stone, and he knows you. Is he your relative?" she asked concernedly.

"Yes. Frank is my cousin, but we don't know each other. I'm a farm boy and he's a very high class gentleman. So you see Miss Stewart, what I have to do, I'll do it for myself," John told her bluntly.

"I also feel that this story is going to be very explosive, and when the press and the other media get hold of it, they'll hound you night and day," she told him quickly. "And I'm also authorized to pay you for your story if it becomes front page news," she told him.

"I'm sure if I'm involved this story will hit the roof, as I'll give it all that I have to give," he told her quickly.

"Now we'll have to come up with an agenda for your story. First, we'll get that face on the tubes, with short details. You should be the one to relate those details in your own words to the public, and how this face came to be. You must be the one to tell your story. We may have to dress you up and change your image a little. How does that sound to you, John?"

"It sounds good, but I don't need my image changed. I need to be myself. The person I have turned into. I have to make the viewers understand why I have turned into this person, a bum."

"Good thinking, John. But I don't see you as a bum. I see you as a handsome gentleman. This may even be better than I thought. You seem to have a natural gift to make things happen. That's what I like about you, John."

"What can I say, it's my nature. And thank you for believing in me," John said softly.

"Well, John, be here at ten tomorrow and we'll have the cameras on you. So think what you're going to say in clear and a concise language," she told John, smiling.

"Well, see you tomorrow, Norma, and we'll continue the good work," John said and left.

The next morning John arrived at the Channel 8 television station. He was taken to one of the studios, where he was placed in front several cameras. He went through a quick rehearsal, and he was nearly perfect in the first instance, then it was for real. He was given the signal.

"I'm appealing to you nice viewers out there. My name is John Stone. Philadelphia was once my home. I lived there with my family, my wife, Mary, my son, David, and my beautiful daughter, Cindy. They were all murdered by a man with a face I'm about to show you. This is the face of an evil murderer. He killed my beloved family in cold blood. I want him caught and sentenced to the electric chair for the serious crimes he has committed.

"This composite sketch was composed recently of how this man looked over six years ago, and there might be little change to his face. I saw this man going up the Hoboken Subway Station. I'm sure he's residing and robbing people in the New York area.

"This man killed my family and shot me twice in the chest, and left me for dead, but I survived. I was charged for the crimes and sentenced to fifteen years in the State's prison. And after serving six years, certain unforeseen evidence came to light, and I was released. I'm a free man, but I'm left with a big scar inside of me, which cannot be wiped away for a very long time.

"I'm asking you nice viewers out there to please phone into this station if you have seen this murderer who is still at large, and may strike again at any moment.

"Thank you very much for listening to me. And I am grateful to Channel 8 for giving me this air time to tell you my story. Thank you again."

John went to Norma Stewart. She was looking on carefully.

"That was great, John. You're a real natural. You were so confident in front of the two cameras."

"So you really liked it?"

"Yes. It's not what you said, but the way you said it. You were really appealing to those people out there. We'll put your video on the air and see what response we get. We may have to open a special phone line for callers," Norma explained to John. "And once this hits the air, the reporters will be hounding you for a story. So be prepared," she added.

"I didn't need reporters at my trial, but maybe now I need them to get my message across to the whole world," he told her sternly.

"You'll have to come in at 10.00 tomorrow, and by that time we may have some news on that wanted face," she told him.

"Well, let's hope we have many phone calls in respect of that ugly face," John snapped.

"You do have a way with words, John. See you tomorrow," she said, and left the room. John stayed for a few more minutes, and in that time he thought about the whole situation. He was now playing on very dangerous ground, but he had no choice. He had to go full speed ahead. He heard footsteps behind him. He got up and turned around to see who it was. He came face to face with this tall, slim gentleman. He was dressed in a dark suit. John knew at once he was an executive of the station. John gazed steadily at the smiling stranger in front of him, then he recognized the man's face.

"John, how are you?" the tall, dark stranger said to John, then he pushed out his hand to him. "Frank Stone, at your service, John," he said, shaking John's hand.

"Cousin Frank, so you finally came out of the woodwork to meet me. I suppose my story will be explosive enough for us to meet like this," John told him bluntly.

"You must understand, John, that I didn't want my name connected with yours, but we're blood and we should stick together. I'm sorry. Linda was your friend and she told me all about you. The way you brought her and her real mother together, then you looked after the funeral of her mother. She considered you as a friend and a relative, and I'd like to be your cousin and also your friend," Frank Stone said, and pushed out his hand again to John. John shook his hand.

"Right about now I really need a friend, Frank."

"This station will be yours as long as I'm the director, and we'll see this through together," Frank told him. "I'll tell Linda about you. I'm quite sure she'll want to see you after all these years," Frank added.

"I'd love to see her when all this is over."

"Well, all the best. Call me if you need me, " Frank said and departed from the room. John walked slowly out of the building. He didn't know what to think. His long lost cousin wanted to be his friend now. This was only because he was now playing a dangerous game on television, and everyone would be riveted to their television sets to see what would happen next. This would be good business for Channel 8 Television, and the director would get all the credit, but John didn't care about the credit, he only cared about the results he'd get from the game of cat and mouse.

The next morning John had breakfast early. Aunt Mildred came into the kitchen.

"Good morning, John. I see you are going out again," she told him with a smile.

"I'm afraid things are getting a little rough and I may have to move away very soon. These videos I'm making will put me in the limelight. My life will be in danger when these videos are put on the air," John told her.

"I understand, John. This is something you have to do to clear yourself and your conscience. I'll pray for you, John, so the Great One above will keep you safe," she said sadly.

"Don't worry, I'll be around to see you, and I'll give you any help you need," he told her softly.

"To be honest with you, you're the son I never had," she said and went over to John and gave him a motherly hug. "And thank you for being here for me, John," she added.

John arrived in front of Channel 8 television station that morning. He saw a crowd in front of the station, and he stopped short, then after a few second he decided to face them. He knew they were reporters and had seen his video on the television. They came toward him and stopped. He stood in front of them and waited for one of them to speak. Then a tall and broad shouldered gentleman came forward to face him.

"Mr. Stone, what do you hope to gain by this video with the face of a man, whom you claimed killed your family? The Philadelphia police couldn't find this so called person, so you were convicted for the murders of your family. We feel you're creating this publicity to clear your conscience," the reporter told John bluntly.

"Good morning, ladies and gentlemen. I don't blame you for distrusting me at this stage. The jury in 1986 convicted me of the murders of my family and I was sent away to prison. Now you're doing the same thing. I was innocent all along. I didn't kill my family. I loved them. The ugly face on the television screen was the one who killed them. He shot each one of them in the chest with my gun. I was left for dead with two shots in my chest. I'm alive and I must prove to the world that the killer is still out there, ready to rob, murder and rape again.

"Ladies and gentlemen, thank you for listening. And I hope the next time we meet, you'll be convinced that I was innocent all along.

"One last note. You must understand that I'm fighting for my very life, and that's why this mad killer out there must be caught. I'm the only one to bring this rat out into the open. I saw him recently in the Hoboken area, and I'm sure he lives here in New York. Now all of you have a nice day," John told them sternly, then pushed his way through the crowd, and into the building. He just kept on going, and he didn't look back.

John entered the reception area and Norma Stewart was waiting for him.

"Good morning, John. I'm sorry about that. All those reporters were waiting for you outside," she told him.

"Well, they saw the video. They think this is just a publicity stunt, so I can clear my conscience. They all think I'm guilty," John said.

She took John by the hand and led him into an office at the back of the building.

"Where are you taking me, Norma?" he asked.

"There is someone here to meet you. He has some very important information for you," she told him as they entered the office. John came face to face with his visitor. The tall and slim gentleman got up from behind the desk to face John. John realized right away he was a cop.

"John, this is Detective Sergeant Bartlett from Homicide Division," Norma told John. Then the two men shook hands. "I'll see you later, John. I'll leave you two to speak," she said and left the office.

"Have a seat and we'll discuss this," Sergeant Bartlett said and sat behind the desk. He had a file in front of him. John sat down and looked at him steadily.

"What is this all about?" John asked.

"I'm sure you are going to be pleased to hear of what I'm going to tell you. I've seen your video and I have put together a file on it, so bear with me," the sergeant explained.

"Well, Sergeant, I'm all ears," John said with a smile.

"What I'm about to tell you will be in confidence. I followed your case in Philadelphia closely. I was attached to the homicide division there. Sergeant Lang had charged you with the murders of your family. He knew you were not guilty. He was just pushing for his promotion to lieutenant."

"A very interesting story, Sergeant Bartlett," John interrupted. "Please go on."

"You see, shortly after you were convicted, the same burglar appeared in several other places. He robbed several women and raped two of them. It was the same description of the burglar you had given and no one took any notice of it. Sergeant Lang was obsessed and he took matters in his own hands. He wanted that burglar dead, so he set a trap for him, but the whole plan backfired. Sergeant Lang dressed as a woman to kill the burglar. The burglar was one step in front of him. Sergeant Lang was found behind a building with a knife in his back. I have a strong feeling it was the burglar who plunged the knife in his back," Sergeant Bartlett explained.

"It gets even better," John interrupted again. "Please do go on."

"The composite sketch of the burglar's face in your video, is the burglar who killed your family. I know who he is from your sketch."

"Who is he?" John asked.

"His name is Richard Thompson. He lives somewhere here in New York. He is wanted dead or alive and a reward of $250,000 is offered for his capture. He knows every trick in the book, and every time we got near to him, he'd disappear. I'm sure what you are doing, John, will bring him out into the open. But you'll be playing a very dangerous game, and you are going to require my skillful help," Sergeant Bartlett told John sternly.

"I'm going to need your help, but we'll have to keep this our little secret, otherwise, our man will not show himself," John told him. His fingers clenched together.

"I agree with you, John. We'll have to meet in secret. In the meanwhile you'll have to provoke him in your next video. Call his bluff and that will upset him. I'll be in touch with you through the station. I'm glad we're on the same footing," Sergeant Bartlett said.

"And thank you for coming," John said as Sergeant Bartlett went out of the office.

John waited a few minutes, then Norma Stewart came into the office and stood in front of him.

"The good sergeant has left us a file on our face. Now we have a name. Richard Thompson. Quite a nice name," John told her.

"That was a good break for us, John, but I'm sure we'll have more information on this case. You can go home and I'll see you on Monday. Then we'll make our next video."

"I can't wait to make another video," John said and pounded his fist lightly on the desk. "I'll read the file and I'll see you on Monday morning," he said and left.

When John got outside he breathed the fresh air in and out. He couldn't believe he was having so much publicity, and that was just the start of things to come. In a way, he liked being in the limelight. He went on the subway, then on the bus to Main Street, where he went to Meg's house on Foster Street. Her father opened the door and let him in, then led him into the kitchen, where Meg was preparing a meal. John had become just like one of the family.

"Please sit down, John," she said. John sat down at the kitchen table. Mr. Smith smiled at him and went out of the kitchen. John gazed at Meg. She wore short cut-off jeans and a green T-shirt. She moved around the kitchen as if she knew where everything was. She poured John a cup of coffee, then sat down with him. She pushed her hand out on the table. John held her hand and bent over and kissed her lightly on the lips.

"I missed you, John. Papa saw your video on the television. How is it going?"

"Fine. Now that I'm here," he said softly and squeezed her hand. I've come into some money, and I want to take you shopping. I want you to be the most beautiful girl in the whole wide world. I love you so much, Meg," he said to her. His voice close to her face.

"I love you too, John. I'll be happy to go out with you, but you'll have to be my eyes and I'll be your ears. Take me to a movie, John. Papa used to take me and my brother when we were little. We used to go to the children's matinee. Now I don't know what movies they make now. I know I can't see, but I can follow the storyline very carefully, if you know what I mean," Meg explained, holding John's arm tightly.

"I'll do my best Miss Smith," he said, smiling.

"You're so good to me."

"And it will get even better," he told her and touched her face.

"Spend the afternoon with me, John. I haven't seen you for the whole week and we'll have to make up for lost time," she said quickly.

"I like that, Meg, but no hanky-panky," he told her.

"I agree. When I'm with you, John, it is like a dream world I'm in, and I can't escape," she said with a giggle.

"What you said about that room, I may take you up on the offer, but I'll pay rent and help to fix up this place."

"Sounds good, John. When do you expect to move in with us?" she asked cheerfully.

"Soon, Meg," he said, then he pulled her over into his lap, and held her in his arms.

"Move in with me, John," she said softly, then placed her lips close to his. "You are the first man I ever loved. That's why I feel the way I do. You must understand that I have never been with a man before. I want to experience it with you only at the right time," she explained nervously.

"All I can give you now is a kiss," he said and their lips met.

A short while after, John looked up and saw Mr. Smith. He had come up quietly in the kitchen and stood there looking at John and Meg. She was still in John's lap and close to him.

"Mr. Smith," John said quickly when he saw him.

"Call me, Pops, John. You're like one of the family now. You love my daughter, Meg. She's always happy when you're here. I'm glad she has you as a friend," Mr. Smith explained, waving his right hand.

"I love her, Pops, and I want to take good care of her," John told him.

"I know you love her, but she is a big responsibility. You'll have to be her eyes all the time," Mr. Smith tried to make him understand.

"I want her to get her sight back, so she can see me for the first time," John said quickly.

"I know you mean good, John. But where are you going to get that much money for an eye operation?"

"I'll get the money. You'll see, she'll see again," John told Mr. Smith sternly. Mr. Smith smiled at him and shook his head.

"You're just dreaming, John," he said distastefully and left.

"Meg will see you again," John shouted behind Mr. Smith, then he held Meg tight in his arms. "You'll see again, Meg," he whispered into her ear.

John left the Smith's home just after 10.00 p.m. He headed down Main Street. Half way down that street, he found himself walking quickly. He suddenly felt uneasy, but he didn't look back. He felt it was bad luck to look back, and he just kept on walking. It was as if someone was following him. He reached Atlantic Avenue, and at that point he decided to trot the balance of the way to the rooming house. He arrived there and let himself into the building, then he went into the kitchen. Aunt Mildred was sitting at the kitchen table. John sat with her and he didn't say anything. She poured him a cup of coffee.

"Well, what do you have on your mind, John?" she asked.

"You seem to know me like a book, Aunt Mildred. That's why I'm going to miss you. I'll be leaving tomorrow. I'll pay you a few more weeks' rent so you can hold the room for Mike. He'll be out soon," John explained.

"I'll miss you too, John. At first when you came, I didn't think we'd make it, but you have been the best. Where are you going to live?"

"I'm going to live with the Smiths at 46 Foster Street, just off Main Street. Meg Smith is blind and her father is an old age pensioner. I have to move in to help them," John told her.

"That's just like you. You're always the Good Samaritan," she said.

"If you want to get hold of me, I'll be at that address," John said and went up to his room.

He looked through the window. He had a strong feeling that someone was looking at him from down below. He saw a shadow between the two houses next door. Then he remembered that someone on Main Street had followed him to the house. But who? It couldn't be who he thought it was. Maybe it was just his imagination. It was too soon for his enemy to make contact with him, but he realized it was possible.

He threw himself onto his bed, then pulled out the reward check from his shirt pocket. He looked at it and kissed it. "We're going to have a wonderful time, Meg. I'm going to take you to a beauty salon, then shopping for new clothes, and you'll be transformed into a beautiful princess," he said to himself. Then he looked at himself in the mirror. "I guess I'll also have to transform myself into a handsome prince," he said with a smile, and threw himself back onto his bed.

Chapter Seventeen

It was Friday and John headed to the Western Bank on Main Street. It was just after eleven o'clock in the morning. It was the same bank that held Aunt Mildred's mortgage on her rooming house. He entered the bank, and by chance the manager came out of his office at the same time John was about to go to a cashier.

"Mr. Stone," the manager called out to John.

"Mr. Martin, I'm here to start an account," John told him when they were near.

"I'd like to discuss this account with you," Mr. Martin told him, and led him into his office. "Please have a seat, Mr. Stone," Mr. Martin said and went behind his desk. John sat down in front of the manager's desk. He didn't know why the bank manager was trying to be so nice to him.

"Mr. Stone, the money from your trust account in Moorestown came through all right. I was told it's quite a large sum. If you ever thought of transferring it, we'd certainly like to handle the money for you," the manager explained.

"I'll certainly think about that," John said. "I have this check to start an account," he added and gave the check to Mr. Martin. The manager looked at it, then at John.

"You certainly get around, Mr. Stone. I suppose this is the check for saving the woman's life in the river," he said.

"Yes. It's a small reward, and I intend to use it wisely. I need to deposit it and I need some cash to help out a friend," he explained. "You may be able to help me in another matter. My friend is blind. I was told if she had an eye operation, she might regain her sight. But this will cost big bucks. I'm not sure if my trust fund will be sufficient to pay for such an operation," John explained to Mr. Martin.

"Mr. Stone, I'll get some details for you and maybe we can do something to help you," the manager said, smiling.

"Thank you, Mr. Martin," John said politely.

"Well, now to your check. I'll deposit it and you require some cash."

"About $1000 for spending money," John told him.

"At your service, sir. I'll be back in a jiffy," Mr. Martin told John and left his office. The office door was left open and John observed a tall, slim man wearing a raincoat and there was a bulge under it. John realized at once that the man was a robber. The man went into the bank quickly and pulled out the shotgun in front of the cashier. The other people in the bank got scared and went to the other side of the bank.

"Don't anyone move," he said loudly, and pointed the gun at the cashier, looked quickly at the customers on the other side of the bank, then at the cashier. The bank manager, Mr. Martin, just stood there looking at the bandit. He was unable to do anything.

John immediately went to the manager's desk and pressed the silent alarm.

"That will get the police here in a jiffy," he whispered to himself. Then he had to think fast. He had to come up with a plan immediately. Suddenly he knew what he had to do. He had to be a drunk. He realized that he had never drunk hard liquor or smoked a cigarette before in his life, and it would be hard for him to pull off such an act, but he had to try.

John ruffled his hair, pulled his shirt out of his pants and made his face look funny. He came out of the office staggering as if he were drunk. He knew he had to put on his very best performance if he were going to capture that bandit single-handedly. He kept a steady eye on the thief. He knew if he made a wrong move it would cost his life.

"Stuff the cash in this bag, Miss, and be quick," the robber said, then he saw John. His attention was now focused on the staggering drunk, and the gun was now pointing at John. Everyone looked on in suspense as if it were just a stage show, or a situation that wasn't real.

"Stop right there!" the bandit shouted at John. But John still staggered slowly toward him. At one stage John stumbled over as if he was going to fall to the floor. The bandit smiled at him. "A drunk in a bank," the bandit said. John stopped, then he turned to the bank manager, Mr. Martin, and made winking eyes at him. John was trying to give him a signal.

"Mr. Martin, I gave you my check. Where's my money?" John shouted slowly. "You forgot to give me my money. I want my money," he told him in a drunken voice. John turned to the bandit. "They didn't give me my money. They're trying to rob me. I need my money," John said, with some spit coming from his mouth.

"You're drunk," the bandit said quickly. Then he turned his attention to the cashier.

"Fill her up, Miss, and be quick about it," the bandit snapped.

"They're giving you money and they don't want to give me any," John said to the bandit.

"They're giving me money because I'm a robber," he told John with a smile. The cashier put all the money into the plastic bag and gave it to the bandit. "Here you are, sir, it's all there," she told him nervously.

"Thank you, kindly, Miss," he said and took the bag with the money. John timed the man carefully. The bandit lowered his gun when he went for the bag of money. John got his chance and threw himself hard against the bandit. His gun went off. Then everyone went for cover. Then John kicked him in the head. The bandit fell against the counter and John hit him several times on the face until he fell onto the floor. He kicked the gun away from the bandit. Then he picked up the bag with the money and gave it to the nervous cashier.

"I believe you'll find it's all there, Miss," he said with a smile. She took the bag without taking her eyes off John. "Ladies and gentlemen, this bank is now open again for business. The police will be here shortly for this rat who is lying on the floor." Then John turned to the bandit on the floor. "I'm sorry, Sucker, but I couldn't let you take our money. You should find yourself a decent job when you get out of prison," John told him.

The bandit opened his eyes slowly and gazed at John.

"You are the drunk," he said in a squeaky voice, pointing his right index finger at John.

"No, sir, I'm very much sober. I never had a hard drink in my life. Now you know my little secret, Brother. Now, I must inform you that I'm making a citizen's arrest until the police get here," John told the bandit. Then he looked up and saw two police officers rushing through the door. He waved at them. "Officers, here is your robber. I've made a citizen's arrest on your behalf," John said to them quickly. Mr. Martin came out from behind the counter.

"I'm the manager, Ted Martin. This man tried to rob us and Mr. Stone was able to capture him single-handedly," he told the officers. The officers cuffed the bandit, then carefully picked up the gun for evidence.

"You did a fine job, sir, taking out that robber. I'm glad that there're abiding citizens like you around," said the officer.

"He was drunk," the bandit kept saying and looking at John. Then he was dragged off by one of the officers.

"We'll send someone over to get a statement later," the other officer shouted at the manager.

The manager turned to John. "Mr. Stone, I must thank you. You saved the day. You put on such a great show. I never saw anything like that before," the manager told him. "Well, where were we?"

John smiled at Mr. Martin. Deposit my check and let me have $1000 in cash. I have a date with a very pretty girl this afternoon," John replied.

"Let's go into my office and get your little matter sorted out. I've kept you long enough."

"That's a good idea," John said with a smile.

After a short while, Mr. Martin returned with the money, and gave it to John. "It's all there. Don't spend it all at once," Mr. Martin said jokingly.

"If I do I'll know where to find some more," John said, smiling.

"Well, good luck with that young lady."

"I'll be in touch, Mr. Martin," John said and stuffed the money into his pants pocket and left.

"Be careful out there," Mr. Martin shouted behind him.

He arrived twenty minutes later at the Smiths' residence. He had left his holdall at the house with his belongings before he went to the bank. Mr. Smith opened the front door for him. "Hi, Pops," John said, then entered the house. Meg Smith came into the passageway and held John's arm.

"John, I was worried about you. I saw danger in the bank. What happened?" she asked nervously. John put his left arm around her waist.

"It's nothing to worry about. I was speaking to the bank manager to start my account," he told her as they went into the living room.

"I was worried about you. I don't want anything to happen to you. You and Papa are all I have," she said gently.

"I have some money and I'm going to take you out," he said happily.

"Where are you taking me?" she asked anxiously.

"Well, I'm taking you shopping and perhaps to some other places on the way," he told her casually.

"When do we leave, John?" she asked with a giggle.

"After we have some lunch," he replied.

"Yes. Lunch." Then she turned to her father. "Papa, John is going to take me out."

"You need to get out into the fresh air," he told her.

"There, Papa approved. Now to fix you guys some lunch," she told John and went into the kitchen. John followed her, then he sat down at the kitchen table. He wanted to look at her work. She quickly prepared some cheese sandwiches and soup, then she placed them on the table.

After lunch John waited for Meg in the living room. When she arrived in the living room, he gazed at her. She looked like a schoolgirl. She wore a short blue skirt and a white T-shirt, and brown shoes. Her hair was tied with a blue ribbon. John got up and approached her.

"Well, Miss Smith, are you ready?" he asked her, smiling.

"Yes, sir, I'm ready. How do I look?"

"You look beautiful," he told her and took her right hand. She didn't wear her dark glasses. Mr. Smith went to the door with them.

"You have a good time," he said to them as they went down the stairs.

"I have a key in my bag in case Papa goes out, John," she said as they headed down on Main Street.

"It's a beautiful day, Meg."

"Yes, I can feel the sun on my face, even though I can't see it. You'll be my eyes, John."

"Your eyes and everything else, Meg," he said, then he squeezed her hand to get his message across.

It was 1.30 when they arrived at the beauty salon. John went and spoke to the chief hairdresser. Then he went back to Meg.

"We'll have to wait a while, Meg."

He led her in the waiting area, then they sat down. There were a few other women in the waiting area.

"We're in a beauty salon. I can smell the hair products," she said to John, as the other people looked on curiously.

"We have some nice ladies sitting next to us, Meg, so you'll have to wait a good while before the hairdresser gets to you," he explained to her, then glanced at the other ladies, who were looking at them.

"Sir, my name is Lisa, and I'd like your friend to take my place. She looks a real darling," she told John.

"Thank you, ma'am. Meg will be grateful to you," he told Lisa, smiling. Shortly afterward the hairdresser came and got Meg, and placed her into the barber's chair. John waved at the hairdresser, and she came to him.

"Please give her the full treatment, Miss," John told her.

"Don't worry, sir, I'll make her look beautiful for you, and that's what we're here for," she told him and went back to her customer.

John was left with the two ladies who were sitting next to him. He saw them eyeing him curiously.

"Well, ladies, I feel you have some questions for me," he told them frankly.

"How did your girlfriend end up like that?" Lisa asked.

"You mean blind?"

"Yes."

"She had an accident when she was sixteen in a friend's car. Her friend died. She lost her sight. She's been alone since I met her."

"That's terrible. How did you meet her?" the other lady asked.

"It's a long story. She was about to cross Main Street that afternoon. I was on the other side of the road, when she started crossing. I saw the truck coming straight at her. I ran as quickly as I could and got hold of her just in the nick of time. We became friends from that day," he told them.

"Quite a dramatic story, sir."

"You see, Meg can't see, but she sees things in her head and not with her eyes."

"That's remarkable," remarked Lisa.

"Well, you're not the only one to feel that way," John told Lisa.

"Will she ever see again?" asked the other lady.

"I really don't know. She'll have to see an eye specialist. If she did see again, it would be a miracle," John said softly.

Then John remembered what Meg's father had told him – that Meg might regain her sight if she had an eye operation. But it was only the money that kept Meg from that operation. He knew the amount would be substantial for any poor family to pay, and no one was going to help them. And the amount would depend on the sort of specialist who would perform the operation.

"The money," John whispered.

"Money?" Lisa asked.

"Yes, money for an eye operation. My father is my last and only hope. He's going to leave me some money, and I'll donate that money to her," he told Lisa. Then John remembered his father who was in a nursing home, and he'd have to call his brother, Harold, to find out what was happening.

The other lady came in front of John and had a closer look at his face, and pointed at him. "You're the man on the television. What is your name?" she asked.

"John Stone, at your service, ma'am," he told her.

"You poor man. That horrible man killed your family, and he deserves to be caught and punished. Don't you know his name as yet? My name is Margaret Ford," she said, looking over him.

"Now I know his name and on Monday his name will be made public," John told her.

"I see now that Miss Meg is in good hands," Lisa said. "And some time ago I saw you on the Brooklyn Bridge. You went up to save that woman. You're a real hero," she told him quickly.

"I'm always glad to help," John said to them.

The other hairdresser came over and looked at the two ladies and at John.

"Who is next?" she asked. The two ladies pointed at John. The hairdresser looked at John and smiled. John smiled back at her.

"Well, it's a long time since I had any beauty treatment. What the heck. Throw in the works," he told her.

"Good for you, John," Lisa told him. The hairdresser led John to the barber's chair. The two other ladies looked on and smiled.

"He's handsome," Margaret said to Lisa.

"Well, sir, how would you like your hair?"

"John, please."

"And I am Olive. It seems you and your girlfriend have livened up the salon. I'll give you a special, John," she told him.

"Thank you, Olive."

Twenty minutes later, John had a shampoo and a special haircut, then he went back to his seat. Ten minutes later, Meg came to the waiting area and stood in front of John.

"Well, how do I look?" she asked.

"You look beautiful," all voices said to her.

"Thank you," she said with a smile.

John got up and paid Olive for himself and Meg, and gave her a big tip for herself. "Thank you John and Meg for coming. Please come again. And you have a nice day," she told them. John led Meg out.

"Good-bye ladies and thank you again," he told Lisa and Margaret.

"We wish you and Meg lots of luck," Lisa shouted behind him.

John and Meg walked slowly hand in hand on Main Street. All the passers-by eyed them curiously. John smiled at anyone who looked at them.

"Where are we going, John," Meg asked.

"The shopping center," he replied. But he didn't know exactly where he was heading.

"We'll go up on Main Street, then turn right on High Street until we come to the Northgate Shopping Mall," she said with a smile.

"I thought I was leading you, Miss, but it's the other way around," he said, smiling.

They arrived at the mall just after three o'clock, and John led Meg into a department clothing store for men and women. The saleswoman came to them.

"Hi, can I help you?" she asked, looking at Meg. "Yes, Miss, my friend, Meg really needs your help. She needs some dresses, skirts, blouses, stockings, shoes and any other clothes to go with it," he told her.

"My name is Silvie."

"John and Meg."

"Is she...?" Silvie asked.

"Yes, Meg can't see, but she can see you by touch. I'll lend you her for the time being and thank you. I'll browse around in the men's department for some stuff for myself," he told her. Then Silvie took Meg into the women's department. John smiled at them, then he went in the men's department. He couldn't help thinking about Meg. Maybe she was feeling like Cinderella. She was now being transformed into a beautiful person and John was her handsome prince. But John realized that much work was needed to make the story complete, and it would never be completed until his princess got her sight back. John shook his head, so as to bring himself back to reality. He knew it was just a dream. He was dreaming with his eyes wide open.

"Sir, can I help you?" the salesman asked.

"I'm sorry, I was far away," he told the salesman.

"I wanted to know if I can help you."

"Well, I was going to help myself, but since you're here and offering your help, I accept. I am John."

"Roy, at your service, John. How can I help you?"

"I have been away for a long time, so I'm out of touch with the latest clothing for men."

"What you are thinking of getting?"

"Well, some pants, shirts, socks, underpants, and a sports summer jacket, also some shoes," John told Roy.

"Were you out of the country, John?"

"You might say that," John replied.

John bought all the clothing he needed, then he paid for it and it was placed into a bag.

"Well, thank you, Roy, you have been very helpful," John said to him, then he went over to the women's department, and sat down. Silvie came to John.

"Meg is still trying on some more dresses. She's found some skirts and blouses and some very nice underwear and stockings. She likes the low heel shoes. She has tried on some dresses and she is trying to choose," Silvie told John.

"Well, she need your eyes. Please help her, Miss."

"She's such a nice person," Silvie said and went into the changing room to help Meg.

Soon after that Meg came out with Silvie.

"John, how do I look?" she asked with a smile.

"Is that you, Meg?" John asked.

"Who do you think it is?" Meg replied quickly.

"Well, you look beautiful from where I am."

"Then you like it?"

"Yes," he said. "Meg, please keep that dress on," he told her. "Meg will take three of those dresses in different colors."

"Well, that completes everything," Silvie said and punched all the items on the cash register, then she placed all the items into a carry bag, including Meg's old clothing.

John paid for all the clothing.

"Thank you for helping Meg," John said and took the two bags in his left hand, then he led Meg on with his right hand.

"I hope you'll come again," Silvie said behind them.

"Well, sir, where to now?" Meg asked.

"That dress looks great on you. Now back to your question. I think I know just the place. Are you hungry?"

"Yes. I now deserve a break. Some burgers and fries," she said as they walked through the mall.

"I'll do better than that, I'll take you to a real restaurant that serves real delicious meals," he told her.

"But that will cost too much."

"Nothing is too much for you, Meg. Today I'll give you the full treatment, for tomorrow we'll be back to our usual selves," he said, smiling.

"Just like Cinder's story. Now I'm at the ball and tomorrow I'll be slaving over a hot stove," she told him with a smile.

"Nice story, Meg. I read it when I was a boy."

"And I guess all the girls gazed at you," she told him jokingly.

"Yes, but I only had eyes for one girl, Mary Young," he told her.

"And you really loved her."

"Too much, Meg. But that's all in the past now. I never thought I could love anyone again, but when we met, you made me feel alive again. You made my life worthwhile, and I fell in love with you; it's a special love, a very, very special love," John told her slowly.

"Now, you're being sentimental about me. I know it was hard on you all those years, your family were taken away from you. Then after all those terrible years, you met me by a strange coincidence. I'm nearly half your age, not beautiful, and most of all, I'm just a poor little girl from Brooklyn. You've rescued me and now you're my hero and my prince," she explained to John.

"That's quite a story. You should take up writing," he told her with a smile. "Now where are we?" he asked.

"If we turn to the right, we'll get to that restaurant, sir," she said and pulled him to the right.

"After you, ma'am. I don't know what I'd do without you." John couldn't understand. He was supposed to be leading Meg, but she was leading him.

"You'll think of something, sir, once we get home," she said with a giggle.

"Here we are," he said as they entered the restaurant. A young waitress came and welcomed them inside the dining room, then she took them to a table in the corner.

"How can I help you, sir?" the waitress asked.

"We'll have your special of the day," John told her.

"Anything to drink?" she asked.

"Yes. Some coffee for me, and a soda for Meg."

The waitress looked at Meg for a few seconds, but didn't say anything, then she left to get their order.

"John, this is the first time I've been into a real restaurant. Papa used to take me and my brother to McDonald's for burgers and fries, and that's the nearest I have got to a restaurant," she said cheerfully.

The attractive waitress brought coffee and soda and placed them on the table.

"Is there anything else I can do?" the waitress asked.

"Now that you mention it, Miss, Meg would like to use your washroom. It would be nice if you could show her there please," John told her.

"I understand. I'll take her," the waitress said and helped Meg up. "Have you been like this all your life?"

"No. I had a car accident six years ago," Meg told her. "I'm Meg and John is my friend."

"My name is Gloria, and I have only been here for the past two months," she told her and led her to the women's washroom. John sipped his coffee and looked around the restaurant. He saw that several tables were taken, but it seemed as if he and Meg were the only customers in the large dining room.

Meg arrived back at the table and the waitress helped her back into her chair.

"Thank you, Gloria," Meg said, looking up.

"You're welcome. I'll get your specials now."

"Miss, can you make that another special to take away."

"Okay," she said and left.

Ten minutes later, the waitress brought the two specials and placed them on the table. "Enjoy your meal."

"Thank you, Miss," John told her with a smile.

Meg smiled at John. "Smells good," she said. "John, please cut up my food for me. I don't want to use my hand. Other persons might be looking at me," she told him.

"I understand," he said, then he cut all the meat up, then the vegetables. "Here you are, Meg, six pieces of meat to the right and vegetables to the left," he told her softly.

"Thank you, sir," she said and started eating. John looked at her for a few seconds, then he realized that Meg needed lots of love and attention. He also knew that in her own way she was able to look after herself, but now she had him to lean on.

"This is beautiful, John. The burning candles and you at my side. It's so remarkable, or maybe so romantic."

"If you can say such nice things at this stage, you'll blow me off my feet when you can see," he told her quickly.

"Do you really think I'm going to see again?" she asked slowly.

"I'm almost sure you will, Meg, even if I have to give you my sight," he told her seriously.

"Does it mean that much to you that I see again?" she asked with a smile.

"It's my earnest wish, so don't you forget that. You have to have faith in yourself. You have to tell yourself that you'll see again," he said convincingly.

After their meal, John paid the waitress and left her a tip. Then they took a taxi home. John paid the driver and they went up the stairs with the bags and a special for Mr. Smith. Mr. Smith opened the door for them and closed it when they were inside. They all went into the living room, then he turned to his daughter and looked at her.

"Meg, you look so beautiful. You have a nice new dress, and your hair!" he said, smiling.

"Papa, John bought you a special. I'm sorry I wasn't here to prepare your supper," she told him cheerfully.

"Thank you, John, for supper," Mr. Smith said and went into the kitchen with the food.

"You enjoy, Pops," John shouted after him.

Meg went to John and he took her into his arms and kissed her.

"I knew you would think of something," she said with a giggle. He held her tight in his arms.

"I want you to see, you'll see, you'll see," he whispered into her ear.

Chapter Eighteen

John had moved into the Smiths' residence. He had his own room on the second floor and he felt at home. Meg and her father had now become his family, and he felt comfortable with them. He knew he'd have do all in his power to take care of them. Meg went into his room.

"John, how do you like your room?" she asked.

"I like my new room fine," he told her, and he took her into his arms and kissed her.

"And how do you like your new family?" she asked into his ear.

"Do I have to tell you that? You know the answer already," he told her and kissed her again.

"Yes, I know," she said with a giggle. "Well, Papa usually goes grocery shopping today, but I want you to take me instead, John," she said in a pleasing way.

"Fine with me, Miss Smith," John said and they both went downstairs.

"I'm dressed, John, so let's make an early start," she said.

"Okay, I'll get my jacket."

John took Meg to the Super Store on Main Street, which was just two miles away from the house. He obtained a cart, then they both went from aisle to aisle selecting items. John would tell Meg what was on the shelves and she would tell him what to buy from the shelves. When they came to the meat, dairy and vegetable sections, John knew what to buy in those departments because he grew up on a farm.

"Are you tired, Meg?" John asked.

"Yes. We went around six times in the store. It was not the shopping that mattered, but being with you, John," she said as she held his arm.

"Don't get sentimental on me now, Meg. We're only grocery shopping," John told her as they entered the queue to the cashier.

"I hope you have enough money to pay for all those groceries," she told him.

"Yes, I do. We'll prepare a nice supper today. Maybe I'll cook," he told her. John looked back and he realized that the other customers in the queue were listening to what they were saying, but he didn't care.

"Well, I'll just put my feet up and let you do the cooking, John."

"Good for you, Miss," the woman customer behind John said. John looked at the lady and smiled.

"I wish they were more guys like you to do the cooking for us," she said to John.

"Why, thank you, ma'am," he told her with a smile.

John reached the cashier and all the groceries were punched up on the cash register. John paid for them and they were placed into five plastic bags.

"Well, Miss Smith, you'll have to carry the two lightest bags," he told her. "We could take a taxi home," he added.

"No. We'll walk. It's only two miles to the house," she said as they made their way out of the store.

Meg used her key to get into the house. Her father had left to visit his friend in the apartment complex. So Meg and John were all alone. John put away all the stuff. Meg went upstairs and when she didn't return, John went to search for her. The door of her room was open. He went in quietly into her room, and found her fast asleep in bed. "You were really tired," he whispered to himself, then went back downstairs. He got some vegetables and meat he needed to prepare a meal. Then he started to peel the vegetables and sliced the meat with a sharp knife. He had to cook something that was easy and delicious for himself and Meg.

Two hours later, Meg arrived in the kitchen. John looked at her.

"Did you had a good sleep, Meg?"

"How long have I been out?" she asked, then she started to sniff.

"About two hours," John told her.

"That long? It must have been all that grocery shopping," she told him. "I'm smelling something good," she added.

"You're just in time, ma'am, for my special. So you sit down my beautiful princess, and I'll serve you for a change," he said and led her to the kitchen table.

"What did you cook?" she asked.

John placed his special meal in front of Meg. It consisted of stewed beef, vegetables and some rice. Meg tasted the meal before she started to eat. "This is very good, John. Who taught you to cook like this?"

"My mother, then Mary. They all taught me something," he said as he ate with Meg. It's still bright outside and I can take you to the park if you feel up to it," he told her.

"I'd love to go to the park. Papa used to take me there when I was a little girl."

"And I'm going to take you there now that you're a big girl," he teased her.

"You think I'm a big girl now?" she asked with a smile.

"Yes, you have all the fillings of a big girl," he told her frankly.

"But yet you haven't taken advantage of me. You have been a perfect gentleman. But sometimes I wish you'd take advantage of me. I realize that you're not that sort of person. You are a very caring person," she explained.

That afternoon John took Meg to the local park. It was just after six and it was still bright. He found a bench to sit on under a pine tree, which was on the far side of the park. Meg wore her short pants, T-shirt and sandals. She held the left side of her cheek.

"It's so cool here. It beats being locked up in the house," she said. "I used to come here when I was a little girl when Mom was alive. I could see all over the park and the people in it," she explained sadly. "Now I can't see those things any more," she added.

"I know it brings back those happy and sad memories," he told her and held her hand.

"Before you came along, John, I used to dream that someone like you would come along and sweep me off my feet," she confessed.

John took a good look at Meg and she seemed so childlike in most of her ways. He felt that she was teaching him how to be a youth again. He didn't have the chance to be a youth and to enjoy himself He had become a husband at eighteen, then a father at nineteen and a father again at twenty. Meg Smith was changing his whole life. She was teaching him how to love again, and most of all, how to be a youth again. She had that powerful effect on him, and he knew for sure that he couldn't let anything happen to his newborn family. He would fight to the death to keep them safe and happy. Then he felt a surge of anger when he remembered how his last family was murdered, and he was not conscious to save them from the bad man.

"John, you are thinking again," she said and shook him. "I can feel it. You feel that I'm a child who needs lots of attention," she added quickly.

"To be frank with you, Meg, I'm the person who enjoys your innocent attention."

"You're teasing me now," she said and hit John softly on his shoulder.

John kept a careful eye on the two white youths who were coming toward him. They came and stood in front of Meg, then they looked steadily at her bare legs.

"Who is there?" Meg asked. She sensed someone was in front of her. Then she held onto John's arm.

"It's just two guys looking at your legs, Meg," John told her. "Nothing to be afraid of," he added.

"What do they want?" she asked.

"We're going to find that out very soon. Please, guys, my girlfriend is getting a bit nervous with you guys standing in front of her. She can't see you, but she can certainly smell you guys, and you stink," John told them sternly.

"Well, what's such a nice girl doing with an old and ugly guy like you," the big youth told John.

"We're going to take your girl away from you and there's nothing you can do about it," the other youth told John, then pointed his finger in his face.

"John, be careful," Meg said, releasing his arm.

"Well, guys, why don't you make it easier for me? Beat it!" John told them, clenching both of his fists.

"He wants us to beat it. What a laugh. And for your information, brother, we're going to beat you up," the big youth hinted, showing his right fist.

"Which one of you dudes want to come first?" John asked, then he slowly stood up to face his aggressors.

"John, be careful," Meg said nervously.

"You should listen to your blind girlfriend. We're both going to beat you up and take your blind girl away from you," the big youth threatened John. John moved slowly to the left of their bench, away from Meg, then he stood there and waited for them to attack. They then rushed him, then he swiftly moved away, and they fell onto the grass. John turned around to face them. They rushed him again. He then jumped high enough with both feet in the air, hitting each of them in the head, then he stood over them with his hands clenched, ready to fight. The two youths stood up quickly, then they ran away.

"And you have a nice day too," John shouted after them.

"What's happening, John?" Meg shouted at him.

"I'm here, Meg," he said and took her into his arms. She was trembling, and he held her tight in his arms to comfort her.

"Those bad guys are gone," he told her. "No need to be afraid," he added.

"I was afraid they'd hurt you, then hurt me," she cried.

"No chance of that. I lost my family once, and that will not happen again. I'll fight to defend you," he said quickly.

"John, you have to let it go."

"I can't let it go until I find the man who killed my family. In the meanwhile, I have to defend my new family. That's the way I feel," John told her sharply. "Do you understand?"

"Yes, I think I do. You must do what you have to do so you can be free from the anger you feel deep inside of you. John, I love you, and I'm also afraid for you. Any day may be your last," she said still in his arms.

"I love you too, and that's why I have to fight even harder. My love for you makes me stronger," John confessed.

"I didn't know whether I was coming or going, as my life was scattered all over the place. When I met you it was as if I was awakened from a deep sleep," she told him softly.

"I didn't know I had such a deep affect on you," he told her softly.

"You do, John," she said looking at him, with tears coming down her cheeks.

"Don't cry," he told her, then he wiped the tears away with his hand from her face, then he kissed her on the forehead. "My one and only wish is for you to get your sight back," he told her gently.

"You really think that I'm going to see again, John?"

"Yes, I have faith that you'll see again, Meg," he told her bluntly.

"John, it's so good you believe in me. Papa told me that I'll never see again. He doesn't have any faith in me, but you make me feel good. I believe in you too, and you are all I have," she told him frankly.

"Well, now that we have shared each other's feelings, let's go home," he said and took her by the hand and led her out of the park. Then they came upon an ice-cream truck. John then bought Meg and himself a large ice-cream cone. He watched her with interest as she sucked and ate her ice-cream cone. She was a young woman who was fighting deep inside of her to be happy.

On Sunday John called his brother, Harold, to find out how his father was. Harold told him that their father has taken a turn for the worse, and he should come as soon as possible. John told him he'd come the following day. He knew he had to make his second video the next morning, and he didn't want to miss out on that.

John arrived on Monday morning at 9.30 at the television station. Norma Stewart met him at the reception desk, and took him into her office.

"John, we've had lots of calls and nice letters in respect of your video, and two publishers called. They're interested in your story, and are willing to pay big bucks for it," she told him from behind her desk.

"Well, right now I'm only interested in going ahead with the videos. I want to get this rat out of wherever he is hiding," John told her sternly.

"Well, John, we'll go that way for now," she told him with a smile. "My director wants me to go all the way with you. I suspect you must have had a stern talk with him," she added.

"I have to do this video this morning. I'll be going to Moorestown this afternoon because my father had taken a turn for the worse. I believe he is dying," he told her sadly.

"I'm sorry about your father," she told her softly.

John smiled at her. "That's life. Now to our video."

"Yes. Studio B is set up for you, so we'll go there."

In Studio B John went through his lines quickly before they were put on video. Then he was given the go ahead.

"Hi, viewers. My name is John Stone. You have seen my first video. It was about the face of a man who killed my family in 1985.

"We have had lots of replies in respect of this face of a killer. I thank all of you who have sent in these replies.

"It has recently come to my attention from a very reliable source that the name of this man is Richard Thompson. He lives somewhere in New York City. He's out there somewhere. Please call in if you have seen this man by the name of Richard Thompson.

"A personal message from me: you're a rat, Richard Thompson. You killed my family and you should give yourself up to the nearest police station. And only then you'll release the pain for all the murders you've committed.

"Richard Thompson this is one last message specially for you. You killed my family. I want you to see their faces again so you can remember what they looked like. I brought their photos with me. This was my loving wife, Mary. This was my handsome son, David, just ten. This was my beautiful daughter, Cindy, just eight. Take a good look at them. You killed them with my gun. And soon your turn to die will come," John said with the tears coming down his cheeks.

"Thank you for listening to me. And I thank Channel 8 for the air time."

Norma Stewart went to John. "That was great, John. I thought at first you were getting a little carried away, but afterwards I saw where you were going," she said sadly.

John wiped the tears away from his face. "It brought back sad memories of the past. I'm sorry I had to cry," he told Norma Stewart.

"But, John, that's what makes it so dramatic. You showed the way you felt, and that's what matters. The viewers will love you for that," she explained.

"Let's hope so, Norma, otherwise I can make another video."

"No. We'll use that video," she insisted.

"Well, I have to catch a bus. So I'll see you in a few days."

"Yes John, and good luck," she told him.

John arrived in Moorestown just after 5.30 p.m. His brother Harold picked him up at the bus stop, and drove him immediately to the nursing home. He went into his father's room. The nurse was there in the room. She shook her head when she saw John.

"He's just holding on for you, Mr. Stone," she told John quickly and left the room.

John pulled up a chair and sat at his father's side. He held his father's hand as he felt tears rolling down his face. "Dad, I'm here," he said slowly.

His father opened his eyes slowly. "John," he said softly. "I knew you'd come," he said, looking at him.

"Yes, Dad, I'm here. I'm sorry I couldn't get here earlier," he cried.

"I want you to have that money from my life insurance, and I want you to do something good with it. It's my way of saying I love you, son," he said slowly. "You didn't want to be the master of the farm, but you became something much greater; you became master of your own destiny," he said, then smiled. Then he took his last breath. John held his father's hand tightly.

"Goodbye, Dad. I love you and I always will, wherever you are," John said, then closed his eyes and said a small prayer. Then he got up and went out to Harold. John shook his head to Harold, then Harold shook his head back to John.

"He was holding onto life just to see you, John. I was afraid you'd get here too late, but you got here just in the nick of time," Harold said, then they both hugged each other. "I have made most of the funeral arrangements, so we'll set the funeral date for tomorrow and you can go back on Wednesday," Harold told him.

The Stone family gathered in the cemetery. They had to pay their last respects to James Stone. They gathered around the casket.

The priest gave his eulogy and said a final prayer for James Stone, then John had to say his final words.

"Goodbye, Dad. We all love you and we'll never see you again. Now you're with Mom and I know you both will be happy together again. We love you, Dad. May God bless your soul wherever you are," John said, looking at the casket, with the tears running down his cheeks.

The casket was lowered into the grave. John picked up some of the earth in his right hand, then he threw it on the casket. "Goodbye, Dad, I love you," John whispered, then he turned away and went to his mother's grave.

"Mom, this is John, your son. I love you too, Mom. Dad is now with you in heaven. I'm really glad you are there to keep him company. Mom, I'm in love with a very nice girl, but she is blind. And with Dad's insurance money, she maybe able to see again. Good-bye, Mom. I love you," John said slowly as he wiped his eyes from the tears.

John went horseback riding on Wednesday. He went to his favorite spot on the northern side of the farm. This was the spot he and his father used to go to. He looked around sadly. The very spot his father had told him he'd be master of the farm. And that same spot he'd kissed Mary for the first time. All the memories came back to him. It made his head spin. He couldn't understand how his life had changed so much, and now he could be killed at any time, and no one would be there to help him. It was him or the man who killed his family. He knew it was easier said than done, but it had to be done sooner or later, meeting Mr. Richard Thompson.

John spent the rest of the day with his family. They tried to get him to stay on the farm for a few more days, but he told them he had to go back to Brooklyn to finish his business with the man who killed his family, and the girl whom he loved.

The next day Harold drove John to the bus stop.

"Well, John, as soon as the insurance check comes through, I'll transfer it to your bank in Brooklyn. I really wish that your girlfriend gets back her sight. And one last warning from your big brother; you are playing a very dangerous game with those videos you're making. So be careful," Harold told him quickly.

"I'll do that, Big Brother," John said and gave him a hug.

"I'm the big brother, but you have always been the leader. So good luck, John, and come and visit us again. Bring that nice girl with you," Harold told him sadly.

John jumped on the bus and found himself a seat. Then the bus pulled off and Harold was still standing by his truck. John waved to him at the window as the bus passed. He sat next to an elderly lady. He looked at her and smiled, then he closed his eyes and started to think. He had to make arrangements for Meg to see again. It was more important for her to see than for him to catch the killer of his family.

John arrived at 7.30 that evening at the house, and before he could knock on the door, the door opened. Meg stood there in front of him. He looked a her for a few seconds and she was a pretty sight to see. He went in and closed the front door and took her into his arms and kissed her. "I knew it was you, John," she said excitedly.

"I miss you too, Meg. On the bus all I could think of was you," he told her, then led her into the living room.

"Hi, Pops, I'm back," he said and sat with Meg on the sofa. "I got there just in time and my father went peacefully," he told them sadly.

"I'm sorry, John," Meg told him and held his hand.

"Sorry about your Papa, John," Mr. Smith told John.

"Well, I saw it coming. Dad was in poor health. He died in my arms and now he's in heaven," John said.

"Thank heaven that Papa is still here with me," Meg said.

"That's why I want to talk to you and Pops," John said and looked at Mr. Smith.

"What do you want to talk about, John?" Meg asked.

"My father has left me a gift and I have to use it wisely. This gift is money and I want to use it for an eye operation for Meg. I'm going to make some arrangements just in case anything should happen to me. As you know I have made two videos and this killer may be after me. I know he's been following me for some time," John explained.

"I felt it too, John. I felt his presence outside. You'll have to be careful," Meg said.

"I'm not afraid for myself, but for both of you. I don't want you to open the door for anyone you don't know. I'll make arrangements for a phone to be installed," John explained.

Mr. Smith got up and looked at John. "I like that John. You really take charge," he said and went up to his room.

"Well, John, you're a take charge guy. Now take charge of me," Meg teased.

"What do you have in mind, ma'am?" he asked.

"Kiss me in a way that you missed me," she said and placed her lips close to his. He kissed her hard on the lips. "Now that's over," she said. Then she got up and pulled him up and led him to the kitchen. He turned on the light and sat down at the table.

"You must be hungry after that long bus ride from your home town. I have some special soup and bread," she told him. Then she turned on the stove and heated up the pot with the soup. She took out slices of bread and buttered them and placed them on a plate. She poured the soup into a bowl and placed it in front of John.

John looked at each movement Meg made. She did everything like a person with perfect sight.

"You see, I can do everything as if I had my sight. So you don't have to waste all that money on an eye operation. I know how much it cost six years ago, and now it must be double the amount," Meg told John as he ate. John just looked at her as she spoke.

"I have made up my mind, Meg, and your sight is all that matters. I'm going to make an appointment for you to see an eye specialist next week in New York City. And we'll make a day of it when we're there," he said and touched her hand, and gazed at her. "I want something to happen very soon, Miss. I want you to say each minute of the day, I'll see again," he told her convincingly.

"Oh, John, when I'm with you my whole world seems so easy. It's as if there's no tomorrow, and I only live for today! I love you so much, that I can see you with all the love you're giving me. How can I repay you?" she said slowly.

John smiled at her. "You can do that by being able to see. That's my one and only wish," he whispered to her.

Chapter Nineteen

John woke up that morning and was determined to get things going for Meg. He arrived at the Western Bank just after 10.30 a.m. The manager, Mr. Martin, took him into his office.

"Mr. Stone, I got the information you required. I also got an appointment for Meg Smith next Tuesday at 11.00 a.m. This is the address," Mr. Martin said to John from behind his desk.

"Bless you, Mr. Martin. I'll sign over my trust fund to be transferred to your bank. My father has passed away recently and left me his insurance money, which will be sent here, also," John told him.

"I'll see to that for you," Mr. Martin told him. "You have made a wise choice," he added.

"I need to make out a will. Have you seen my videos? They told me I'm playing a dangerous game. I want to make out a will in case anything should happen to me. I'd want all my money to go to Meg Smith of 46 Foster Street, Brooklyn. The money would be for an eye operation, no matter what happens," John told Mr. Martin.

"I'll have a will drawn up for you as soon as possible, Mr. Stone. You can come in later today to sign it."

"Thank you, Mr. Martin," John told him, then left.

John went to the hardware store. He bought some building supplies, plaster and several tins of paint. He wanted to make a start on the Smiths' house. He also bought a set of tools to fix the leaky faucets and toilet. John paid for all the stuff. Then he took the light stuff with him, and the rest was to be delivered to the Smiths' house later that day.

John arrived back at the house and used his pass key to get in. He went into the kitchen.

"John, you are back," Meg said. John put the bag with supplies on the table, then took Meg in his arms and kissed her. "You missed me?" he asked.

"Yes, I miss you, John," she said and went back to her cooking on the stove. "Before I forget, one of your friends came to see you. I didn't open the door. I told him you were out and you'd be back soon. He said his name was Mike," she told him.

"Good girl, you didn't open the door."

"Do you know a Mike?" she asked.

"I certainly do. He used to be my cellmate, if it is the same Mike," he said to her. "I'll have to get some plaster and tape and start on your room. I want to make your room beautiful, when you can see it."

"That will be the day, me see," she said with a giggle.

Later that afternoon, John heard a loud knock on the front door. He came down quickly from the second floor to answer the door. He had a feeling it was Mike. He opened the door quickly and Mike Williams stood in front of him.

"Speak of the devil, Mike," John said loudly.

"I'm still the same Mike. Aunt Mildred gave me your address and I wanted to see you. I got out this week and it's all because of you, John. You had a great effect on the warden," Mike told him, smiling.

"Don't stand there. Come in and meet the folks."

Mike entered the passageway, then gave John a friendly hug. John closed the door and led Mike into the kitchen.

"I'm really glad to see you, Mike," John said and turned to Meg who was at the stove. "Meg, this is my friend, Mike." Meg turned around to face them then she pushed out her hand.

"Nice to meet you, Mike," she said as Mike shook her hand. He looked at her for a few seconds, then he turned to John.

"Is this the lady in your dreams, John?" Mike asked softly. John didn't say anything for a few seconds. "Yes, the one and only. It happened just as in my dream," he answered.

"And you had to save her from that truck?" Mike asked, looking at John. Meg had gone back to what she was doing on the stove.

"Yes. It happened on Main Street, by the big billboard, with that beautiful girl smiling down at everyone," John explained.

"You remember when you were released, I made a joke with you. I told you to hold onto that beautiful girl when you saved her, and that's exactly what you have done," Mike explained to John.

"It sounds like a story out of a book," Meg told Mike. "You see, Mike, by some strange reason myself and John are connected. We can feel certain things that are about to happen. Well, I have said my piece, now back to work. And I'll get you gentlemen some coffee as soon as the water boils," Meg said and went back to the stove.

"Sit down, Mike and we'll talk. I need your help to fix up this place," John told him. Then they sat around the kitchen table.

"Well, I'm doing nothing right now, so I can give you a hand."

"I'll pay you for your time, Mike. I want to see you go straight, and not back to that ugly place. We brothers must stick together," John told him.

Mike shook his head. "To tell you the truth, John, I am really lucky to have you as a friend. Aunt Mildred told me about all the things you did for her. She's very grateful. She really likes you, and that's surprising," Mike told John, tapping his index finger on the table.

"Why's that?" John asked.

"Well, she has always given me a hard time. We never got on since my mother passed away," Mike told him.

"You must remember that family is forever," John told him.

"John, you did a great job on the rooming house, and you paid Aunt Mildred bills for six months. Now, I'm going to help you. Whatever you need, Brother," Mike told John.

Meg placed two cups on the table, then she poured the coffee from a small mug. Mike watched her carefully, then he pointed to John. John shook his head in reply to Mike's question.

Then Meg turned to Mike and smiled. "In answer to your silent question, I'm only able to do this by careful practice," she told Mike.

"How did she know that?" Mike whispered to John.

John shook his head. "Do you have any jobs lined up as yet, Mike?"

Mike looked at John shyly. "Who's going to hire me?"

"Don't you ever say that. You're a good person. You have made a wrong turn and you've paid for it. There are lot of places out there who would be glad to hire you. All you need is a chance to show what you can do," he explained.

"Well, I'll try it your way," Mike said.

"I taught you how to be white and you taught me how to be black, so we can deal with each other equally. I'm not saying it's easy. It takes a lot of work to make things happen," John told Mike.

"It might be easy for you, but this is something very new to me. I'm willing to get involved," he said confidently.

"That's the spirit. If you get stuck, I have two places you may get some work; they owe me favors."

"That's what I like about you, John, you're always willing to help anyone. I wish I were like that. It would be nice," Mike said softly.

"That's the Mike I know."

"John I'm afraid for you. Those videos on the television will surely get you killed. That dude is really a dangerous person. I don't want to lose you at this stage of our friendship," Mike told him quickly.

"I keep telling him the same thing. But this is something that John will have to finish. I know he will not rest until that bad man is behind bars or dead or either of them is dead. We'll just have to wait and see," Meg said forcefully. John got up and took her in his arms.

"Meg, don't get all upset on me now. Let's think of all the good things," he told her and attempted to calm her down. Mike got up and John led him to the front door.

"I'm sorry about that, Mike."

"John, I must say this, you have a good woman there. Take good care of her. And don't die on me," Mike said with a smile.

"Yes. I'll get some paint and we can start painting this place next Monday," John told him, clapping Mike on the shoulder.

"I'll be around, John. Be good," Mike said and left.

On Monday a telephone was installed in the Smiths' house. John tried it out and called Norma Stewart. He told her that he'd be in on Wednesday morning.

It was a bright and sunny morning on the 4th of August. John felt good; he knew his wish was coming true. He took Meg Smith on the bus to the Hoboken Subway Station, then they joined the subway and continued to 7th Avenue. Then they got off and headed to the Medical Building on 2006, 7th Avenue. John held Meg's hand as they went up the lift to 20th floor. He felt like a father who was taking his child to a doctor for a checkup.

"Meg, we're nearly there, nineteen and twenty," he told her.

"It seems like a journey of no return. Up and down," she told John with a giggle.

"Now all we have to do is to find Dr. Morrison's office," he told her as they headed down the passageway, then they came to the doctor's office. They entered it and reported to the receptionist.

"Please take a seat and Dr. Morrison will be with you shortly," the receptionist told them.

Twenty minutes later, the receptionist took John and Meg into the doctor's office, and went back to her post. Dr. Morrison shook hands with John and Meg. They took a seat in front of his desk. He went to a drawer and took out a file and went back behind his desk.

"Miss Smith, I managed to get a copy of your medical file from your doctor. You lost your eye sight over six years ago. If you had an eye operation then, you might have regained your sight or part of your sight. We don't know for sure, but now it would be impossible to carry out such an operation," Dr. Morrison explained.

"Why would it be impossible, Doctor?" John asked.

"Well, in a case like this, Miss Smith's eyes were badly damaged, and at this stage it would be impossible to carry out an eye operation to repair them. I'd be taking your money under false pretenses, and such an operation is very costly. First, I'll carry out an eye examination on Miss Smith," he told them with a faint smile.

"Well, Doctor, I'll be grateful for any help you can give Meg. I want her to see," John said with his finger clenched together.

"Ted Martin at the bank told me all about you and I'm very impressed. I want to help Miss Smith in whatever way I can."

"Doctor, if you can use any new method on Meg for her to see, then you'll have lots of clients after," John remarked.

"I know what you mean, Mr. Stone," Dr. Morrison said and shook his head. "If you'll wait outside. I'll borrow Miss Smith for a while," he told John.

"See you in a while, Meg," John told her and went outside, then he sat in the waiting area. He looked up and saw the receptionist, and she smiled back at him. He sat there and kept his fingers crossed. "Meg, I want you to see," he whispered several times to himself. He felt since he had come this far, he wanted to go all the way to make his only wish come true.

Twenty-five minutes later, Dr. Morrison led Meg out of his office and into the waiting area where John was waiting. John got up and led Meg to a chair, then he went to Dr. Morrison.

"I just want to have a quick word with you in the office," Dr. Morrison told John, leading him into his office. He closed the door and went behind his desk. John took a seat in front of the doctor's desk.

"What's the news, Doctor?" John asked.

"The news is not good. As I told you before, her eyes are too far gone, and no operation can bring back her sight. I'm sorry to say it, Mr. Stone, but you have to face the facts," Dr. Morrison explained.

"Is there no way Meg can see again?"

"She might be able to regain her sight if she got new eyes."

"What do you mean?" John asked urgently.

"She need eyes from a young donor, then she may have a 70% chance of seeing again," Dr. Morrison explained, tapping his finger on his desk.

"How do we go about such a task?"

"You have to be really lucky. And it would help if you had a fairy godmother," the doctor said quickly.

"That bad?"

"Yes," the doctor said.

"What if I used the media?"

"That's a good idea, Mr. Stone. From what I have heard of you, Miss Smith is in good hands. If there's anyone to pull this off, it's you."

"What do you mean, Doctor?"

"I mean that you will be her fairy godfather. If you know what I mean."

"Yes, I think I know what you mean," John said and got up from his seat. "Thank you, Doctor Morrison."

"I wish you and Miss Smith all the luck. Take good care of her," the doctor said, then shook John's hand.

"We'll be in touch, Doctor," John said and left the office.

John collected Meg and took her into the lift. He held her hand and it was cold.

"Cold hand, warm heart," he told her.

"John, I'm not going to see again," Meg said sadly.

"Don't you ever say that again. You have to have faith in yourself. You'll see again, even if I have to give you my sight. I love you and I believe in you, Meg," John told her quickly as the lift traveled from floor to floor.

"What did Dr. Morrison tell you, John?" she asked.

"He said that your eyes were too badly damaged to be operated on," he said to her softly.

There were two other people in the lift and John didn't want them to hear what he was saying to Meg.

"What now, John?"

"Let me do the thinking. I'll come up with something. Now let me take you to lunch, Miss Smith," he said and squeezed her hand. "It's nice to have a date with a beautiful young lady," he said to her. The two other people looked at John and Meg and smiled.

John led Meg out of the lift when it came to the first floor and out of the building.

"Oh, it's nice out here in the open," she told John. "Where are you taking me for lunch?" she asked excitedly.'

"When we get there I'll tell you," he said.

They walked about six blocks down 7th Avenue, then John came to a Chinese restaurant; he led Meg into it.

"How did you know I wanted Chinese food?" Meg asked.

"How did you know this is a Chinese restaurant?"

"I can smell. You still haven't answered my question."

"Well, it was the nearest restaurant around here," he told her. Then they were led to their table by an attractive Chinese waitress. Minutes afterwards John ordered fried rice, roast pork, noodles, and ice-cream for dessert.

After lunch John took Meg walking.

"Where are you taking me now, John?" She asked, as a schoolgirl would ask her father.

"When we are there I'll tell you, Miss Smith." John told her and led her several blocks away.

"You want to surprise me," she said, smiling.

"That's right," he said and squeezed her hand. "We're there," he said.

"Where?" she asked.

"We are on 34th Street. You remember that famous street in New York City?" he asked.

"Yes, John. But why are we here?"

"Well, Meg, I'm a little sentimental."

"You're a lot sentimental, and I can really get accustomed to it," she said as they walked.

"I brought you here for a reason. Do you remember the movie, *Miracle On 34th Street*?"

"Yes, I saw that movie before I lost my sight. The little girl got her wish for Christmas. I remembered. I cried when I saw that movie," Meg said sadly and started to wipe the tears from her eyes.

"Don't cry, Meg," John told her in a soothing voice.

"I will never get my wish," she mumbled.

"You'll get your wish. This is the miracle street," he told her softly.

They walked along slowly, then John saw an old man stumbling toward them. He presumed the man was a beggar. They stopped and the man also stopped in front of them. The old man held out his hand and John realized what he wanted. He pushed his hand in his pocket, pulled out a banknote and gave it to the old man.

"Thank you, son, and bless you child. You'll see again," the old man said and went his way.

"Why did you stop, John?" Meg asked.

"Did you hear the old man thanking me for the money I gave him?"

"No. But I felt a strange light in front of my eyes," she told him and pulled him on. John looked back quickly and there was no old man in sight, then he realized the street was called the miracle street, so anything could have happened.

"Oh no, it couldn't be," he whispered to himself.

"Did you say something, John?"

"I was just talking to myself," he said with a smile.

"Don't you forget it. I'm here and you can talk to me," she said to John cheerfully.

When John and Meg arrived home, John told Mr. Smith the outcome of what had happened.

"I know my Meg will not see again, just as I told you before. It would take a miracle for my poor Meg to see again," he said discouragingly. Meg burst out into tears and ran up to her room. John went after her. He found her in her room, then she immediately went into his arms.

"There, now you are safe," he told her softly in her ear.

"I feel so safe with you, and no one else. You're the only one who believes in me," she said and held back her head to John. "I love you, John," she said softly and placed her lips close to his.

"I love you too, Meg," he said quickly and kissed her. "Now come downstairs and I'll make a light supper for us. And after all that walking you need to get your strength up," he told her.

"Okay. I'll change and I'll be down shortly," she said and pushed John out of her room.

John had installed a telephone on the Monday before, so if there was any trouble, Meg could call 911 for help.

The next day John went to Channel 8 Television and he spoke to Norma Stewart. He told her about Meg Smith.

"John, it's a beautiful story. I was told to give you all the assistance I can, so you go ahead with that video," she told him.

"Thank you, Norma."

"Don't thank me. Thank your lucky stars."

Twenty minutes later, John went to Studio B, where he would read his lines.

"Hi, viewers. My name is John Stone. I have brought this photo of a very pretty face. This young lady is a friend of mine. A few weeks ago she nearly lost her very life. I came along in the nick of time to save her from a moving truck on Main Street. This came about all because she is blind. She unfortunately lost her sight in an accident six years ago. When I came into her life, I wanted her to see, so I made arrangements for her to see a specialist.

"A few days ago, Miss Smith had an eye examination. She was told that she needed new eyes from a donor. My father died a few weeks ago and all the money he left me, I donated it to an eye operation.

"Miss Smith needs a donor. She is twenty years old, with brown eyes. She needs eyes, black, brown or blue or any eyes so she can once again see the sunset.

"Please help Meg Smith. She wants to see badly.

Thank you for listening. And I thank Channel 8 for the air time."

On Friday morning John received a message on the telephone to be at Channel 8 Television at one o'clock. He didn't know why.

He arrived just before one o'clock at Channel 8 Television. Norma Stewart met him at the reception desk.

"Mrs. Proctor is waiting for you in the waiting room at the back. I think you're going to be very pleased with what she has to say. I'm going to have a crew to record the whole conversation. I'm sure it's going to make a great story," she explained to John while they walked to the waiting room. Norma Stewart introduced John to Mrs. Proctor, then he sat down in front of her. She was an elderly lady, tall, slim and very nervous. John saw that her hand shook as she sat down. Norma Stewart gave the signal to start the cameras.

"Mr. Stone, my daughter Debra is just nineteen and she is dying from a rare disease. She only has days to live," Mrs. Proctor said nervously, the tears running down her cheeks.

"I'm sorry, ma'am," John said, and put his left hand under his chin. He actually knew what Mrs. Proctor was going to say before she did.

"Your girlfriend Meg Smith reminds me so much of my own daughter. I went to see my daughter after I saw your video, and I told her the plight your girlfriend was in. She held my hand and smiled at me. I've never seen her smile like that before, and it made me happy. 'Mama,' she said softly, 'when I go to heaven, give that poor girl my eyes so she can see the sunset again.' That was my daughter's wish, Mr. Stone. My daughter's eyes are blue. Tell your girlfriend that she'll inherit Debra's two blue eyes," Mrs. Proctor said sadly. "My daughter is in the St. Joseph's Hospital in New York. I'll sign the papers and you can make all the arrangements with your doctor, because she doesn't have long to live," Mrs. Proctor added.

"I never knew this would happen so soon, Mrs. Proctor. Thank you and thank your daughter, Debra. Meg and I would like to thank her personally. I love Meg and it's my earnest wish for her to see again," John said slowly.

"I hope everything works out for the best with your girlfriend," she said.

John got up and shook her hand. "Thank you again, Mrs. Proctor. We'll keep in touch. I'm grateful to you," John said, then left. He couldn't believe what was happening. It was just like a miracle. Then he remembered when he took Meg to 34th Street. Maybe the miracle happened then, and that's because he wished for a miracle to happen, but he didn't believe it would really happen. Now he had to face all the facts and put them together; even then they wouldn't make sense to anyone else but himself.

Norma Stewart took John into her office. "John, that was great and we'll like to follow up on your story. It's a very dramatic story. But anything to do with you is dramatic. It would be nice to have you here full time," she told him, smiling.

"I may take you up on that if I live long enough to tell my real story. That man is following me and sooner or later I'll have to meet him face to face. Norma, only then will you have a real story. I'll try my best to get it done in such a way that you'd be able to carry it on the air live. Only then I'll be able to prove to the whole world who really killed my family on that cold winter morning," John told her sternly.

"I wish I could have recorded what you said," she told him, then touched his shoulder. "I'm with you all the way, John," she added.

Chapter Twenty

John received a telephone call from Norma Stewart on Saturday morning that he should take Meg to St. Joseph's Hospital immediately. Her donor was going to become available shortly.

John called Dr. Morrison to give him all the details, and they arranged to meet at the hospital. Meg got dressed and she packed a small bag with stuff she'd need. John took her by taxi to the hospital. They got there just in time to see Debra Proctor. She was the young woman who was donating her eyes to Meg Smith.

They got to the hospital just after 1.30 p.m. Mrs. Proctor came to the reception area, and took them into her daughter's room.

"You're just in time," she told them softly. Meg sat at the side of Debra Proctor's bed, and John stood at her side. Mrs. Proctor sat at the side of the bed, then she patted her daughter's forehead.

"Deb, you have a visitor," she told her daughter softly. John looked on carefully as Debra opened her eyes slowly, then she turned her head towards Meg.

"Hi, Meg, I'm Debra," she said slowly and pushed out her hand towards Meg. Mrs. Proctor took Meg's hand and slowly guided it towards her daughter's hand, then they both held hands.

"Debra, I want to thank you for your generosity. If I'm able to see with your sight, I'll be seeing for you," Meg said with the tears coming down her cheeks.

"Don't cry, Meg. I want you to be happy with what I'm about to give you. Thank you for coming. You'll have your new sight shortly," Debra told her softly. Then John took Meg's hand, and they left the room. He wanted Debra and her mother to be left alone when the moment of truth came.

John met Dr. Morrison at the reception desk.

"They told me you were visiting Miss Proctor, and her end is very near. I'll have to make all the arrangements now for the eye operation on Miss Smith this afternoon," Dr. Morrison explained.

"We were prepared so I told Meg to bring some of her stuff with her," John told him.

Meg held on close to John. "John, I'm afraid. New eyes will be something I will never have experienced before," she said nervously.

"I'll be here so you won't be alone."

"Everything has happened so fast and I don't have time to think!" she said quickly. Then she was taken away by a nurse to her room.

"I'll be here, Meg," John shouted behind her. "And I love you," he whispered to himself.

"I'll have to get ready, so I'll see you later," Dr. Morrison told John, then he left. John went to the waiting area and sat down. He knew he would have a long, long wait.

Fifteen minutes later John saw Mrs. Proctor coming towards him. She was in tears and she kept shaking her head. John got up and went to meet her, then he put his arms around her in a comforting and a friendly way.

"My Debra is gone, Mr. Stone. They took her away so as to get her eyes," Mrs. Proctor sobbed.

"I'm sorry for your loss, but I'm glad she will be able to give Meg her sight. Well, Mrs. Proctor, some part of your daughter will live on in Meg Smith," he told her softly.

"You're right, Mr. Stone. Her eyes will live on. I must go home and make all the arrangements for Debra," Mrs. Proctor told John and left.

John went to comfort Meg when she was pushed into the operating room at 5.30 p.m.

"I'll be here, Meg. Everything will be all right. I'll keep my fingers crossed for you," he told her, then they wheeled her into the operating room.

John went to a public telephone and phoned Mr. Smith. He explained to him that the doctor would be operating shortly on Meg's eyes, so she could see again.

"I don't think my Meg will be able to see again. John, you're wasting your money," he said and hung up. John didn't think much of what Mr. Smith had said, but he realized the man was old, and he certainly didn't believe in modern medicine, or modern methods.

John sat and waited patiently in the waiting room. He tried to read, but he couldn't read; he tried to think, but he couldn't think. All he did was to gaze at the blank space in front of him, and wished

Meg's operation would be a success. Then he closed his eyes for a short while, and suddenly an old man's face appeared to him in his memory. He certainly didn't know why. Then he remembered that was the same old beggar whom he had met on 34th Street. He tried his best to remember what the man had told him, then he repeated those words to himself. "Thank you, son and bless you child, you'll see again," the old man said to him in a delightful way. Meg was with him at the time, yet she didn't hear a single word the old man said to him. He just couldn't understand why. "Not unless the old man was an angel. No, it couldn't be," he said to himself. "What couldn't be, Mr. Stone?" Dr. Morrison asked.

John opened his eyes and looked up. "Oh, I was only talking to myself. How is Meg?" John asked, holding his hands together.

"Your Miss Smith is a very brave young lady. The operation went well, and I feel she has a very good chance of seeing again. We'll just have to wait and see. Keep our fingers crossed," Dr. Morrison explained.

"When can I see her, Doctor?"

"She's resting now. Maybe in the next few hours from now. The nurse will come and get you."

"My wish has come true. Thank you, Doctor," John told him cheerfully.

"You're welcome. Don't thank me just yet; wait until you get my bill." Dr. Morrison said and left.

Several hours later, a nurse came for John and took him into Meg's room. He pulled up a chair and sat at her bedside, then he held her left hand.

"I'm here, Meg; I'm here for you," he said softly. Meg turned her bandaged head towards him.

"Oh, John, I feel so light headed as if I'm floating in air. My new eyes feel so strange. I feel like a new person," Meg said slowly.

"I called Pops and told him about you."

"I'm sure he said that my Meg will not see again," she said and shook her head slowly. "But you're the only one who believes in me. I can ask for nothing more," she said and squeezed his hand.

"They'll take good care of you here, Meg," John told her. "I'll be back tomorrow to see you," he said and bent over and kissed her.

"See you, John," she uttered as John left the room.

John and Mike did some work on the house while Meg was in the hospital. They decorated Meg's room first, and installed a new carpet on the floor.

"John, we have been working on this house for the past five days and you haven't said five words to me in that time. What's the matter?" Mike asked.

"I'm sorry, Mike. I have a lot on my mind. I don't know if Meg will see again. I keep telling her that she is going to see again, but yet I have my doubts to whether she'll see again. It will be a great blow to us if she doesn't," John told Mike as they painted the passage upstairs.

"What about that dude, Thompson? Did you hear anything more about him?" Mike asked.

"Nothing as yet; just as well. I don't have the time for him as yet, but I'm sure that I'll have to face him sooner or later. The later, the better. I want to concentrate on Meg. She's all that matters right now."

"That dude is dangerous, so beware, John."

"I have been speaking to Norma Stewart at Channel 8 Television. She told me there may be an opening for you very soon, as a cameraman."

"A job for me?" Mike asked with a smile on his face.

"Yes, but you'll have to start from the bottom and work your way up," John told him.

"John, you're quite a character. You have time to find me a job after all the things you're going through. You're quite a friend," Mike told him, still smiling.

"Well, what are friends for?" John asked.

"John, what will happen if Meg doesn't see?"

"I don't know, but I feel responsible for her. I'll most probably get married to her as soon as I get my life straightened out. I wish there was an easy way, but there isn't," John told him.

"I wish you all the luck, John."

"Thank you. I'll need it. Now back to work."

That evening John went to see Meg. He sat at her bedside. She didn't say anything to him at first. He knew she was depressed. Then he started to tell her stories of when he was a boy on the farm. And how his father wanted him the be master of the farm. And if he had stayed as master of the farm, he wouldn't have met her. After a while she smiled at him and gave him her left hand.

"I don't know how you put up with me. I'm ugly and I don't seem to appreciate what you're doing for me," she told him humbly.

"Well, we're two of a kind. I don't have anyone else to put up with. You're my one and only," he told her softly, still holding her hand.

"You're good to me and you're the best thing that has ever happened to me. I know that I should think positively. You always tell me that," she said quickly.

"That's my girl. Tomorrow is the big day and I'll be here."

"That's what I'm afraid of," she told him quickly.

"Mike and I redecorated your room. It looks very nice."

"I hope I'll be able to see it when this bandage comes off my eyes," she said softly.

The following day was Friday. John arrived at the hospital at 12.30 p.m. Dr. Morrison arrived just after him and they went to Meg's room.

"Well, Miss Smith, I'll take off the bandage from your eyes," he told her. She sat up on the side of the bed, while Dr. Morrison cut off the bandage. Then she opened her new eyes slowly. She blinked them up and down.

"Well, Miss Smith. Can you see anything?" Dr. Morrison asked anxiously.

"I can only see a dim light, Doctor. That's all," she said nervously. "Why can't I see, Doctor?" she asked nervously.

"Well, Miss Smith, don't get discouraged. Your sight will come back slowly or maybe all at once," he explained.

"Take me home, John. I want to go home where I belong," she said, discouraged.

John took Meg home in a taxi. Her father came to her when she was inside the house and gave her a hug. John looked on carefully.

"Meg, you're back. Can you see me?" he asked, looking at her steadily.

"No, Papa, not yet. But I will, you'll see," she told him sadly.

"The doctor messes with your eyes and you still can't see," he told her, and shook his head in disgust.

"She'll see, Pops. You wait and see," John told him.

"Always 'Meg will see', but Meg will never see again," he said and went into the kitchen.

John took Meg up to her room and he held her in his arms and kissed her.

"Welcome home, Miss Meg. Your room is all done up. You'll see it very soon," he told her.

"Well, all I have to do is think positive," she told him softly.

"That's my girl. Get some rest and I'll get you some supper," he told her and left.

"Love you," she shouted behind him.

On Saturday Norma Stewart called John on the phone that something important had come up and he should come down immediately to the studio. Three hours later he arrived at Channel 8 Television. Norma Stewart met him at the reception desk, and took him into her office.

"We received a video this morning from Richard Thompson. This is a reply to your videos, John," she told him as they walked to her office. "Have a seat," she said and turned on the video cassette recorder. John gazed steadily at the television screen, then the face of his enemy appeared on it. That was the ugly face that he could never forget.

"John Stone, here is your most awaited reply from me, Richard Thompson.

"You've been blabbering your big mouth on the television about me. Well, here I am. I'm out of my hiding place, and it's my turn to speak.

"I see you have put on some flesh onto your puny body since we last met. Pity you didn't die when I shot you twice, but the next time you'll die by these strong arms I have here.

"You were let out of prison because your neighbor saw me coming out of your house, otherwise, you would have rotted in that stinking prison.

"Now you're in another prison. You won't be able to sleep nights. You'll see my face, the face that wiped out your beloved family. How does it feel, John Stone. I'll kill you when I'm good and ready and you won't know when, where or how. Only then you'll be put out of your misery.

"Ha, ha, ha ha! Have a nice day, Stone."

"What do you think, John?" Norma Stewart asked.

232

"A very intriguing video which I'll reply to immediately," John told her sternly.

"Yes, I think that's best. He seems to mean business, John. We'll have to work fast. We'll go into Studio C and I'll operate the television camera," she told him.

In Studio C Norma Stewart got the television camera ready and gave John the signal to go ahead.

"Richard Thompson, I saw your very intriguing video. Now we know where we stand. You want me and most of all, I want you. In a way we are just alike. You're bad as they come, and I'm, on the other hand, as good as they come.

"I want you so badly that I can't sleep nights. I see your ugly face everywhere I turn. You're the devil itself and I want to wipe you off the face of this earth completely.

"I have to meet you alone. This is between you and me - a duel to the death. Take me up on my offer if you're not a chicken. I know you're brave enough to rob and kill other helpless people. Don't take my word for it. Look into the mirror and see your horrible face. The ugly face I wish that I had never seen before.

"I have to do this for my family whom you killed. You have to pay and that you'll do. Pay, pay, pay!

"I'm your worse enemy, John Stone."

"John, that was perfect," Norma Stewart told him.

"I'm glad you like it. Let's see if he'll reply," John told her, smiling.

"I hope you didn't mean everything you said. A duel to the death. That's terrible!" she hinted.

"I said that to get him out of his empty shell. Let's hope he takes the bait," John said quickly.

Chapter Twenty-One

On Monday morning John went to his karate lesson. He realized he had to work out before his big fight with Richard Thompson. That was if 'Dick' took him up on his challenge to a duel. John realized that a duel was a thing of the past. Men would fight for their pride in the past, and the best man who was left alive was in fact the winner. John felt the same way as those brave men of the past, and that was why he had to take a chance to fight for his pride. He'd fight and die if possible like a brave man. He had to do that for the family he once knew and loved.

"If you can't beat someone fairly, and you're pushed into a corner against all odds, then you'll have to fight dirty. You kick your opponent between the legs where it hurts most," his instructor, Mr. Fu had told him with a smile. John knew that he'd have to use every trick up his sleeve to fight his enemy when the time came.

On Tuesday morning John took Meg out for a run and a walk. He knew she was depressed since she came out of the hospital a few days before. He wanted to get her out of the house for some fresh air. He knew she was disappointed because she didn't get her sight back, and especially now that she was fitted with someone else's eyes.

They ran two miles, then walked briskly back to the house.

"Thank you, John. I really enjoyed that," she told him, smiling.

John saw her smile for the first time in few days, and he knew she was coming to grips with her disappointment about not been able to see again.

"We'll have to do this more often," he told her and led her into the house.

On Wednesday afternoon John received a telephone message from Norma Stewart. She explained to him that Richard Thompson had taken him up on his offer to fight a duel to the death. He'd give the time and place tomorrow morning. John knew at that moment he'd now have to face the man whom he hated for so many years.

That evening John got Meg alone in the living room.

"I'll be meeting that bad man who killed my family tomorrow," John told Meg.

"John, he'll kill you and I'll have no one to lean on! You've brought so much light into my life and also some into my eyes. John, don't do this! Don't leave me that way! I love you too much to lose you that way," she said through her sobbing.

"I love you too much, Meg. That's why I have to come out of this alive. Your love will give me the strength that I need to bring this giant down to his knees," he told her quickly.

"You wouldn't have any help, John. I wish I can be there to help you to fight your battle," she told him nervously.

"Sergeant Bartlett will be there as a backup. I don't want to get the police involved, otherwise Richard Thompson may not turn up. That will be my only chance to get him. Only this way we can have a happy life for the future. Do you understand, Meg?"

"Yes, John, I understand. You have to do what you have to do, no matter what," she said sadly, and held onto him.

"You've given me everything I ever wanted in such a short while, and in another short while, it will be all taken away from me," she said, sobbing.

"I know it's hard on you. I wish I could make it easier on you, but I can't. We'll just have to face the facts," he told her bluntly.

"Yes, it's even harder that I can't see your face," she said and started to feel John's face for a few seconds. "Now, I know what your face feels like," she said with a little giggle.

"I'm sure soon you'll be able to see my ugly face," he told her softly, then kissed her and held her in his arms.

"Before I met you, my wish was to die, and when I met you, my will was to live," he told her cheerfully.

On Thursday morning Norma Stewart called John up on the phone. "John, he wants to meet you at Hoboken Subway Station at 3.00 p.m. The northern side of the upper part of the station will be cordoned off for you both. Cameras will be hidden in the walls and you'll be wearing a wire so we can hear everything you say. You have just over three hours to get ready, John. Good luck, John," she told him.

"I'll be there. I hope he'll be there too," John said and hung up.

Then John called Sergeant Bartlett. He told him what was about to happen at 3.00 p.m., and he should wear his bullet-proof vest just in case there was trouble with Richard Thompson.

When John hung up from speaking to Sergeant Bartlett, he turned around and saw Meg in the doorway of the living room. She was listening to him on the telephone.

"You're really going after that bad man? John, don't go, he'll kill you," she said nervously.

John went over to her and held her in his arms. "Nothing will happen to me. Sergeant Bartlett will be there at Hoboken Station as my backup man," he told her softly.

"You don't understand. I know he'll kill you. I can feel it. Please, John, don't go," she pleaded.

"I love you, Meg. I'll be back," he said and kissed her. "Stay here, I'll be back," he told her sharply.

John entered the passage and looked back at Meg.

"I wish I could see so I could help you," she said and slapped her head with both hands. "I want to see!" she shouted. John gazed at her sadly and went out of the house. Meg ran to the front door and opened it. "John, I love you," she shouted behind him. "I love you, John," she cried and went back into the house.

John arrived just after 2.30 p.m. He went straight to the section that was cordoned off and allotted to them. He stood there and for some strange reason he felt nervous. He looked around the area to see where the cameras were concealed, and he was unable to observe where they were hidden in the surrounding walls.

"Where are you, Dick? I'm here waiting patiently for you," John whispered to himself. Because the area was cordoned off, some of the passers-by in the station looked curiously at John, who was standing there by himself. He started walking up and down in the area. He felt it would help to keep his nerves intact. He didn't know if Richard Thompson would show up, otherwise, he'd look like a fool. The television cameras would start up as soon as his arch enemy came face to face with him. He couldn't help thinking about Meg. He remembered her cries when he left the house. "John, I love you, John I love you," she kept shouting behind him, but he just kept on going. He didn't turn back to face her. He knew he had an appointment with danger, and there was no turning back. He was now forced to face his own destiny at Hoboken Station.

At 3.00 p.m. sharp John saw a tall, dark, well built man coming towards him. Then he recognized that man to be Richard Thompson. John stood there and waited for his opponent to arrive. Then his whole body felt stiff, and he became more intense. He started to breathe in and out slowly. That was the moment for which he had waited for a long time, and there was no turning back on his part. He kept his eyes fixed on the tall figure approaching him. It was supposed to be a short wait for his opponent to reach him, but instead it was the longest wait of his whole life. The two men came face to face with each other. The tall, strong, seven footer stood like a giant over John. The big man had a small scar on his left cheek, and a small beard on his chin. He wore blue jeans, a blue shirt, a leather jacket and leather boots.

"Well, Stone, I'm sorry to keep you waiting, but I had to make sure that you were alone. So we meet again for the second time," Richard Thompson told him with a smug smile on his face.

"That's right, Dick, for the second and last time. This time it will make a great difference, you'll see," John blurted out. John wore tight blue jeans, a brown shirt, a pullover, and leather boots.

"You really look well, Stone. Jail has agreed with you. You must have exercised well to have developed that body. But just take a look at my muscles to your puny muscles," Richard Thompson said, pumping up his right arm.

"You may be bigger than I am, Dick, but I'll bring you down one way or the other," John told him sternly, with both fists clenched.

"You're sure you're going to bring me down, Stone?" he asked with a sudden laugh.

"Yes. You brought down my family. Now it's my turn to bring you down," John told him quickly.

"Easier said than done, Stone. Enjoy yourself while you are still alive," he told him in a crisp voice.

"Tell me why you had to kill my family?" John asked bluntly.

"If it would make you feel any better, I'll tell you why I killed your family that morning. You need to know this before you die at my hands," Richard Thompson explained.

"Go on – I'm all ears," John interrupted.

"That morning I used my special passkey to enter your house on Blexley Avenue. Then I hit you on the head when you came after me downstairs with your handgun. I took your gun and made my way upstairs. When the lights suddenly came on, and I was caught off guard. When I got to the bedroom door, your wife sprang on me like a tigress. She wasn't afraid of the gun I held in my hand. 'What did you do with my husband,' she shouted angrily at me, then she pulled the ski-mask off my face. She wasn't afraid of me. She attacked me again. I panicked and that's when I pulled the trigger on her. She fell slowly to the floor. I bent over and touched her face. She was beautiful. What a pity I had to kill her. While I bent over your wife, two small figures came from behind me, pounding on my back. 'What did you do with my Mommy?' the little boy cried out at me. I threw him off my back. Then I turned around and the children saw my face. I had no choice. It was a tough decision, but I had to pull the trigger. I shot them. Then I made my way down the stairs, then I met you again at the bottom of the stairs. You saw my face and I shot you twice, but you lived to tell the tale. Now I must finish the job. You must die, Stone. Sad! Sad!"

"Thank you, Dick. That's all I wanted to know. Now that you have confessed, I'm hereby making a citizen's arrest on you, Richard Thompson," John told him quickly.

Richard Thompson laughed loudly at John. "You're going to arrest me? A little puny thing like you?" he said, looking at John. John couldn't take it any more; he had to break loose. Then he punched hard at Richard Thompson, but his opponent didn't wince. He just looked down at him and smiled.

"I'm tough as they come. You can't hurt me with those puny little hands," he said sternly, then he punched John in the face, knocking him to the ground.

"That's a real punch, Stone. If I were you, I'd stay down," he told him. John tried to get up and he was kicked again down to the ground. "Stay down," Richard Thompson shouted at John. "You're a weakling, and you're no match for my strength," Richard Thompson blurted out at John. John wiped the blood from his lips.

"You can't win Dick. You're a loser. I'll bring you down yet, sucker," John said quickly, looking up at his arch enemy.

"You can't bring me down if you're on your back, Stone. What a laugh," he said and laughed out at John.

John knew what he had to do; he had to do what he was good at and make it work for him. He went back quickly in a somersault, then quickly on a forward somersault, kicking Richard Thompson in the groin, sticking it to him where it hurt most of all between his legs.

Richard Thompson fell to the ground, holding between his legs, and howling with pain. It was a powerful blow he never expected. At this point viewers were looking on from a distance on the scene that was taking place. The area was cordoned off so to them it was just a stunt taking place, and not anything real.

John stood up in front of Richard Thompson, looking down at him. "Now who's down?" John asked slowly, looking down at Richard Thompson as he panted and held his balls with his left hand. 'If you can't fight them fairly; fight them dirty,' John's instructor had told him. And that's exactly what he had done to his arch enemy.

Richard Thompson looked up angrily at John, then he pulled out a handgun from under his jacket and stood up slowly. John took a sudden step backward and gazed at him.

"I have a good mind to shoot you right now for kicking me up the balls," he shouted angrily at John.

"We both have to do what we have to do," John told him sternly. Richard Thompson took a quick step forward and hit John with the gun on his head. John fell to the ground.

"How does it feel, Stone? I can shoot you now," Richard Thompson said, pointing the gun at him.

John lay on the ground half dazed, then he looked up at Richard Thompson. "You are quite a big man with that gun in your hand," John told him slowly.

"Yes, I can pull the trigger and you'll be dead as a door nail," he said with a little laugh.

"I hope the cameras are getting all of this. It will make quite a good story," John said and shook his head, as if he were trying to keep himself awake.

"You mean to say we're been recorded by cameras? Television cameras? This was all a set up to catch me with my pants down, and you did a good job in doing so, but the cameras will also be able to record your death. The same death your family met with," Richard Thompson told him.

"Yes. So this time everyone will see you doing the kill, and you will not get away with it, Dick," John said quickly.

"You're trying to pull my leg. I don't see any cameras. We're all alone, Stone. The only thing that is pointing at you is my gun," Richard Thompson said with a half grin on his face.

The way John was lying on the ground, he observed Sergeant Bartlett, who was supposed to be his backup man, was approaching Richard Thompson from the back. He had a gun in his hand. When he was close enough, he shouted, "Halt, this is the police." Richard Thompson turned around quickly and fired twice at Sergeant Bartlett. The sergeant fell to the ground. John got up quickly and the two men faced each other.

"That takes care of your friend. Now it is just you and me, Stone, And I have the edge over you," he said with a pump up face.

"Now for sure the police will be after you. You have shot one of them," he told him casually.

Richard Thompson took two steps backward, looking at John steadily.

"Well, Stone, I'll shoot you first. You are not going to escape me again. Well, it was nice knowing you. Good-bye, Stone," Richard Thompson said bluntly, then he took careful aim with the gun at John's head.

"Dick, Dick," a woman's voice shouted from the side of Richard Thompson. He turned quickly and fired twice at the figure that was rolling over on the ground. Then two shots rang out from the rolling figure, hitting Richard Thompson in his side. Richard Thompson turned the gun onto John. John kicked him hard in the groin to the ground, then he slammed his foot on his opponent's hand, and kicked the gun away from him. He stood over him with his fists clenched. "That kick was for my family," he told him bluntly. Then John was able to focus his attention on the figure in a raincoat and hat, who was still lying on the ground. The person had shot Richard Thompson twice in the nick of time, and saved his life. John went over quickly to investigate, and then he knew who the familiar voice belonged to.

"Oh, no, it couldn't be," he whispered and shook his head, as if he was waking himself up from a deep sleep. He realized who his heroine was and bent down and picked her up.

"I told you to stay at home, Meg," he said to her softly and took the gun away from her hand, and put it on the ground. Meg gazed at him steadily with a big smile on her face.

"I knew you'd be glad to see me," she said nervously.

"How did you see to get here?" he asked.

"I followed you and you do need a shave, John," she told him quickly.

"You can see?" he said cheerfully.

"Yes. I hit my head on the door because I felt mad with the whole situation, and the impact made me dazed, but afterwards my sight came back to me gradually. I had to come to help you, John," Meg told him quickly. Her new blue eyes were all lit up.

"Luckily, you came just in the nick of time. But where did you learn to shoot like that?" John asked.

"I learnt that from the old western movies. Papa used to take me and my brother. It really came in handy. I thought I'd lose you, John. After all you have done for me, I couldn't let that happen," she told him, holding his arm tightly.

"It's so strange. The prince usually saves the princess, but in this case the beautiful princess saved her prince," John said to Meg cheerfully.

"Well, it was my turn to save my handsome prince," she said with a smile.

They went over to Sergeant Bartlett and he was now moving. He was hit twice on his bulletproof vest and had been knocked cold.

"He's alive," John said. Then they went over to Richard Thompson and looked down at him. He was bleeding from the side and chest. The police and paramedics arrived soon after and were able to mop up the whole situation.

John took Meg into the center of the area. "You risked your own life for me, Meg. That's why I love you so much," he told her, holding her in his arms.

Meg smiled at John. "I'm seeing your ugly face for the first time, John. Will you marry me now that we're equal?" she asked softly.

"Oh, no!" he blurted.

"Oh, no, what?" she asked quickly.

"We're still on the air. This is supposed to be a live broadcast," he told her quickly.

"All the better. The whole world will know how we feel about each other," she said, edging closer to him.

"What the heck. Yes, Meg. I love you. And I will marry you," he said and kissed Meg Smith to seal his words.

John heard the clapping all around them. He didn't realized they had an audience, an audience who felt that John and Meg were lovable characters.

The broadcaster stepped a few paces away from Meg and John, towards the camera, to show it was the end of the story.

"You've been watching a live broadcast from the Hoboken Subway Station. This was a duel between John Stone and Richard Thompson. Thompson was the man who killed John's family in cold blood in 1985.

"And now to bring you up to date. Sergeant Bartlett of the New York Police Department went to the assistance of John Stone and he was shot twice by Richard Thompson. Luckily, he wore his bullet-proof vest and was only concussed.

"A lone figure in a raincoat and hat came up at the last second, and shot Richard Thompson twice with Sergeant Bartlett's gun. Richard Thompson was just about to shoot John Stone. That lone figure was Meg Smith. She was blind up to two hours before she arrived at Hoboken Subway Station. Her love for John brought her sight back, and she saved his life from the gun of Richard Thompson.

"Richard Thompson was taken to hospital under police escort. Sergeant Bartlett was treated and released on the spot.

"Well, for John and Meg, I do wish you a happy life together. I am sorry. I am so happy. I am crying. It was a very happy ending to a very tragic beginning.

"This is Norma Stewart signing off for Channel 8 Television in New York City."